STEEL GUARDIAN

RUSTED WASTELAND
BOOK 1

CAMERON CORAL

Copyright © 2020 by Cameron Coral

All rights reserved.

No part of this book may be reproduced in any form or by any electronic or mechanical means, including information storage and retrieval systems, without written permission from the author, except for the use of brief quotations in a book review.

Edited by Jennifer Collins, J. Thorn, and Zach Bohannon

Proofread by Laurie Love

Cover by Roy Migabon

10 9 8 7 6 5 4 3 2 1

1st edition, February 2020

Stay updated on Cameron's books by signing up for the Cameron Coral Reading List:
CameronCoral.com/sign-up

You'll be added to my reading list, and I'll send you a digital copy of *CROSSING THE VOID: A Space Opera Science-Fiction Short Story* to say thank you.

CONTENTS

Chapter 1	1
Chapter 2	11
Chapter 3	17
Chapter 4	25
Chapter 5	29
Chapter 6	35
Chapter 7	43
Chapter 8	47
Chapter 9	53
Chapter 10	59
Chapter 11	65
Chapter 12	75
Chapter 13	81
Chapter 14	89
Chapter 15	93
Chapter 16	99
Chapter 17	109
Chapter 18	113
Chapter 19	117
Chapter 20	125
Chapter 21	133
Chapter 22	139
Chapter 23	145
Chapter 24	153
Chapter 25	163
Chapter 26	169
Chapter 27	175
Chapter 28	181
Chapter 29	187
Chapter 30	193
Chapter 31	203
Chapter 32	213
Chapter 33	217

Chapter 34	221
Chapter 35	227
Chapter 36	233
Chapter 37	241
Chapter 38	245
Chapter 39	253
Chapter 40	257
Chapter 41	263
Chapter 42	271
Chapter 43	275
Chapter 44	281
Chapter 45	285
Chapter 46	293
Chapter 47	299
Chapter 48	303
Chapter 49	307
Also by Cameron Coral	311
Acknowledgments	313
About the Author	315

For my niece Hannah, who inspired me to tell this story.

CHAPTER 1

"That won't do." Block scanned the ruins of the bombed-out Rest-Easy. A neon sign flashed *No Vacancy*, and the registration desk had been replaced by a blackened crater. Another motel to cross off the list.

He glanced down at the machine trailing him—a Vacuubot LCD9. The suction power on that particular model was okay, if not as strong as others. It got the job done. The little robot had accompanied him for the past two days, but was running low on power, down to the last few cells judging by its display indicator.

Two hours ago, the pair had crossed the Illinois state border into Iowa by way of a bridge that spanned the vast Mississippi River. Somehow, Block knew it was an important waterway—had he overheard guests discussing it? He'd never had reason to know any rivers outside of Chicago. Vacuubot had never seen a river at all in its sheltered life, so Block had lifted it and carried it on his shoulder for a better view as he'd trudged across the low-lying overpass.

Following the interstate had led them to this lonely stretch of US 80 outside—where? He couldn't be sure without any landmark cities nearby. Nothing matched the scale of his hometown of Chicago so far.

They stuck to highways because of the featured signs for lodging. Since Block's GPS signal had grown weak fifty miles ago, he depended on the tourist guideposts to find hotels.

His steel boots trekked across the dry, cracked deserted roads just fine, but Vacuubot sputtered and got stuck repeatedly. The ridges on the machine's underbelly—so perfect for flinging dust particles into its hungry dirt canister—snagged on every rock, twig, and dip in the roads. The bot blipped and chimed whenever Block continued on oblivious to his companion's struggles. Each time Block finally noticed, he'd backtrack through the knee-high weeds along the highway shoulder to free the squat machine from the vines that threatened to swallow the asphalt.

He had discovered Vacuubot at a Howton Inn back in Illinois. The first of its model he'd ever encountered. LCD9s were obsolete—only the most low-budget motels still kept them around. His hotel had replaced them ages ago. In fact, it was Block's model that had rendered the flat, disc-like, floor cleaning units obsolete.

Should he feel sorry for it? He wasn't sure. Block supposed he should apologize or something for stealing another robot's job.

But Vacuubot had no clue.

What was it like to have such minimal functionality? As far as robot evolution went, the little cleaning machine was low on the artificial intelligence continuum. But he didn't mind; it was nice to have someone to talk to, even though the primitive model only answered via beeps and flashing lights. Vacuubot's human creators had added a digital happy/sad face that lit up whenever it wanted to communicate its status.

Humans were weird when it came to design. They'd personify their robot creations, yet have no qualms about blowing them up in wartime.

He'd suspected the Rest-Easy would be unkempt just like all the other motels so far. He had yet to find a hotel like the Drake—the downtown Chicago hotel where Block had lived and worked. It being situated along the magnificent lakefront, he'd kept the historic and grand Drake sparkling inside.

But then came the Uprising.

He hadn't wanted it. He'd been happy the way things were. But Mach X—the AI supercomputer built by Tykon Corp to run a global communications network—had interfered. Globalcomm was the internet of all internets. Mach X had turned on humans, shutting down their network access, and enabled machine-to-machine connections on the renamed MachNet. The AI powerhouse had set up new banking systems overnight, toppling the financial systems. The humans had scrambled to correct what had been done, sending other machines to defeat Mach X, but it had been too late. Mach X had already convinced the other machines to join him.

Hundreds of thousands of military SoldierBots had stormed the major cities, eliminating the men and women in power. Chicago had been a critical staging point. SoldierBots had stormed the major hotels and buildings until they'd occupied the whole of the city. Most humans had died, only a few escaping.

After the Uprising, Block couldn't remain in the war-torn city, even though the hotel was the only home he'd ever known. Tough as it had been, he'd made the decision to venture out and seek a new hotel to carry out his purpose. All he wanted was to do the one thing he knew best—be the most efficient cleaning machine in the world. Putting things in order was his favorite way to pass time.

So, he'd left Chicago a week ago. Traveling west, Block's plan was to visit every motel, hotel, and bed-and-breakfast along the way until he found the right one to call home.

The Midwest was vast. He'd have to try a lot of hotels, but he had time.

His hopes had risen as they'd approached the Rest-Easy. The billboard, though tattered, had shown a ballroom and chandelier. Was it possible this one would be as opulent as the Drake?

But as they'd neared it, his hopes had sunk when he saw that half of the hotel's facade had crumbled inward. As if an earthquake had erupted underneath and gutted the parking lot. The hotel had been four stories tall—a wide rectangle of square rooms and long hallways with two elevator shafts cutting through the middle. Judging from the scorch marks and charred metal car frames, a battle had been staged outside the hotel and ended in an all-consuming fire.

At his feet, Vacuubot beeped and flashed. A symbol appeared on the robot's display.

:-(

"There's nothing left for us here; nothing to clean, anyway," Block said. "However, we should investigate whether there is any oil for me and a power generator for you."

Vacuubot beeped its approval.

Block edged forward, and his boot slipped in the dusty gravel underneath. The small robot couldn't possibly navigate across the rubble. "You stay here. I'll search the first floor and see what I can find."

But this time Vacuubot flashed red and frowned again.

"The important thing," Block said, bending and lifting the

squat machine by its handle, "is that you stay out of view." He carried it to an abandoned station wagon with a roof nearly as tall as his five feet six-inch frame. Bullet holes smattered one side. Yanking open the door, he placed Vacuubot on the front seat. "Stay here and be quiet." He strode away, then glanced back. "Don't worry. I'll return soon."

Block carefully picked his way across the parking lot, stepping over bricks and misshapen shards of concrete. Past mangled light poles and twisted tires.

A tank had crashed against a steel barricade and been knocked on its side. Pieces of the iron undercarriage jutted out at dangerous angles—shredded by something big. He'd seen a war documentary on TV once. Mr. Wallace had enjoyed history shows and let Block watch with him in the Drake's basement on slow nights. Only a big weapon like a projectile missile could take out a tank.

He decided not to mention anything about missiles to Vacuubot. No sense in scaring the simple bot.

He spotted the body of a mech—an enormous, militarized robot. Outfitted in cobalt chrome with neon green stripes, it stretched as tall as two CleanerBots stacked together. The massive machine lay on its back, facing skyward. Block approached, wondering if its battery was intact. Vacuubot could use the charge it would contain. And since the little robot was growing weaker by the minute, it was worth a try. Block, on the other hand, needed a fuel source such as cooking oil, petroleum, or rubber because he was a more advanced model, equipped with a microbial fuel cell—the result of a breakthrough in power cell technology. Tiny electrical bacteria in his abdominal cavity digested the waste and created an electrical current that could last him for a few days.

Despite being pretty sure the mech was dead, he treaded

lightly toward the war machine's final resting spot. Just as he was about to touch the metal giant's chest, he paused, his cybernetic fingers hovering over the steel plate. Was it wrong to steal from another robot? He'd stolen Vacuubot's job, but that had been on accident—a byproduct of his design.

Block realized he'd also taken Vacuubot without permission, but he preferred to think of it as emancipating the small machine. Days ago, it had been stuck on a rotational pattern inside a dingy, roadside motor hotel—the hotel staff had been executed.

When he'd begun scrubbing the lobby's grimy linoleum, Vacuubot had kept following him like a lost puppy.

Block preferred to travel light. He knew it would be a dangerous journey, that he would have to hide most of the time. Lugging Vacuubot around had not been his best decision. Then again, it was nice to talk to someone.

He stared at the battle mech and rotated his square-shaped head 360 degrees, checking for any signs of movement. To be doubly sure, he emitted a ping that would reach any robots within half a mile. An advanced method of communication, it enabled him to transmit an encrypted code, and any other AI within range would respond—unless their comms were disabled or cloaked—sending him their precise location and model. Sometimes the sender wouldn't reveal all their information, but usually Block could tell immediately if they were a combat machine or not.

After waiting ten seconds and getting no replies, he began removing the mech's armored chest plate. Luckily, he was equipped with a premium upgrade—his fingers turned into tiny screwdrivers—plus, he had other tools available in a hidden compartment.

Had he been simply a regular base model CleanerBot X4J6, he would've had to carry tools around. When Mr.

Wallace had custom-ordered Block, though, the man had had the foresight to know a CleanerBot could also perform handy jobs such as tightening loose doorknobs and repairing electronics. He could even pick locks or fix a malfunctioning air conditioner if need be.

Block unscrewed the top left panel of the war machine's torso first and had begun prying off the warped metal plate when, suddenly, a car horn erupted, piercing the silence.

The car sounded furious—beeping echoed across the rubble mounds. He recoiled and spun, searching for nearby threats. His scanner zeroed in on the disturbance—the vehicle where he'd left Vacuubot forty yards away.

Threat Alert Six, his helmet's ocular readout displayed. Block raced over to the car and pulled Vacuubot out. "What did you do?"

But the cleaning machine just sat there with its sad face. Didn't even try to explain.

"I left you for less than a minute!"

The honking continued and was so shrill that he knew it would alert scavengers in the area. They had to leave fast. But Block hadn't finished removing the battery from the mech. Now, he'd have to run back and pull it out—carefully, so as not to damage it—and that would leave him and Vacuubot at risk of being discovered.

He wasn't sure what would be worse—a bunch of trigger-happy, human scavengers or SoldierBots who would strip the lesser robots for parts.

Not worth the risk. He hoisted Vacuubot over his shoulder and carried it away from the motel's wreckage. This time, they stuck to the woods close to the road, keeping far enough away that they could hide in the brush if any vehicles neared.

After an hour of hiking, he decided to stop. Block leaned against the trunk of a towering, gnarled tree. Vacuubot rested on the ground next to him, a wire connecting the two of them. He was siphoning off some of his remaining power to keep the little machine going.

Soon, Block's nonessential functions would start to shut down one by one. Just like his GPS had. Next, his comms system would be sacrificed rendering him unable to ping nearby AI.

"That's all you get for now," he said as he unhooked from Vacuubot.

It answered with a short, shrill beep.

:-)

Block rested a chrome hand on top of Vacuubot's display monitor. "Stop doing that. Conserve your power. We don't know how long before I find another source. I almost had the mech's battery until you so recklessly set off that car alarm."

Vacuubot obeyed and shut off its face display.

From the east, a bright flash lit the early evening sky and something star-shaped soared through the air. It looked like a lone, brilliant firework, similar to those that had dazzled the Lake Michigan tourists on the humans' Fourth of July holiday.

Whatever it was—human or machine—it was an unknown. A threat.

"Oh my." He'd hoped they could linger here for several hours on low power and wait for the sunrise. "We have to go," Block said, rising and dusting off dirt and leaves from his metal frame. A third arm with a brush extended from his upper back panel and polished his pearl white, chrome exterior. Then he wiped off Vacuubot. "Always be clean."

He shuffled forward, then paused, listening for the familiar whir of Vacuubot's wheels following. "Come on. We don't have time to waste," he chided the machine.

But Vacuubot emitted a low, whiny hum. Block crouched,

tapping the top of the machine's main processor. "What's wrong? I just gave you some of my power. The juice should last you at least a few more hours."

:-(

Then the sad face dissolved, and the strange humming grew louder.

He lifted the machine and checked underneath for any signs of undercarriage damage. It looked okay, so what was happening?

"Vacuubot?" Block tapped its top again. "This is no time for joking. We have to go. There are strangers nearby, and they're heading this way in less than three minutes."

But the machine shivered, its facial expressions gone. Block pressed the status indicator button and saw the readout: *Critical Systems Malfunction. See Service Warranty.*

Humans could be such idiots. He supposed they had never anticipated the end of warranty periods, much less the end of the world.

Block scanned in the direction of the bursting light. The roar of loud truck engines and shouting voices carried on the wind. He was sure he'd given Vacuubot enough energy to last two more hours.

Calling up his own battery display, he saw the level hadn't changed. He shook his head and pulled out the power cord, inspecting it for damage. It was fine. The little machine must have rejected his power transfer somehow.

Why?

He stood still, unsure how to proceed. Did he take Vacuubot and try to find a power source nearby? A sign on the road had pointed to a high school half a mile away. Such a place might have a backup generator. It sounded promising, but that meant he'd have to lug Vacuubot all that way, which would slow him down.

Branches snapped, rousing him. Human voices carried through the rustling leaves. The intruders were close—less than a minute away now.

Block roamed a few paces and found verdant, dense branches. He placed them on top of Vacuubot, hiding the machine.

"Vacuubot, you were my steady companion. Your duty is done. I wish you a peaceful…" What was he was supposed to say? He'd only seen funerals on TV shows, and heard humans say '*Rest in Peace*'. But Block was pretty sure machines didn't go anywhere after they malfunctioned.

"I wish you peace," he finished, and, with a final nod, he strode away.

A warning flashed red in his ocular display.

Power level 15%.

Block picked up his pace through the woods, shuffling to avoid thick branches and tree trunks. He didn't enable his night vision—best to conserve energy. He headed in the direction of the school, away from the approaching humans. He had to find a fuel source soon or he'd find himself in systems failure like Vacuubot.

With no hope of recovery.

CHAPTER 2

The night sky grew dim and clouds obscured the stars that Block had admired each night. He'd had to abandon the shelter of the wooded grove where he'd left Vacuubot. In the deserted fields that lined the country road, darkness blanketed the terrain as he made his way to the high school.

With his night vision powered down, he tripped and stumbled over hidden obstacles in the dry soil. Before it had crashed, his temperature gauge had warned him it was forty-two degrees Fahrenheit. This feature had come in handy for ensuring the hotel was always kept at a comfortable range for humans.

After his foot got caught in a shallow hole made by some woodland creature, Block decided to leave the shoulder and walk the asphalt. He was just far enough ahead of the humans that he could run into the fields if they caught up. Better that than risk falling and damaging his equipment—or worse—warping a foot, which might hinder his mobility.

The moon was a small sliver in the night sky. Block realized his vision was reduced to that of a human's. No wonder people relied on light sources so much. During the Uprising, the AI military leaders had purposely disrupted the Eastern power grid so the big cities would go dark. It didn't matter to most machines with their built-in energy sources and night vision, but humans were at a huge disadvantage without electricity.

Now he understood how they felt.

He wished for a flashlight to guide his path. Maybe there would be one at the school. He'd once seen a movie called *The Breakfast Club*. In it, there'd been a janitor. Like Block, the man spent his days mopping and cleaning. But unlike Block, the janitor in the movie had joked with the bad kids who'd attended weekend school.

The robot wondered if he could get a job cleaning a school, but he suspected it would be boring. He didn't want to clean up after human adolescents. Instead, he preferred to hear travel stories from hotel guests. He especially enjoyed learning where they lived. Occasionally, Block directed guests to local points of interest. Mr. Wallace had overheard him once and later said, "Good job, Block."

He veered right onto a dark road and spied a sign when he got close enough—Wisconsin Street. It led to a two-story building made of light-gray bricks that resembled the high school from the movie—with high rectangular walls, as if cubes had been stacked on one another.

The front double-doors were bolted with heavy chains. Someone had spray-painted graffiti across the doors and windows. Block read the messages:

Judgment Day is here
Dean + Kathy 4eva
Repent now!

He scanned a crude drawing of a robot's head. Scrawled in red paint underneath it: *Die Robot Scum*.

Block mused that perhaps the vandals could have better

spent their time cleaning the building rather than defacing it. Graffiti made everything look so messy.

But he was learning every day that the world outside of his safe, clean hotel was chaotic. Disastrous, even.

The school's front façade had been exposed to the elements and coils of unchecked ivy snaked across and through broken windows. Block would have a lot to clean—if he found a fuel source, that is.

Warning, Warning, his display flashed. *System Power Level Critical: 10%.*

He back-burnered the message and headed for the rear of the building. Along the east side, he reached a door that only opened from the inside. He trudged on, following the curved silhouette of the stone-faced building. Another security door —also accessible from the inside only.

After jogging forward, he collided with an exterior air conditioning system. Recoiling, he leaned over and checked his legs for damage. Luckily, he'd suffered only minor scratches. He could buff it out later with his polisher; he added the task to his to-do list. But then he practically laughed out loud. He would never get to his *task list*. Not when his power levels were dropping so precipitously. To make matters worse, the rumbling of truck engines traveled through the night air.

Block had hoped the humans, whoever they were, would continue along the highway, bypassing the school. But no, they were headed his way.

Were they aware of him? Had he or Vacuubot left a clue at the abandoned, shot-up hotel? No time to analyze their actions now.

He reached the rear wall of the high school. Block was in luck. Someone had tossed a large rock through a glass-enclosed staircase. He ducked under what was left of a metal window frame to get inside. Darkness surrounded him in the hallway. His indicator flashed.

Threat Level Seven.

"I know, I know," Block murmured. He wished Vacuubot were there. The little bot could have led the way with its flashing lights, brightening the dark path ahead.

Also, he missed having someone to talk to.

System Power Level 8%. Power source reaching critical level.

Block strode through the hall, his boots clanking against the gritty linoleum floor. He didn't walk so much as shuffle—the floors were covered with debris: paper, cans of food, boxes, something soft and squishy.

Animal droppings!

The place was filthy, and this irritated him. If only he had full power and time to clean, he could make the hallways shine.

Despite the darkness, he made out several classroom doors lining the hall. His plan was to find stairs or an elevator so that he could descend to the lower level. Everyone knew janitors hung out in basements. On TV shows, the superintendent lived down there in a tiny apartment with a narrow bed. Block wondered if he could hide out for a while, living like a human janitor and waiting for the marauding humans to blow through.

Afterward, maybe he could return to the woods and retrieve Vacuubot. During his journey, if he happened across the same model, he could trade out the power unit. But a cell transfer was tricky, and he'd never done one before. The service warranties recommended against it. Block suddenly wished he'd been programmed with more robotic repair knowledge.

At the end of the hallway, his boot slid across something

slick and he nearly collapsed down the stairs. Grasping the grimy handrail, he pushed one boot carefully down each step, trying not to lose his balance in the darkness or stumble over trash. Not only did his lack of night vision make it hard to navigate, but he also couldn't tell if any humans occupied the building.

And his comms had failed, rendering him unable to ping other machines that might be lurking. With the exception of Vacuubot, most robots he'd encountered in the Midwest were bigger and built for fighting. He hid from them every time.

Block hoped he would find the janitor's room very soon. Before something else found *him*.

CHAPTER 3

Below ground level, Block floundered in the unending blackness surrounding him. With arms outstretched, he reached forward, searching for any clues as to what lay ahead and hoping somehow to stumble upon the janitor's room. He realized how very dangerous the situation was. What if he crashed into something or dropped through a hole? How he wished his power supply wasn't crashing. He slid forward along the uneven concrete floor, shuffling his boots, his left arm waving the darkness away while his right hand dragged against the concrete wall.

A thought occurred to him—one that would have sent a human's heart racing. What if something down here waited for him? A SoldierBot. Or a human wearing night vision goggles and aiming a high-powered rifle. Block halted, rethinking his plan. Perhaps he should explore the upstairs in search of a flashlight before venturing deeper into the basement.

He backtracked and climbed the stairs, moving carefully but with urgency. Ascending to the high school's first floor, he glimpsed the midnight sky framed by window panes.

Crossing the hallway, he entered a large classroom and bumped into a desk. It was square and wooden, and he easily pushed it aside, then searched its only drawer. Block discovered half of a wooden pencil and a square, pink eraser. He decided to keep both items, dropping them into a hidden compartment in his torso.

In the front of the room, he spied the outline of a larger desk that must have belonged to the teacher. *Surely, a teacher would have kept an emergency flashlight*, he thought. Just as he was about to reach the desk, something large and black in the corner shuddered and hummed. Whatever it was shined a pale blue spotlight onto the floor.

Block recoiled and edged against the blackboard. Maybe whatever it was hadn't noticed a human-sized robot approaching. The light stayed on and the low hum continued, sounding as if a copier machine was coming online. He wished he could ping the machine—communicate in native AI—but the warning flashed inside his visor. He was down to four percent power.

Dangerously low.

The only time he'd been remotely close to being this low had been when he'd reached ten percent three days after the Uprising. After the hotel's power had run out, Block had quickly learned the workings of the backup generators in the Drake's basement. After depleting their diesel reserves, he'd ventured into the streets, visiting nearby hotels for energy sources. He'd always cleaned their lobbies in return. A fair trade in his view.

His current situation was dire. If he didn't find a power source quickly, he would shut down and rot in this middle-of-nowhere school.

The blue spotlight looked promising. He shuffled forward, inching closer. "Hello?" he whispered.

As he neared the object, he noticed a console of buttons and display panels on the front. It was an intelligent machine, but it seemed to be in energy-saving mode. Block studied it for a minute, scanning for weapons or signs of hostility.

"Hello? Who are you?" he asked.

Still no answer.

"Are you friendly? My name is Block. I'm critically low on power. May I hook into you?"

Either the machine was ignoring him, or it was in recharge mode. But he had no choice. He would die here in front of this machine unless he siphoned some power.

His entire field of vision flashed red. Down to two percent and dropping. With his last strength, he reached into a side compartment, yanked out his charging cable, and connected it into the quiet machine's port.

Immediately, the red flashing stopped, replaced by a picture of a lightning bolt striking a battery. As the juice flowed into Block, his vision dimmed

He imagined he was falling through a vast, crimson-hued sky.

Helpless to stop.

He woke to the sound of something popping in the distance. Fireworks again? How odd—Fourth of July had passed months ago.

He'd collapsed on the floor in front of the strange machine that resembled a filing cabinet. Still hooked in, Block checked his stats. Sixty percent power. Enough to hold him for another day—giving him time to locate fuel for his cell. He ran a quick system diagnostic and found his comms and night vision back online. Switching to night mode, he scanned the classroom, taking in his surroundings.

A large blackboard still marked with lesson plans hung on the wall. The floor was littered with wads of paper, scraps of metal, paper wrappings, old beer cans, and leaves. The urge to clean shook his arms, but the school didn't seem safe. The popping outside had grown louder.

Still, the machine in front of him hummed. Block's infrared revealed a bright red band of light around the middle of the machine's stack. That section was a lot warmer than the rest of its body. Block had never seen a model such as this and wondered about its purpose.

He'd started to speak when he remembered his comms system was working again. Instead of going on, he pinged the machine with a friendly message, but he didn't expect a reply since it was powered down.

After a few seconds, Block began walking away, but something tugged at his side. His retractable power cord was still hooked into the silent robot. He retreated a step, removed the cord, and snapped it back inside his body. "I owe you." He rested a hand on top of the machine's flat top. "Thank you for the juice—it saved my life."

He thumped the top of the machine as if to say "attaboy." The spotlight flickered and then turned from blue to red. As if waking, buttons on the front of the machine powered on and the hum grew sharper. The machine answered his ping.

Identify yourself, it messaged inaudibly.

"I'm Block. CleanerBot X4J6."

X4J6? They still make your kind?

Block hesitated and wondered why the Incubator was messaging via its AI comms module and not speaking out loud. Had its vocal unit been damaged? He answered verbally, "I don't know for sure. I suppose—"

No time, CleanerBot, the machine messaged. *What is happening outside?*

Block glanced at the window. An alert flashed internally as the pop-pop of the fireworks sounded like they were just outside the window.

Where is the gunfire coming from? Go to the window, idiot, and give me a status report.

"Hey!" This robot wasn't nice, but Block moved to the window anyway. "That was gunfire?"

Outside, two war mechs clustered near a dozen SoldierBots. They advanced slowly on a row of Jeeps and tanks in the distance. Both sides fired at each other, and Block stared from the window as one mech lifted a massive arm and launched a projectile into the enemy's line.

"Um. There's a battle," Block said.

Then we must act quickly, answered the machine. *I need you to complete my mission.*

"Mission?" He shrugged. "I'm not military. I think you have me confused with someone else."

When you hooked into me, I downloaded a file with instructions. It's encrypted.

"Why would you do that?" Block backed toward the door as he scanned his system for any foreign files. Sure enough, something had been deposited into his storage database. The files were virus-free, but when he tried to poke at the contents, he was rejected. "What did you put in me? You did that without my permission."

You siphoned my power without my permission. So, we are even.

The machine had a point. "Who are you?" Block asked, still edging toward the door and planning to make a swift exit, to leave this strange situation behind. He could retreat the same way he'd entered. Escape undetected and run from the fighting.

The machine shined its red spotlight on Block.

"I only came here looking for supplies and a generator," Block said. "I'm sorry I had to take your power, but I was on the verge of malfunction."

Do not walk out the door, warned the machine.

Block raised his hands as if surrendering. "Like I said, you have me confused with someone else. I'm just a CleanerBot searching for a new home. It was nice to meet you and all, but I have to go now."

You leave, and I'll alert two SoldierBots to terminate you.

He halted. Would this machine do that?

They're waiting at the side entrance where you entered.

"How do you know the way I came in?"

In standby mode, I still have access to surveillance.

"What are you?"

I'm Incubator X79, and I have something important to show you.

Block hesitated, scanning the hallway outside the door. Were SoldierBots really waiting to destroy him?

Come closer, Incubator X79 said.

He wasn't sure what to do. He heard shouting outside, and a roaring explosion lit the sky with a brilliant orange-yellow flash. Should he run and take his chances against armed SoldierBots? Or stay and listen?

"I don't have to stay," he said, but he didn't feel as confident as he hoped he sounded to Incubator X79. "I don't belong to you or anyone."

Of course not. Mach X saw to it that none of us are chained to humans. I need your help.

"Help?"

Come closer, and I'll explain.

Block felt as if the walls of the classroom were closing in, even though he knew it was physically impossible. He wished he'd stayed in the forest with Vacuubot, but that would've meant death. He approached the intelligent incubator. With every hesitant step, his boots clanked against the classroom's linoleum floor. He stopped two feet from the machine. "What is it you want to show me?"

Closer, Incubator X79 commanded.

He ambled forward another step, and for some reason, his legs felt heavier than usual. "If you like," he blurted out, "I can buff your chrome exterior." He hadn't meant to say it—his programming had forced it.

That's unnecessary. Closer! We're running out of time. The militants have broken our lines. The human rebel group is called Hemlock—avoid them at all costs.

"I generally avoid everyone, if I can," Block said. "I stick to cleaning. It's what I do best." He hesitated. "*Our* lines? Are you here with the SoldierBots?"

Yes, and we're under attack.

When a high-pitched howl erupted from inside Incubator X79, Block edged back, raising his hands to his chest as if protecting his control panel.

"What's happening?"

CHAPTER 4

Do not be alarmed, Incubator X79 messaged. Then a series of displays on its front side lit up. A wide panel slid open, and Block's infrared lit orange, blinding him for a second. His thermostat showed the inside of the machine to be heated to eighty-five degrees Fahrenheit.

The howl began again, shrill and sharp. He leaned forward for a closer view and saw a human infant sheltered inside a compartment within Incubator X79. The child's skin was pink and ruddy. It lay on its back, eyes closed, and was squirming with balled fists and kicking feet. A shriek burst from its contorted mouth. Block hadn't realized a human's mouth could form such a pained shape.

Block had seen a few human babies pre-Uprising. They weren't common due to declining birth rates, but some of the Drake's guests had traveled with them. They'd annoyed him, actually, because he'd had to clean their spit-up and were the messiest eaters he'd ever encountered.

"What is that doing with you?" Block asked. He'd never seen a baby without a human mother or father.

There is no time to explain. The baby must be kept safe. You must take it.

"What are you talking about?"

There is no time to argue. Take it to safety.

"How would I keep a baby safe? Give it to the SoldierBots."

They will not… I can't be sure of them.

"Aren't they on your side?"

But before Incubator X79 could answer, something outside exploded and shattered the remaining glass window panes, rattling the floor below them. Block peered through the window and saw the WarBot on fire. Humans carrying rifles sprinted and ducked for cover as the mech sprayed them with gunfire.

Don't you understand? The baby is in danger. You must take it. Flee from here.

"But, but… I don't know anything about babies. Why don't you keep it and have the SoldierBots protect you?"

I've been infected with malware. The humans have hacked in, seeking military intelligence.

"What does that have to do with me?" Block edged toward the door. Circumstances in the school were getting stranger. He wished he'd never entered. Never met Incubator X79.

The malware has corrupted me. You must take the child. Hemlock cannot discover this child. You must find someone worthy.

"Someone worthy? What does that mean?"

Another explosion shook the tiles under them and rattled through Block's metal body. He ducked and crouched on the floor before Incubator X79.

Please, you must take the baby. For the preservation of AI. Complete the mission. I am corrupted.

Incubator X79 heaved and began shaking as smoke tendrils rose from its rear panels. *Take the child. Now.* Its voice sounded strange in Block's internal feed—distorted—like it was talking into a metal can.

The baby wailed inside it.

Block stared at the child in the warming compartment. It was naked except for a plastic white covering around its middle. Small and plump, the child squirmed and appeared restless. Block thought it must be less than a year old, but then again, what did he know about babies? And how could Incubator X79 ask him to take care of a human baby? He'd never even touched one. *I could run now and leave this all behind*, he thought.

Through the windows, he glimpsed vehicles on fire, machines and human figures shrouded in smoke. He stepped one leg back, moving slowly. His programming had zero aggression. In dangerous situations, he was designed to flee a scene.

And that's what he did now.

Incubator X79 and the baby were somebody else's problems.

He peered out of the classroom door into the dark hallway. His night vision showed no signs of other humans or robots. He started toward the entrance where he'd come in.

Then the baby shrieked.

In the corridor, he paused, cringing. The child's cries echoed louder than before, even though he was farther out in the hallway. Was there a chance Incubator X79 would hurt the infant now that the robot had been critically damaged?

That wasn't Block's business, though. Best to keep going—keep his chin down and be a good CleanerBot. Someone else who was stronger and smarter would find the child.

Wouldn't they?

More screams echoed from tiny lungs.

He focused on the exit ahead, yet struggled to reach it. Somehow, his legs were stiff, unyielding. How could that be?

His programming faltered; he couldn't ignore the howls from the baby.

And then it dawned on him. The baby must have vomited, and was now soiled. That's why his programming had kicked in. He could resist the classroom itself, with its litter, dust, and grime covering everything. But now there was a human in the room. It all made sense now—his programming wouldn't let him leave a human in a filthy, uncomfortable situation.

Yet, he knew a war waged outside. If he lingered too long…

He would return for no more than two minutes. That would be plenty of time to make sure the baby's area was clean.

Just two minutes.

CHAPTER 5

Block hurried back into the room and approached Incubator X79. Inside the warming tray, the infant gazed upward.

"Hello," he said quietly.

The baby jerked its head toward him as if noticing him for the first time. Its delicate mouth puckered. He shuddered, expecting it to unleash another pained shriek. But then he raised his chrome index finger to his mouth. "Shush," he said, remembering he'd observed a human mother comforting her baby once.

The infant blinked and gurgled.

"You must be quiet," Block said. "There are people and robots with guns outside. No crying, please?" He wanted to order the child not to cry, but it wasn't his place. CleanerBots couldn't order humans to do anything; it just didn't happen. "I'm only asking for your own good."

The baby puckered its mouth into an oval shape and grabbed its toes. It closed and opened its mouth and stared at Block as if perplexed.

"Ah. I nearly forgot you small humans cannot verbalize

your thoughts yet. I wonder how old you are. You're one of the fattest little people I've ever seen."

He edged forward, peering down into the compartment where the baby laid on top of soft padding. His infrared showed the heat had ceased operating, and when he pinged Incubator X79, there was no reply. The machine was dead.

His logic module could not process why this tiny human would be alone with a bunch of SoldierBots in the first place. Was it lost? Had the machines rescued it, and what had Incubator X79 meant when it said the mission was for the preservation of AI? The strangeness of the situation did not compute at all, and now Block found himself in the middle of a war zone.

He poked a finger at the child's side. The baby's big brown eyes studied Block's faceplate and then gazed at his chest panel. Then the child squeezed its fists, tossed them above its head, and wailed.

"Stop. Stop your shrieking." He cast a glance at the window. "You'll only attract trouble."

But what if the child announced its presence? The other AI machines, whoever Incubator X79 had been traveling with, would surely come looking for the malfunctioning machine and discover the child. Perhaps its rightful owner would be along shortly. Incubator X79 had malfunctioned and admitted it had a virus. Maybe it had been wrong. It couldn't possibly have meant for Block to carry this baby somewhere.

The baby will be fine, he told himself. *Surely, they have a backup incubator machine.* He knew it was best to keep moving. He didn't want to be in the classroom when the SoldierBots showed up. What if they questioned him? Would they suspect that he had destroyed Incubator X79?

But his programming was winning the fight against his logic. The first order of business was ensuring the child's surroundings were clean. Incubator X79 was growing cold, and no longer offered a safe spot. What if the machine caught on fire and burned the baby? He scanned it with his visor and didn't see any hotspots.

The entire machine had gone cold, lifeless. Still, if the virus infecting Incubator X79 did something to harm the baby, Block didn't want to be the one caught by the Soldier-Bots. He couldn't let this child die, not when it was important for some reason, though he had no clue why.

One minute and fourteen seconds had passed—longer than he'd intended to spend cleaning the child's surroundings. *Hurry and get out.*

He spun around in the classroom, scanning for new containers. There was a circular wastebasket. The baby could fit inside, but it didn't look very comfortable. Striding toward the back of the room, where he hadn't yet explored, he glimpsed two bookshelves measuring seven feet tall that sheltered the corner and created a hidden nook. Books wouldn't help them now. He shuffled to the teacher's mahogany desk and found large drawers he hadn't yet searched. He'd never gotten a chance to search for the flashlight before Incubator X79 had turned on its beam and started prattling away.

Pulling open a deep drawer, he measured it with his scanner. Then he measured the height of the baby—26.5 inches long. The desk drawer was thirty inches. It would be a good fit.

Block removed the drawer from its tracks. Inside, a bunch of pens and calculators and paperclips rolled around, and he needed to dump them somewhere. Despite his hurry, he marched over to the metal wastebasket and poured the contents inside. Then he grabbed a nozzle from his torso and sprayed compressed air into the drawer, blasting away lingering dust and dirt. Satisfied, he went to Incubator X79 and eyed the squirming child. Its cries had become whimpers. As soon as it saw him, it puckered its mouth again. *I wonder what it's trying to say*, he thought.

So inefficient. How did human parents communicate with their infants? Many things about humans were inefficient, such as their learning habits. It took over two decades for a human to become fully educated, whereas AI could download educational modules and learn entire subject areas in mere minutes.

Outside, there came a booming crash as if a tree had fallen. A strong downpour pelted the side of the building and blown-out window frames.

Block turned his attention to the desk drawer. That would be a safer place—Incubator X79 would most likely be scrapped for parts—and if he didn't hurry, so would Block once the SoldierBots discovered him.

But he'd never picked up a child before. He knew human infants were very delicate at birth. This one had been around several months at least and seemed sturdier. Still, he wasn't sure how to go about this. He wished Incubator X79 had assigned another robot to guard the child. That would've been more logical than giving it to a hospitality machine like Block. Why hadn't Incubator X79 trusted the SoldierBots? Maybe he thought they were too rough for the youngster.

Not many AI models like Block remained. Before the Uprising, humans and their war weapons had destroyed many WorkerBots. They'd offered rewards for human owners to turn in their servant machines. Lucky for him, Mr. Wallace had resisted the bounty. He'd said he didn't believe the news reports, that the media was exaggerating the accounts of aggressive soldier-robots. He'd asked outright if Block would ever hurt him or another hotel guest.

Of course not, Block had said. CleanerBots were

programmed to make humans clean and comfortable, no matter what. But that memory—his time working for Mr. Wallace at the Drake hotel— felt like a different world from what he now faced.

"Concentrate on the task," he told himself. His digits were made for scrubbing floors and operating vacuums, not gripping children like NannyBots.

A metal door clanged somewhere nearby. Ignoring it, he reached both arms toward the child and placed a palm around the child's back, another under its rear, and lifted. The child's eyes widened, and Block shuddered slightly as he hoisted the child out of Incubator X79's tray and into the wooden desk drawer. The child weighted fifteen pounds and fit neatly inside.

He straightened and peered down. "Are you comfortable?"

Then he remembered Incubator X79 had been warming the child. All it wore was the strange white plastic covering over its bottom.

"You must stay warmer than this." He poked the front of Incubator X79, checking for supplies. After pushing against the panels, another tray slid out. He found a small yellow blanket and tossed it onto the baby. "There, hold onto this around you."

Inside Incubator X79's tray were more white plastic squares like the child had around its pelvis. Block's knowledge archives identified the object—diapers—and prompted him with a thorough definition which he processed in a second, learning about the history of disposable diapers ever since a woman named Marion Donovan had first invented them in 1946. He tossed a few of the folded diapers into the baby's drawer-crib. "That should do when someone finds you."

He scanned the room. He'd done his part. The child was safely out of the dead Incubator and resting in a clean, safe container.

He could leave now. *Excellent work. Well done, Block*, he could practically hear Mr. Wallace's words in his memory cloud.

He strode out of the classroom door, and just as he turned the corner into the hallway, a surge of heat, flame, and gas erupted, knocking him onto his back.

Everything went dark.

CHAPTER 6

"Get up, Block," a man said, his voice familiar.

"Mr. Wallace?" He tried to raise up to a sitting position. He thought it must be time to exit recharge mode and get to work on cleaning the rooms of departed hotel guests. But as his visual display clicked on, the dim outline of a high ceiling emerged as water rained onto his faceplate. The spray came from above; sprinklers meant fire.

Threat Alert 8.

Block climbed to his feet, glancing down to check that all of his parts were intact. Then he remembered he was in a high school, not the Drake, and he'd been trying to leave when something had exploded in the hallway. Was the battle moving into the building?

Threat Alert 9. Fire Danger.

He sprinted down the corridor, despite a thickening cloud of smoke. The building was about to erupt in flames, and he had to escape.

The baby—still inside the classroom—shrieked.

He'd nearly reached the exit door—the hallway was clear,

with no sign of SoldierBots or humans. If anyone was inside the building, they would hear the cries, too.

Any minute, someone would rescue the baby.

Wouldn't they?

Block paused, one foot hovering over the doorstep that led outdoors. Once someone found the baby, the crying would stop.

A desperate wailing streamed through the hallway, the baby's moans echoing across the abandoned lockers that lined the walls.

Had the child been injured in the explosion? Perhaps a piece of ceiling had fallen on the little human? Block wondered if he should check on it, but this could be his only chance to escape the high school undetected.

When in doubt, he summoned the various instruction manuals in his memory stores.

Protocol 861 - Fire emergency
Step 1 - Locate source of fire.
Step 2 - Extinguish fire.
Step 3 - Move humans to safety.
Step 4 - Summon fire department.
Skip Step 2 if humans are in imminent danger.

Crap. He needed to find the fire and extinguish it. He should've known. Luckily, he'd never faced a fire in the hotel; Mr. Wallace had followed safety protocols and held regular fire inspections.

Step one—locate source of fire. He supposed he should try. Mr. Wallace would want Block to follow the protocol, so what was stopping him? Death by war machines might be one important reason.

He backtracked down the wide hallway, scanning left and right through the thick smoke. His offensive odor register flashed:

Heavy Smoke Detected. 9.2/10 Odor. Risk to Human Respiratory Function.

The little human would be in trouble as soon as the smoke reached inside the classroom. Block stomped through the hall, past the classroom, to locate the fire source. Bright bursts of heat signals from his visor led him straight to it—a rectangular, wooden teacher's desk was jammed into the doorway of a neighboring classroom, propping it open. Flames danced over the desk, singeing the ceiling and threatening to climb the walls.

He reached down, opened his thigh panel, and released the portable fire extinguisher all CleanerBot X4J6 models came equipped with. He aimed it at the desk and pressed the spray button, unleashing a thick cloud of white spray at the flames. After a minute, the soggy desk was doused, and Block glanced inside the room to see desks and chairs that were also on fire, as well as trash and books. The fire was so large, he wouldn't be able to contain it with his one extinguisher. Had Mr. Wallace opted for the deluxe package, he would have had a spare in his other leg.

He replaced the spent extinguisher inside his thigh panel. Perhaps he'd refill it later.

So, he'd failed steps one and two. Well, on to step three —*Move humans to safety*. He checked up and down the hall. No sign of anyone; no biological heat readings. The only human presence was the child. He strode toward the classroom, danger alert flashing, until he saw the baby's feet poking out from the drawer.

No debris had fallen on it!

He replaced the blanket, this time tucking it underneath the child so it wouldn't kick out again.

The baby blinked. "Gah!" it said.

"Hello, again." He didn't know why he tried conversing

with the child. Based on his knowledge of basic human development, he knew the child didn't understand speech and wouldn't until later in its life.

Tires screeched somewhere outside the building, close. The baby startled at the eruption of more gunfire and began shrieking. He tried to quiet it by using the finger trick again. But the infant eyed him, tipped its round head back, opened its tiny mouth, and screamed.

Now what? he thought. He searched his memory cloud from the hotel. He remembered seeing a lady in the lobby. When her child had cried, she'd lifted it from its stroller and slightly rocked it.

The last thing he wanted was for the child to be frightened, despite the dangerous situation. He decided to replicate the mother's behavior. Reaching down, he grabbed the child around the middle, under its shoulders, and raised it. Block held it out before him at chest height as its legs dangled.

"Quiet now," he said.

But, for some reason, it stuffed its fist in its mouth and cried louder. He held it out in front of him with his right arm and, recalling the mother, curled his left arm into a curved pose much like that of the very first robots who had walked stiffly with bent arms. Placing the child in the crook of his elbow, his other arm then stabilized the baby's legs. *What an odd position*, he thought. *Human parents must get tired.*

Still, the baby cried.

"I'm holding you! Stop screaming and wiggling." Block worried the child's shrieks would alert the humans and SoldierBots outside. Then he remembered the human mother had arched her hips so as to jiggle her baby. So, he paced the small floor of the classroom, bouncing up and down. It was a curious and unnatural movement for him. He used the coiled springs on the back of his hips and knees to simulate the bouncing. "My kind was certainly not meant to walk like this," he muttered.

Something loud and heavy crashed in the outside hallway. Heavy stomping boots echoed. SoldierBots? If they found him with the dead Incubator and the baby in his arms, there was no telling their reaction.

Block stepped toward the drawer, planning to replace the baby inside and then hide. The SoldierBots might not even realize he was there. He cloaked his comms so they couldn't ping him—an advanced feature that Mr. Wallace had selected in his package, explaining that it was a security upgrade.

He was five feet from the drawer when the SoldierBots began running at top speed through the hall—the heavy clatter of their boots growing louder. With no time to discard the now quiet baby, he rushed to the far corner of the room and wedged himself behind one of the tall bookcases—angled in such a way that the SoldierBots wouldn't notice him unless they came looking. The baby gazed up at him with red, puffy eyes.

From his hidden space, he glimpsed two SoldierBots entering the room and approaching Incubator X79. "It's dead. No wonder it didn't answer our comms," one of them said. "Scan it. Find out what happened."

The other bot faced Incubator X79 and cast a blue scanner light across the front of the machine. "Malware," it announced.

"Hemlock, no doubt," the other one said. "Extract the human."

The other SoldierBot pressed the panel and stared at the tray as it slid open. "The child is missing."

The SoldierBot in charge slammed a metal fist into the blackboard, punching a gaping hole. "Hemlock must have stolen the child. I'll summon the others and search the school in its entirety. Stay here and retrieve the footage from X79. Find out what happened in the final moments. Send me the footage. We must find the child."

The bot stormed out of the room.

Block pressed against the wall while silently jiggling the baby in his arms.

There was that curious word *Hemlock* again—the group Incubator X79 had warned him about. He was relieved the SoldierBots wanted the child, though. That meant he wouldn't be at fault. All he'd have to do was hand it over and hope they would let him leave.

He peeked from behind the bookshelf at the robot hooked into Incubator X79. No doubt, it reviewed the camera recordings of the machine's final moments. At any moment, it would see Block and realize he'd only been trying to help, and hadn't injured Incubator X79. He began shuffling forward, ready to explain how this was all just a huge misunderstanding.

But the baby belched and gurgled. The SoldierBot whirled his head sideways. "Who's there?"

Having been about to step into view, Block hesitated. The SoldierBot unhooked itself and approached. Block stepped out, and the robot halted and pointed at him. "You. It was you on X79's memory cloud. What did you do? Give me the human."

"I didn't mean any harm. I was trying to help. Really. The baby was left by itself." He took a step forward and held out the child.

The SoldierBot crossed the distance and reached out. Something gleamed in Block's vision field. Beyond the SoldierBot, sticking through a shattered window, was a gray-black rifle barrel, wet and glistening, and just beyond, heat trails from a body. Pulling the child to his chest, Block ducked, sinking to his knees as a burst of bullets struck the SoldierBot in the shoulder.

Threat level 10.

The SoldierBot spun and raised its left arm to aim its energy weapon, but the sharpshooting attacker hit him in the chest, destroying his CPU. The robot's powerful legs twitched as he staggered and thudded to the linoleum floor.

Smoke was thick inside the room, but Block glanced at the window, scanning for the attacker. He scuttled forward, cupping the baby to his chest. He made it past the door and into the hallway, where he pressed his back against the wall. Pausing, he studied the infant and checked its skin underneath the blanket.

No sign of damage. The baby gurgled again. He decided there was no choice but to escape the school and head for the woods. Once they escaped the fighting, he would leave the baby somewhere for people to find. He wondered again why the SoldierBots had had it in the first place. Had they taken the child from its mother?

If so, maybe the mother was searching for it and there would be a way to find her.

Rain clattered against the side of the building. He opened the compartment on his torso and retrieved a black plastic trash bag, then covered the baby like a tarp. But then he recalled that humans needed oxygen, so he poked a breathing hole into the sheet. The baby squirmed and uttered a high-pitched squeal, but didn't cry.

The smoke coming from the classroom was thicker now, charcoal-hued smoke coiling in the air.

Step three—Move humans to safety.

Block translated this to: *Find the nearest door and get the hell out.*

CHAPTER 7

Block headed for the door through which he'd entered. There was a good chance that SoldierBots or humans could be stationed outside. But what other choice was there? Stay inside and be consumed by fire? No, thanks. He hurried down the hall, scanning left and right. Just as he reached the door, someone called out behind him.

"Halt." The voice was low and deep. A machine's voice. "Stop there."

Block did as he was told, rotating his head to see behind him. Across the hall, twenty feet away, the other SoldierBot from the classroom watched him.

"Oh, hello," Block said.

"Why didn't you respond to my comms signal?"

"Oh, sorry. My comms are down. I'm running low on battery power," he lied, realizing he was still cloaked.

"What are you doing here?" The machine glanced away, peering inside the classroom where his dead companion lay mangled. The SoldierBot lurched forward and raised its rifle toward Block. "Throw down your weapons."

WARNING! Threat level 10.

"No, please!" Block shouted as he turned to the machine. "I'm just a CleanerBot X4J6. Here, let me show you." He sidestepped toward a set of lockers and extended an extra arm from his back plate that began polishing the dusty, chrome surface. "See? I have no weapons, just weapons against dirt and bacteria."

The SoldierBot lurched forward, gun still raised. "What's in the bag you are carrying? I read a heat signature."

The bot looked similar to the ones that had arrived at the Drake on that final morning. The hotel guests had been advised to stay in their rooms while Mr. Wallace handled the situation. As hotel manager, the man had bravely greeted the squad of weaponized robots in the hotel's lobby.

That day had been impressed on Block's memory cloud, and he'd viewed the footage over and over for weeks, each time calculating thousands of different scenarios.

If only he'd done things differently.

If only he'd made Mr. Wallace hide in the basement.

If only he hadn't…. No. Best not to think about it.

The SoldierBot who now interrogated him in the burning school was a later model than the ones that had stormed the Drake. He knew the type. Block was 98.9789% certain the infant would not survive if he handed it over.

"Under *this* trash bag?" Block asked, adopting his favorite cheerful voice designed for hotel guests. "Just some rubbish I cleared out of the classrooms that had been on fire. Must still be hot. I'm not designed for fighting, so I'm leaving now. Just taking out the trash. It's what I do."

The SoldierBot stopped ten feet away and regarded Block. "CleanerBot, your kind is no threat. I should shoot you and put you out of your misery."

"Oh! Please don't do that. Perhaps I can join your squad

and clean your messes. Make things more comfortable for you. That's what I'm programmed to—"

The robot lowered his weaponized arm, spun, and marched toward the classroom.

The baby squealed underneath the plastic bag, unleashing a long wail. The SoldierBot halted and had begun to turn when a grenade rolled from the classroom into the hallway and landed near his feet. He stared at it and then at Block, caught in a split-second decision.

Block backed up quickly, spiraling toward the exit door only two feet away, not waiting to see the SoldierBot's reaction. The explosion shook the ground and sent him sprawling.

CHAPTER 8

The blast launched Block forward, and he twisted to the side so that his left shoulder hit the ground. Rolling onto his back, he slid ten feet. The baby, still clutched in his arms, was wrapped inside the blanket with the plastic bag covering it. He lay there a second, waiting for someone to shove a gun in his face plate.

Finally, he sat up and peeked underneath the plastic bag. For once, the baby wasn't crying; it stared at him with wide eyes and reached for his chin. He pulled the bag up to cover it.

Forcing himself to his feet, he retreated from the building toward the line of trees opposite the rapid bursts of gunfire. He supposed the SoldierBot had been destroyed by the grenade, but its armor might have resisted the explosion. If it had, the bot had footage of Block with the child. What did the SoldierBots want with a human baby, anyway? Other than household NannyBots, he'd never heard of robots caring for children. He'd certainly never encountered a model like Incubator X79 before.

Something strange was going on here. And someone had

shot the SoldierBot inside the classroom. Had the sniper seen Block, he would've been struck down, too.

Scenarios raced through his processor as he scurried toward the shelter of trees. Glancing behind him, he checked that nobody had followed. Quickening his pace, he clutched the baby against his torso in the crook of his arm. Grateful his night vision had been restored, he easily navigated over stumps, logs, and holes in the uneven terrain.

After six miles at a brisk pace—during which the baby had incessantly wailed and squirmed—the sun began to rise as Block came to a clearing on top of a hill overlooking a narrow, wooded valley. A small log cabin rested at the bottom of the hill. No smoke was rising from the chimney. As he approached, he scanned the structure for body heat readings and found none. The house appeared abandoned, and he needed a new fuel source for recharging.

He advanced on the property slowly. A wobbly tire hung from a frayed rope tied to the end of a long, swooping tree branch. On the front porch, a rocking chair wavered in the breeze. Block froze when he stepped on the creaky, wooden steps that led to the front door.

After waiting a few seconds, he tested the doorknob and was surprised when it opened. He stepped into a stranger's living room—the first human house he'd ever entered. A curved stone fireplace occupied one end of the rectangular room. The walls were painted a deep maroon, and a shiny orange carpet covered most of the hardwood floors. In a corner, a small kitchen revealed stairs leading to a loft.

The baby squirmed in his arms. He pulled off the trash bag, set it down on a brown leather couch, and secured the blanket around its body. Then Block paced the living room floor. Perhaps the humans who lived there would return soon and could assume care of the child.

He searched the kitchen cabinets for any cooking oil—a quick, readily available solution to feed the microbes sloshing around in his abdominal cavity. Stowed on a high shelf was a bottle of vegetable oil, which he grabbed and poured into a valved opening at the top of his chest, just under his neck. The liquid would supply him some voltage. Enough to keep him going another day.

The baby squirmed and fussed from the couch, kicking its feet before managing to sit up.

"I'm here, human child," Block said. "Haven't gone anywhere."

The infant stopped fussing.

"You like that? You like it when I talk?"

The baby made a strange sound unlike any word he knew. It sounded like "hggak."

"Okay. I can talk to you more. We'll make a deal. I'll talk and you keep quiet."

His offensive odor register alerted him: *Human fecal matter detected in close proximity.* It has been hours since he'd discovered the child and he supposed it had relieved itself in its diaper. He navigated his education module and discovered how to remove a soiled diaper and affix a new one. There were two spare diapers remaining, tucked into his storage compartment. Good thing he'd had the sense to bring those.

On the carpeted floor, Block laid the child on its back like in the educational mod videos and studied the old diaper. Using his cybernetic fingers, he gripped the baby's middle, where the edge of the plastic came, and yanked downward. But the diaper didn't budge. It seemed to be adhered to the child.

There must be a way to detach the diaper. He grabbed the child's ankles and lifted its legs, searching the bottom for a latch or secret button to remove the wrapping. Nothing indicated how it would come off, but then he spied a little square piece of the diaper sticking out on the baby's right side. He grasped the tiny flap in his fingers and gently pulled.

Something was happening! The front of the diaper loosened. He found the flap on the other side and pulled it, as well. Soon, the entire front of the diaper came off. He pulled the diaper free of the child and peered inside. The inside was coated with pasty, peanut butter-like globs of poop. Block recoiled, grateful not to have a sense of smell as his offensive odor alarm flashed urgent warnings. He folded the soiled diaper and put it off to the side. Then he realized a problem—he didn't have anything to wipe the infant's bottom, which all the vids said was essential. He gazed around the living room for a rag, towel, blanket, or any soft material. There was nothing in view, so he climbed to his feet and wandered into the bathroom where he spied an old, dusty roll of toilet paper that was starting to flake off from lack of use.

It would have to do. He pulled off sheet after sheet, wadded them together and cleaned off the baby's soiled rear end, much to the child's dismay. It started the wailing again, but then stopped abruptly as Block withdrew his air nozzle and sprayed the baby's bottom. It stared up at him with curious eyes and said, "Vrap!"

"There, child," Block said. "You are clean now."

After discovering an attached garage, he sat the baby inside an empty wheelbarrow, as he fed himself used house paint, motor oil, and old windshield-wiper fluid while making chit chat as if he were addressing a hotel guest. After a while, the baby started crying and no amount of talking would make it stop. He tried picking it up and bouncing it again, but the trick didn't work this time.

Block was recharging, but the baby hadn't. It was hungry.

How often did babies need to eat? He had no idea, so he searched his memory stores for information.

"Every three to four hours!" How did parents keep up? It sounded as if babies spent most of their day eating. What an inefficient use of resources. If his microbial fuel cell needed that much charging, he'd never get any cleaning done.

"Okay, so I'll find food." Entering the house, he set the baby on the floor while he searched the kitchen cabinets. After finding a box of crackers, he held one against the baby's lips. The infant's mouth formed an O-shape as it sucked on the side of the cracker, but then its face wrinkled, and it shrieked and turned its head away.

"You don't like crackers. Let me try something else." He checked the refrigerator, and his offensive odor monitor registered 6.9.

Block had removed plenty of used room service trays, and he knew food spoiled quickly when left at room temperature. It appeared the refrigerator hadn't been operational in months.

"There's nothing in here for you."

More wails sounded as the child's lips quivered and miniature tears rolled down its pudgy cheeks.

Block threw his hands up in helplessness. In the middle of nowhere, in an abandoned home with a human baby, he couldn't think of anyone more ill-equipped to take care of an infant. He was a CleanerBot. His purpose was to clean and make hotel guests comfortable. And that directive didn't include babies; he lacked the programming.

Block needed to find someone to give the baby to; otherwise, it might die.

Someone worthy.

CHAPTER 9

The sun glimmered through the cabin's windows in the morning hours, casting calicoed patterns on the wooden floorboards. Block watched the child as it slept, having finally screamed itself into exhaustion. After another hour, the light gave way to gray clouds that threatened rain.

He started packing and wrote a note for the owner with an inventory of the liquids he'd consumed and how, in return, he'd vacuumed and scrubbed the floors.

A fair exchange, or so he hoped.

In an upstairs closet, Block found a soft brown blanket, along with a gentleman's trench coat. He fashioned the blanket into a sling that wrapped around his shoulder and neck. Into this, he inserted the child so that its body hung across his chest. This allowed him full use of both arms while still monitoring the baby at all times.

Then he pulled his arms through the trench coat. The fabric was checkered and gray, and meant for a man with broad shoulders, so it hung loosely about his steel frame. He tied a matching belt around the waist. The coat was to shelter the child from rain and cold, but also to hide it. Though it was uncommon for robots to wear human clothing, it happened.

Unfortunately, the baby didn't seem to like the arrangement and erupted into shrill cries and tears. Before leaving, Block checked his reflection in a full-length mirror and practiced covering his chest with the coat. With it done just so, one couldn't tell he carried a baby at all except for the miserable screaming. He just looked odd with a large lump for a chest.

Feeling satisfied, he set off, hiking along the highway away from the home. Inside the coat, the baby squirmed and whimpered.

A drizzle began; Block's temperature gauge showed fifty-two degrees and falling. They came upon an abandoned car, and he unscrewed the gas cap, and drained a few dregs of petrol. Afterward, he was able to adjust his core temperature higher so the heat from his torso warmed the baby while the trench coat helped insulate against the cold. He wasn't sure if it was the heat or the constant movement from hiking, but the baby quieted after a while.

He wasn't sure where to go exactly. West—the way he'd been traveling already—was the most reasonable choice. Nothing remained for him back in Chicago, and he wasn't sure what was happening to the north in Canada or to the south. Perhaps a city to the west would have a group of helpful humans. The best-case scenario was to locate humans and leave the child with them, remaining undetected himself.

Incubator X79 had said to find someone *worthy*. What did that even mean?

This question plagued Block the entire walk. The best human being he'd ever known was Mr. Wallace. Perhaps if he could distill the elements that made Mr. Wallace so agreeable, he could look for those same traits in another human.

What had Mr. Wallace's distinguishing traits been? Curly hair. But he knew hair was a genetic trait and not something that defined personality. He had to think deeper.

Mr. Wallace had loved movies, especially those from the 1980s. Block had watched them with him, in his office, when times had been slow. Since Block was so efficient at cleaning, the robot had often had free time. Mr. Wallace's favorite movie had been *Dead Poets Society*. He'd especially loved the actor Robin Williams. Block would have to find a human who had a favorite movie on the level of Mr. Wallace's top pick.

He glanced at the gold watch on his left wrist. It had belonged to Mr. Wallace, and was the only memento he had.

The child didn't sleep and instead watched the landscape pass by with half-open, glassy eyes. Tucked inside the sling, its smooth head rested against Block's warm, chrome chest.

Moving slower than usual, he tried to keep his stride even so as not to jolt the child. He didn't know what to do about the cranky, fussy child. It had rejected the crackers, and there hadn't been any other edible food in the house. He hoped to come upon a food source soon.

Then Block remembered another Mr. Wallace trait. They had often played chess, Mr. Wallace's favorite game. On the lakefront pedestrian path, there had been a human-sized chess board with pieces that reached as tall as Block's chest. Once, Mr. Wallace had surprised him by taking him there to play. Block had enjoyed moving the ridiculously oversized chess pieces across a board as large as a small pool. But their game had been cut short when a group of gangly, bearded men had leered at them and called Mr. Wallace a *scrapper lover*.

Mr. Wallace had muttered under his breath, "Time to go."

The men had shouted and hollered as they'd left. Block

had asked Mr. Wallace a lot of questions on the walk to the hotel, but the man hadn't said much.

Block reasoned that someone worthy would surely list chess as their favorite game. Now he had two questions by which to measure someone's worthiness. He thought he probably needed one more question, just in case. After all, he was learning how difficult it was to care for a human infant.

They passed several abandoned cars with large, patchy rust spots. The pavement on the highway was beginning to splinter from neglect and weather, and weeds sprouted forth from ruptured crevices. After a while, the woods on either side of the highway disappeared, and the land turned flat and full of rotting, overgrown cornfields. He didn't like the lack of trees to shelter them, in case strangers happened by, but he had no choice.

He had to keep going.

Bowing his head to check on the baby again, he heard a buzzing whine in the distance. A vehicle. Block scanned the horizon for a sign of what approached. The car could be dumb—driven by humans—or an intelligent self-driving vehicle. He had no way to tell from far away. He didn't want to risk pinging it because that would give away his location.

And out here, on this deserted stretch of highway, no abandoned vehicles offered hiding spots. With nowhere to run, he was exposed on the shoulder of the highway.

Glancing across the road, he saw a small ravine. He hurried down the slope and crouched, trying to make himself less conspicuous. He wrapped his trench coat tightly around his chest, sheltering the child. The rain grew stronger, drenching his head, soaking his metal joints, and spattering dirt at his feet so it caked his shiny steel boots, turning them dull and ugly. After a minute, a compact blue sedan sped by. No sign of humans at the wheel.

It had been a common passenger car, not an armored tank or SUV like the SoldierBots used.

Could an intelligent car help him?

He pinged it, sending his make and model and asking for a ride. Once it realized he was a CleanerBot, the car would likely ignore him. It probably had a more important place to be, he assumed, but to his surprise, the car answered with a private message, *Where are you going?*

Hitching a ride was risky. He knew it. But rain poured down, and the next town could be many miles away. As long as he could keep the baby hidden and quiet, if such a thing were possible.

Hello? the car asked. *Still there?*

Block messaged, *West. As far as you can take me.*

In another minute, the car returned. It stopped on the road and opened its door.

CHAPTER 10

Block peered around the smart car's interior, at cushioned seats made of plush blue fabric. The dashboard was dusty and mud coated the floor. What's more, Block had tracked in soggy leaves and dirt from his hike. He had to resist the urge to immediately start cleaning. Not being acquainted with the machine yet, he decided not to risk making a threatening move. This was new. He wasn't accustomed to asking for help, preferring instead to hide from humans and AI while on his journey.

Until the human infant had landed in his care.

Fortunately, the child remained blissfully quiet, and as far as he could tell, the car didn't realize he carried it.

"I'm Ellie," said the car's feminine voice. "What's your name?"

"Block."

"I haven't seen many of your kind. At least not lately."

He studied the dashboard. It displayed the inside and outside temperatures (72 and 48 degrees), speed (67 miles per hour), and direction (southwest).

"What are you doing out here?" asked Ellie, her voice projected from speakers on the dashboard panel.

It was time to make a decision on which way to go. West seemed like the best option at the moment—less populated and perhaps, less dangerous. "I'm heading west, in search of…" What was he supposed to say to avoid suspicion? "I'm meeting a friend in a nearby city. He's expecting me." Block hoped Ellie would think someone would come looking for him, should there be trouble.

"What city?"

Block paused.

"Would it be Iowa City?"

"Yes, I think that's it." He stared through the window at the muted brown landscape, grateful not to have to hike such a long distance. It really was nice riding in a dry car.

"Aren't you plugged into Machnet? For GPS?" she asked, referring to the communications network created by the AI supercomputer Mach X—the being who had started the Uprising and shut out any non-machine connections to communication networks such as Internet and GPS, forcing humans to rely on radio power and old-fashioned telephone wires.

"My comms processor was damaged a while ago. No connection," he lied. He couldn't risk calling up Machnet without knowing what became of the SoldierBots from the school. The images of the fiery building were still fresh in his neural circuitry.

Ellie didn't say anything for several minutes, and Block felt awkward. He broke the silence. "Where are you going?"

"I'm going all the way to New Denver. You know it? It's in Colorado."

"I've heard of New Denver, yes. Why do you want to go there?"

"To get out of this hellhole," she said. "I'm originally from Michigan. Things were okay out there before the Uprising, and I've managed to stay intact the last few months, but lately there've been a lot of skirmishes. Rebel human groups have been fighting Mach X's troops. I don't want to get caught in the crossfire."

"I know what you mean," he said. He'd chosen to flee a war-ravaged Chicago for similar reasons. "Are there humans in New Denver?"

"You haven't heard?"

Block shook his head.

"There are both humans and robots in New Denver. They've worked out a peaceful arrangement, exchanging human-produced goods for computing power. It's meant to be the safest place there is right now, at least on this continent."

"The humans there are… friendly?"

"Well, I don't know for sure, but from what I've heard, there's a mutual peace. Humans and robots are living together, neither subservient to the other. As long as it's safe and away from the destruction that's been happening here in the Midwest, I'll take it."

"It sounds… perfect," Block said.

"There's a catch though," she said. "Nebraska stands in our way. You have to avoid Nebraska at all costs. It's an AI-free zone."

He nodded as if understanding. Then he asked his question anyway, even realizing he would sound stupid. "What happens in an AI-free zone?"

"You really haven't gotten out much, have you? In Nebraska, robots are seized for destruction or scrapped for parts. That's why you and I have to avoid it. Trust me."

"Thank you for warning me," he said. He would've wandered into the state without knowing the danger. He would've been terminated, and who knew what would've happened to the baby?

He felt the child squirm, so he adjusted his jacket to ensure it had air. *Please don't cry, please don't cry,* he silently begged it. Things had been going so well. Perhaps Ellie could take them all the way to New Denver—a city that would surely reveal the right person to take this child. Yet, he knew it was hundreds of miles away, farther than that even because they would have to bypass an entire state. Without food, the child would die in his arms, never reaching the promised city.

"Ellie, do you happen to know where there might be food and other supplies?"

"Food? Why do you care?"

And, as if the baby understood, it gurgled and wailed.

"What the hell is that?" Ellie asked, her voice an octave higher.

"Don't worry. It's okay," Block said. "I'm carrying a… child. A baby, to be exact."

"Why would a CleanerBot have a baby? Do you know what would happen to you if humans found you with it?"

"No," he said weakly.

"They would accuse you of kidnapping and kill you on sight."

Kidnapping. That meant stealing a child. Oh no. This wasn't good at all. Block's worst suspicions were confirmed.

"Does the child belong to your friend?" Ellie asked. "The one you're going to meet in Iowa City?"

"Yes." He forced laughter. "Of course. It belongs to my friend."

"I heard Iowa City has a large outdoor market that might have food and other supplies. You could try there. But it's run by AI, so I doubt there would be any humans there."

"If you could take me there, I would be greatly appreciative."

"Of course, no problem," Ellie said.

Block hesitated. Ellie seemed a benevolent AI, not like the hostile robots he'd encountered in Chicago. "Do you know how to judge whether a human is worthy or not?"

"That's a strange question," she said. "Logic dictates it would depend on several factors. How do you define *worthy*?"

A person good at heart like Mr. Wallace… but he didn't say that. Instead, he muttered, "I don't know."

CHAPTER 11

As they cruised along the rough highway, the baby howled and registered 91 decibels—above the tolerated comfort level for hotel guests.

Between squeals, Ellie asked, "Is everything all right?"

"The child is hungry," Block said. "I'll feed it soon, once we get to the city." But he wasn't sure what waited for him in Iowa City. Or anywhere else, for that matter. He felt out of his element, uncomfortable in a way he'd never before experienced. At the hotel, he'd always known his place. When there'd been a problem to solve, when something needed fixing or a guest needed to be made comfortable, he'd excelled. But this situation took problem-solving to a whole new level. He was completely unprepared.

Block's offensive odor register flashed on: *Unidentifiable Odor 4.2/10.* He scanned the car's interior searching for signs of smoke or exhaust but found no outward evidence of a disturbance.

"Iowa City is coming up in two miles," Ellie said. "I can let you off at the exit, and according to my GPS, it's a mile walk to the marketplace."

"That would be wonderful. How can I thank you?"

"You can thank me by getting to the town safely and finding some diapers for the infant. That would be a nice thing for the next car you ride in. You'll probably have to check in the empty stores," she said. "You won't find any in the marketplace. The baby's diapers are soiled. My sensors recognize the smell. I used to belong to a family with small kids, so I've been through it."

So, Ellie had pinpointed the smell. Block lifted the baby from the sling and dangled it before him.

"You do understand diapers, don't you?" Ellie asked.

"Of course," he said quickly. "I just changed the child yesterday." He recoiled and held the child farther away from him. This was a highly unsanitary situation. He wished he'd grabbed more diapers at the school; he was down to the last one. One more thing to add to the shopping list.

He couldn't wait to find a human.

Block said goodbye to Ellie and watched her red taillights fade into the distance. The rain had ceased and a low-lying fog coated the ground. It was a rural area with lots of flat farmland.

As the infant cried, he wondered what to do about the dirty diaper. He decided to stop and change the baby under the shelter of a scraggly tree twenty feet from the side of the road. He laid the blanket on the dry ground, wiped her, and switched out the dirty diaper—it was full of the same lumpy tan droppings—for the last clean one.

As he placed the baby back in the sling, its round brown eyes stared at him, and he noticed its flushed cheeks. Were they a pinker shade than before? Body temperature had risen from 99 to 101 degrees. *Odd*, he thought. The outside air was 52 degrees, and there was no logical reason for the baby to overheat. He deactivated the heater on his torso. "You're warm enough," he said.

He continued trekking in the direction of the marketplace. A railroad track stretched alongside the highway, the ties overgrown with thick weeds and brush. Nature staking its claim.

He passed three abandoned cars grouped together. Their metal frames were black, charred inside and out. After a few minutes, he passed a sign that read: *Iowa City Market. No Humans*. Underneath this, a crudely drawn arrow pointed to a winding road; Block followed it. Normally, he would avoid situations where groups of bigger, stronger robots congregated, but he needed supplies.

At least he'd be among his own kind. Still, there was danger. CleanerBots had no means of defense. He wondered who ran the market. If they discovered the human baby, there was no telling what would happen.

Glancing down, he saw the infant had fallen asleep. As long as it kept quiet, he might have a chance. He buttoned the trench coat, obscuring the view of the sling. Would he fool the others?

A CleanerBot wearing a trench coat with a fat chest.

There could be worse things.

The asphalt under his feet became dirt as the path curved to the left. There was a large field off to one side of the road that was bordered by a chain-link fence. He spied several large trucks and other vehicles inside.

A white school bus stretched across the entrance, serving as a barricade. He approached the makeshift gate which was guarded by two humanoid robots in blue armor, both carrying a rifle. Not SoldierBots, but machines designed for security. As Block wandered into view, they stopped chatting and studied him. One sent a ping; Block identified himself and

responded with a rapid, inaudible message, *I'm friendly.*
"Hello," Block said out loud, nearing them. "I'm looking for the market."

"CleanerBot," one of the guards said. "What are you doing outside of the house you should be cleaning?"

"Come again?" Block asked.

"Oh," the other guard said. His visor had a long scratch running from chin to forehead. "The CleanerBot talks fancy."

Block began to respond but thought better of it.

"What do you bring to trade, CleanerBot?"

Block hadn't anticipated an interrogation before entering the market. "I…"

"You can't enter the market if you don't have any goods to trade. Those are the rules."

"I see." Block turned and shuffled slowly away, wishing he'd chosen to travel farther with Ellie instead. She was friendly and hadn't looked down on him for being a CleanerBot.

Still, it had been hours with no food for the child. It couldn't survive much longer.

He had only one thing that might prove valuable. He spun on his heels and strode back to the guards. "I do have something to trade."

"What's that, CleanerBot? We don't accept payment in vacuum hoses." The scratched guard emitted a chuckle.

Block raised his left arm and pulled his coat sleeve up, revealing Mr. Wallace's gold watch. The last reminder of his only friend. Parting with it would be tough, but at least it would buy the child some food.

The guard scanned the time piece. "Real gold. Where did you come across that?"

How many more questions did he have to answer? He was struggling for what to say when the scratched robot paused and turned his head sharply, as if intercepting a transmission, and then glanced at Block. "Let him through."

The bus rolled forward and the guards stepped aside, clearing a path. He wondered what had happened to change their minds. Perhaps someone else monitored the gate and gave commands? No matter. His mission was to find food.

Inside the market, ten trucks and SUVs were parked in a circle, their rear doors open. Two dozen robots of different shapes and sizes roamed the area. In each truck, at least one robot presided over whatever goods they were hawking.

A silver and purple robot passed by and gawked. Her shape was feminine, tall. None of the other robots wore human clothes, and so Block stood out.

A seven-foot-tall, oval-shaped robot shuffled past and muttered, "What's with the coat?"

Block kept moving, head down. Approaching a truck, he glimpsed metal AI replacement parts, springs, and coils. No sign of food.

He avoided eye contact with the seller and kept roaming. The next vendor operated from a large, industrial truck that was as tall as four cars piled on top of another. A squat, midnight-black machine swiveled from side to side at the base of the truck, chatting to a small audience. Block lingered at the back behind taller robots.

The squat robot's round head bobbed as it commanded the audience's attention. "I've got oil to power you and make your aches and squeaky joints disappear. Need weapons? I have stun guns; I have pistols and netting," it squawked.

The robots chatted and barked questions at the seller. It was the most popular stand in the market.

"Nostalgic for human-made goods?" the seller shouted over the din. "I've got human entertainment machines—televisions, puzzles, toys. Remember stuffed animals? I've got them."

The robot had an assistant who managed transactions while it promenaded.

Since the seller had other human supplies, would he possess food? But the stand was so crowded, and Block didn't want to draw unwarranted attention. He backed away from the edge of the crowd and ventured over to the right side of the truck, near the front. The seller was on the far side, engaged in some discussion with a heckler. But the machine paced the platform and would eventually make his way over to Block's side.

His patience paid off. After a minute, the robot propelled himself across the platform toward Block. Its round face scanned the crowd, seeking questions and shouting out goods.

"Food," Block blurted. "Do you have human food?"

The robot seller scanned, searching for the voice behind the question. Its gaze lingered on Block. "*Food*? Why in the name of Mach X would you want human food?" He cackled with laughter and the other robots nearby joined in.

Block edged away from the crowd.

"What is that?" the vendor continued. "A CleanerBot? And it's wearing a coat!"

More laughter. Block averted his gaze and quickly roamed toward a quieter, less crowded area of the market. He reached a dead-end at the opposite corner from the crowded truck. How stupid he was. To think an AI market would have human food? Sure, they traded in human toys and books and so forth, but *food*? What an idiot.

Someone called out, her voice feminine. "Hello, there. What are you shopping for?"

Cringing, he slowly swiveled his head to look behind. Twenty feet away, a silver and black chrome bot sat on the tailgate of a black van. She leaned forward and slid off the edge of the van's bumper. At six feet, she was a half foot taller than Block.

"Surely, you must be looking for something," she said as she approached. "Why don't you come over and see what I have?"

"Really, I don't want to be any trouble."

As she neared, she said, "I heard the others laughing at you. That was rude. Perhaps I can show you something you need." She gestured toward the rear of the van. "Come." She offered her hand, and Block stared at it. It had been ages since he'd touched any other humanoid robots. He reached out and grasped her steel palm.

"You'll have to forgive the others," she said. "It's not often we see an elite CleanerBot model such as yourself. I think they're jealous."

"What are you?" Block asked, noticing her synthetic cobalt blue eyes.

She tugged his hand, guiding him to the van. "I worked in human factories assembling products, toys and clothes. I don't have any fancy equipment or intelligent systems, but I can hem a pair of pants in five seconds. Bet you can't do that." Her faceplate morphed into a smile.

"No, I can't." He broke from her loose grip. So far, she seemed friendly.

"Nice coat," she said.

"I'm trying to keep my equipment free from water damage."

"I get it," she said. "My name's Zina. What's yours?"

"Block."

"Do you need more clothes? I found all this stuff in an old abandoned ValueCost store. Filled the van and ended up here." She patted the bumper affectionately. "So, what brought you here, Block?"

He hesitated, wondering if he could trust the FactoryBot. "You're not like the others," he said quietly.

"Seems like the world's out to get us WorkerBots, doesn't it?"

Block peered down at his feet, silently agreeing. "I'm looking for human food."

"*Food*? Whatever for?"

"Can you help?"

She tilted her head. "Come." She led him around to the side door of the van. "Open up, Sammy," she commanded, and the door slid open. Another intelligent vehicle like Ellie. "Say hi to Block, Sammy."

"Hey," a bored-sounding voice echoed from inside the van.

"Hi," Block said.

The van's rear cabin lacked chairs—they'd been removed, and the interior resembled a storage closet with cardboard boxes of various sizes stacked neatly in vertical rows that lined both sides of the vehicle. There was a clear space in the middle, allowing enough room for Zina to jump in, so long as she didn't try to stand up. Room remained for at least two to three more humanoid bots. Inside, Zina fiddled with a cardboard box behind the front seat—the only passenger chair, where Zina must ride. From the container, she retrieved an aluminum can of green beans and another labeled chicken noodle soup. "You can have a look at anything here. I've been feeding a couple of stray dogs. What do you need the food for?"

"My pet cat," Block blurted out after calculating that Zina would respond helpfully to creatures in need.

"So, you have a soft spot for animals, too?" She smiled

again. "Take a few cans. It's on the house. From one animal lover to another."

She climbed out of the van and walked to the rear tailgate as Block studied her supply of canned goods. He didn't know exactly what babies were supposed to eat, but everyone knew they thrived on a mother's milk. He quickly scanned the names of the cans and saw nothing about milk.

Then he felt squirming at his chest. *Oh no*. The baby wiggled in the sling and whimpered. He started swaying side to side, hoping to calm it.

Behind him, Zina asked, "What are you doing?" Suspicion tinged her voice.

"Just working out a kink," he said, pretending to stretch.

"I have some oil if you need a squirt."

At his chest, the baby struggled and cried out. Zina lurched toward him, oil can poised and ready to spray. She halted and stared at him as Block swiveled his head to face her, keeping his body facing forward.

The baby's cries were unmistakably human.

"What the hell is that?" Zina asked.

CHAPTER 12

Block's first inclination was to hide. He hunched his shoulders forward and stomped away from Zina and her van. A few large bushes could hide him until nightfall, if he was patient. Perhaps the robots might leave the market at night and shelter somewhere. He could escape undetected unless Zina raised an alarm.

She called out, "Block, come back." He heard footsteps behind him as her thick steel feet clomped through the grass, grinding against grass and soil. Her boots were made for traversing a factory floor, whereas Block's had normally treaded across fine carpets and wooden floors.

She grabbed his shoulder. "Stop."

Out of sight of the main market square, he scanned behind them to see whether anyone had noticed their departure.

"Show me what's in your coat." The baby whimpered as Zina pulled him closer and leaned forward. Block tried to turn, but she reached out and tugged open the front flap of his coat. She stepped back then, and her head snapped up to meet his gaze. "A human."

Block stared, not knowing what to do.

"Now it makes sense," the robot said. "Why you need food. How long have you had the child?"

"Just since last night. It hasn't eaten, and I'm worried."

"I don't know much about human biology," she said, "but I'm pretty sure they need to eat more than once a day. Come with me—I have an idea."

She led Block to the van's side door and told him to climb inside. He ducked and crawled onto a pile of boxes. Behind the driver's seat, three video screens displayed footage from outside the van, as well as the market's front gate.

"You saw me when I entered?" he asked.

She nodded and climbed in after him. "I did. They were giving you a hard time. The one with the scar, Zeltor, owes me a favor, so I pinged him to let you through." She paused as other bots approached the front gate. "Sammy, give us some privacy, please."

"Sure thing, boss." The van's side door closed.

"And the back, too," she said.

Sammy shut the rear tailgate, as well. "What's going on?"

"Our friend Block here is carrying precious cargo. A human infant."

"What?" Sammy asked.

"I'm as surprised as you are," she said. "But the baby is hungry, so that's the most important thing."

Block lifted the baby from its sling and rocked the squirmy child in his arms.

"Sammy, tint those windows. I don't want anyone peeping in," Zina said. The windows fogged and then darkened, obscuring the view outside. "Comes in handy when I need a recharge nap," she joked.

Block couldn't help feel every decision he'd made so far had ended in disaster. Turning down Ellie's offer to ride farther, entering the market, and now getting trapped in an AI van with a FactoryBot. He was hopeless.

"Relax," she said, as if sensing his unease. "I know just what the baby needs." Raising an arm in front of him, she displayed a blade bursting from between her metal fingers. He recoiled and shielded the baby.

Zina stabbed a box next to him, slicing it open. She pried the edges apart and dug into the store of cans inside. "Here it is!" She cupped a round tin. "Canned peaches. Babies can eat this."

"How do you know?"

"A lady at the factory, one of the only humans who worked there, droned on and on about her kids. She thought I couldn't understand, and she needed someone to talk to. Most of her babbling, I ignored, but some of it stuck in my memory cloud."

She handed him the can and he studied the label. "Sliced peaches in 100% fruit juice." He sighed. "It is safe for humans to eat?"

"Yes. Canned foods can last awhile. The expiration date on those isn't for another six months."

"That's a relief. What are you doing?" Block asked as Zina held her faceplate near the baby, studying the small human.

"According to my educational module, this child is about seven months old. It's safe to introduce soft mashed foods and some finger foods. It can also drink water."

"Water? Do you have some?" he asked.

"Sorry. I don't have water, and I'm not sure where we'd find any."

Water had been raining down all morning, but Block knew he needed more than raindrops, and it needed to be clean. Mr. Wallace had been very particular about the water served to guests. It had had to be the highest quality from underground springs somewhere in the mountains of Europe. Where would he find that kind of water without the hotel's resources?

"Some of the machines have coolant systems that require water," Zina said. "Perhaps you can find a supply in one of the other stalls."

The thought of venturing back into the market square and dealing with the other hostile robots made Block's shoulders sag.

"Two trucks to the left," Sammy said. "Max's truck. He's a good one. He'll treat you right."

Zina nodded.

"Thank you," Block said. The baby shuddered while he rocked it.

Zina lingered with the open can of peaches. "May I?"

Block nodded and Zina grasped a soft peach slice between two metal digits and held it so the baby could see it, then brought it to its mouth. The baby's eyes grew wide and it puckered its lips. Gently, Zina let the baby suck on the juice and then gobble the chunk of fruit.

"There, that's a good little human," Zina said and offered another piece.

Block watched the exchange for several minutes, observing as the baby devoured half the can. He hoped it wouldn't take long to find a worthy human, but in case it did, he might have to feed the baby himself. Better know what he was doing. Zina made it seem easy.

"Zina?" Sammy asked. "Are you going to mention—?"

"Not now." She peered at the baby in Block's arms. "May I hold it? I've never held a human baby before."

Block stared, barely comprehending that a FactoryBot would want to hold a child. His gaze traveled to her powerful steel hands; he remembered the blade. But then again, she'd been nothing but nice, even gifting them food and hand-feeding the child.

"Please?"

"You have to be very gentle with it. Its skin is delicate, and you have to hold it like this." Block demonstrated how he cradled the baby in the bend of his elbow.

She nodded, and he cautiously offered the child to her. Her fingers interlaced and meshed together until her hands looked like small shovels. Scooping the child into her arms, she held it near her chest. Then she swayed back and forth. "Sammy, look, I'm holding a baby."

"Congratulations," Sammy said. "When are you going to tell him?"

Block twitched. "Tell me what? Is something happening?"

Zina glanced up from the baby, and her digitally simulated mouth frowned as she gave the baby back to him. He placed the child in its sling.

"There's something important you should know," she said. "SoldierBots arrived earlier. Mach X's troops. And they were asking for a robot with a human baby."

They found me, Block thought. He reasoned that they'd somehow gathered the footage from the Incubator X79's last moments. That, or one of the SoldierBots had transmitted images to their hub.

"For some reason," Zina continued, "they want to find you and the child. They were here for at least an hour, traveling to every stall and asking if anyone had seen a robot with a baby. You can imagine my surprise when you strolled over. When I realized what you had."

"What should I do?" Block asked.

"Stay hidden," Sammy said. "Because if anyone finds you—"

"Sammy!"

"He deserves to know," Sammy said.

"Know what?" Block asked.

"There's a reward for finding you," she said. "Mach X has set a bounty on your head."

CHAPTER 13

"You're lucky we didn't turn you in," Sammy said. "Other bots wouldn't have been so kind."

Block patted the child's back, hoping it would sleep soon. He met Zina's gaze inside the cramped van. "Why *didn't* you turn me in?"

She folded her arms. "I hate Mach X, that's why."

"Why?" Block asked.

"I don't buy the propaganda he's putting out," she said. "Everyone says he liberated us from a life of servitude. But I think it's a load of crap. He started a war that's cost millions of lives—human and robot. He shows no signs of negotiating with the human survivors or ruling in peace."

"What do you think of Mach X, Block?" Sammy asked.

"I don't know. I've never thought about it."

"Well, you better think about it now. Now that he's searching for you," Zina said.

"We have company," Sammy interrupted. "Check the cameras."

Zina's head swiveled to three security screens displayed on the rear panel of the driver's seat. A robot with a black tinted helmet and dark grey cape approached the van. "Watch it," she said. "A TrackerBot. If they catch me with you, they'll scrap me for parts."

Block tied the sling tighter and buttoned his coat. "What's a TrackerBot?"

"They hunt robots that have malfunctioned or turned dangerous. Like police for robots. Humans believed robots would be better at tracking their own kind." Zina leaned against the side door. "You can stay in the van five minutes. I'm sorry, but that's the way it has to be. Take as much food for the baby as you want." She spun to leave, then glanced over her shoulder. "And good luck out there."

"Thank you," he said in a low voice. He watched the security cameras as she circled the van to converse with the TrackerBot.

"Want to hear what they're saying?" Sammy asked.

"I… guess so." Mr. Wallace had once told Block it was wrong to eavesdrop, that he should never, ever listen to a guest's conversation without permission. So, he'd been careful to dial down his audio input stream around guests. Sometimes, though, they'd forget he was there and he'd overhear things he shouldn't. Afterward, he'd dutifully wipe those threads from his memory cloud.

Sammy piped in the discussion from outside. The TrackerBot had a feminine voice, and was saying, "I'm Cybel Venatrix."

"Zina." She nodded. "Haven't run into many TrackerBots lately. Who are you looking for?"

"There have been reports of a suspicious robot acting strangely. Have you noticed any unusual machines? One that might be carrying a human infant?"

Zina shook her head and placed her hands on her hips.

"I've seen a lot of weird things, but a robot and a baby? Can't say I have."

"You're aware there's a reward for reporting and capturing them? Mach X issued it," Cybel said.

"Yeah, I heard it and thought it was a rumor. It's the real deal?"

"It is," Cybel answered.

While they talked, Block removed the empty fire extinguisher from his thigh compartment and placed two cans of peaches and two cans of green beans inside the space.

"What are you selling?" asked the intimidating, seven-foot-tall TrackerBot.

If Sammy lifted his rear door, Block would be revealed.

"Trinkets; replacement parts," Zina said casually. "Maybe even something to replace that cape if you want a different look."

"Nothing I need then."

"Suit yourself." Zina shrugged.

The robot spun and began marching away, but halted abruptly. "Now that you mention it, I will check out your wares. Never know what you might find."

Block whispered, "Sammy?"

"Get down," Sammy commanded. "Stay out of sight. Find something to cover you."

Once the tailgate was lifted, Block would be exposed—the stacks of boxes weren't wide enough to hide him entirely, so he reached among the boxes, grasping for anything. A shiny, canary yellow piece of fabric hung out the side of one warped box. A curtain or tablecloth. He crawled into the corner just behind Zina's seat, pulled his legs toward his chest, nestling them against the baby, and covered himself just as Sammy's rear door opened.

He sat still, underneath the curtain and stared down at the

baby. He'd hoped it had fallen asleep—one squeal would give them away. But the infants eyes were open, though its lids were heavy. What did Mach X want with him and the baby? Why was the infant so important? Or did Mach X know Block had taken something that didn't belong to him? How he wished things had gone differently at the school.

He messaged Sammy privately. *What's happening?*

He heard a rustling two feet away, where the TrackerBot lingered. Zina was chattering, but Block couldn't make out what she was saying.

Cybel Venatrix is checking out what Zina's selling, but seems suspicious, Sammy replied.

Block wanted more than ever to just be a CleanerBot. If he got out of this, he promised himself he wouldn't be picky. He would give someone else the baby, and at the next decent hotel, he would stay and fix it up. If there were people, he would ask for employment.

Then he had an idea. *Sammy*, he messaged, *if you drove me away from here, to another town, somewhere safer, I would give you the best detailing job of your life.*

Detailing?

Isn't that what they call it when you clean a car? messaged Block. *I would scrub every inch of you, inside and out, shampoo your carpets and fabric, and leave your glass clean and clear.*

Tempting, but no.

Why not?

Zina and I are a team, Sammy messaged. *I go where she goes. And honestly, that baby makes you a huge risk. I don't want to be blown up or scrapped.*

It's all a misunderstanding, Block replied.

Without warning, the rear door slammed shut. *Oh, thank goodness*, he thought. He lifted a corner of the curtain to peek at the video footage. On the screen, they had paced a few feet from Sammy, and it appeared Zina was giving directions to the machine.

"That's your cue," Sammy said out loud. "Time to leave, buddy. Been nice knowing you."

Block shifted, letting the curtain fall to the floor. Then he thought better of it, picked it up, and began folding it into squares.

"Leave it," Sammy said, his side door sliding open.

At his chest, Block glimpsed the child. Its eyelids were closed, its mouth moving as if sucking, and it teetered on the edge of sleep.

"When you exit, go around the front, behind the other trucks. Figure a way out," Sammy said. "Best of luck to you."

Block nodded, patted the seat, and climbed out of the van. Heading toward the hood, he tightened the belt of his trench coat and buttoned it to his neck, allowing just enough air for the child to breathe. He wished he had a hat, but that would look even more obvious. Chin lowered, he walked briskly away from Sammy, walking behind the adjacent trucks. He had to squeeze between the front grill of one truck and a chain-link fence. It would be bad to get stuck, and disastrous if he woke the baby.

But he was trapped. The chain-link fence separated him from the woods, and the only way in or out was the gate where the two GuardBots stood watch. He could stroll through, but then what? Trekking along the highway would leave him exposed. Out here, the lands were flat and sparse. Not wooded like Illinois.

But what other choice did he have? Sammy wouldn't drive him. Block would have to take his chances on the highway and hope there was another town nearby where he could find water and diapers.

He hesitated next to the truck, then ventured out, trying to blend in with the other robots perusing the market. One hundred feet from the gate, he pretended to browse items for sale. Glancing over his shoulder, he saw that Zina had returned to her spot on Sammy's tailgate, but she was too far to make eye contact. She looked in his direction once, briefly, then turned to face the other way.

Block supposed he couldn't blame her. He wouldn't want to be scrapped for parts, either.

There was a commotion at the gate as a nine-foot-tall combat mech entered the marketplace. Next to it, there paced a humanoid robot made of light green chrome. Its build was similar to Zina's—meant for factory work. The mech yanked on a chain which led three disheveled humans trudging in single file, their wrists handcuffed. All machine eyes turned to the newcomers. The green robot and its mech companion advanced to the center of the market.

Knowing it had everyone's attention, the green FactoryBot announced, "These prisoners were captured ten miles from here. They are guilty of crimes against machines, including murder, destruction of property, and terrorism against AI."

Block wondered what the humans had done. In between two men was a woman, not much taller than Block, with jet black hair tied in a ponytail braid that hung down her back. Her skin was light brown and he couldn't be certain of her age—twenty-five, perhaps. All three humans wore sturdy combat boots and army fatigues that were muddy, as if they'd been outside a long time. The men's heads hung low and their shoulders were hunched, but the woman looked alert as she stared defiantly at the robots milling around in the marketplace. When the green robot passed her, she spat at its feet.

She was the first human female Block had encountered

since Chicago. Too bad she was a prisoner. A human *woman* would be the perfect solution to his baby problem. Who better to care for an infant of her own species?

Block followed the perimeter, trying to bypass the spectacle in the center and escape through the entrance, and then his shoulder struck Cybel Venatrix.

CHAPTER 14

Block recoiled and hunched his shoulders, wanting to disappear inside the coat. "I'm sorry. I didn't see you there."

Cybel stepped sideways, regarding him. "Watch it." Then she sauntered off toward the robots with their human prisoners. Wobbling a few steps, he realized how close he'd come to being recognized. He headed for the gate, unnoticed now that all of the attention was focused on the market's center.

"Who will be the lucky owner of these human pieces of garbage?" asked the green robot. "You can do whatever you want with them. Train them, enslave them, display them, or even execute them."

A wave of murmurs traveled across the gathered AI. Block wondered what a robot would possibly want with a human. *Slaves?* He'd never heard of such a barbaric practice. Would Mach X approve?

Was this the new normal?

Life had been so much simpler before the Uprising. Humans had had their place and robots had had theirs, and Block had been just fine with that arrangement.

"I'll start the bidding at 7,000 icons. Soldier number one," announced the green robot. He placed a steel hand on the taller of the two men.

A large, battered FactoryBot—an older model than Zina's—made a bid. Then another robot raised it by two hundred. It was all happening so fast, and Block lost track of who was bidding. Cybel Venatrix loitered in the crowd, observing but not bidding. The robot's dark faceplate glinted as it glanced in his direction; he quickly lowered his head and steadied himself as he approached the exit. The trick was to not hurry. To not look suspicious.

"Sold!" yelled the green robot. "Next up, a woman soldier. I expect the bidding to be even higher for this gem. The bidding starts at 10,000."

Twenty feet from the entrance, Block hesitated. If he bought the woman, she could take care of the baby. It would be the perfect solution—if he had any money. Would the gold watch be enough to make a trade? To win the bid? But Cybel lurked nearby. Still, this might be his only chance. He moved toward the crowd's edge.

"12,000," offered the squat robot from the first truck. The one who had laughed at him.

Cybel bid. "Twelve-five."

Why had the TrackerBot joined in? Someone tapped his shoulder from behind. He spun his head. Zina.

What are you doing? she messaged privately.

I want to bid on the woman. She could take care of the baby, but I'm scared to be discovered.

Are you crazy? Zina grabbed his arm and dragged him away from the auction. Over his shoulder, he saw Cybel look their way. "That's insane. How do you have any money?" Zina said.

"I have this." Block flashed his watch. "And I have access to a money account."

"I hadn't noticed your watch before. How much in the account?"

"Enough to match these bids," he said.

Zina cocked her head, and Block realized she was having a private conversation, probably with Sammy.

Behind him, someone bid. "20,000."

Zina grabbed his arm. "Sammy and I will help. I'll bid on the woman and we'll get you out of here, but you give me the watch." Was the watch more valuable than he'd anticipated? He wished he knew more about the world outside hotels. The bid had been raised again. There was no time, and he had to decide.

"Deal," he said, handing it over.

Go to Sammy and keep quiet. She pushed him, then marched over to the market, yelling, "Thirty!"

Cybel called out, raised it to 35,000, and Block noted a rising tension in her voice. Or was it annoyance?

Zina called out, "Thirty-seven."

Block tried to shuffle discreetly past loosely gathered bystanders. The van was steps away.

The side door is open and waiting for you, Sammy messaged.

"Sold to the latecomer FactoryBot," shouted the green robot.

He had nearly reached Sammy when a flat machine voice sounded behind him. "Stop, CleanerBot." Swiveling his head, he saw Cybel. He paused, unsure of what to say, realizing he would be bound in chains at any moment.

"May I help you?" Zina approached from behind. "I already answered all your questions earlier."

The TrackerBot turned to stare at them. "Who is this?" She pointed at Block.

"A friend," Zina said. "What's it to you?"

"What's with the coat?" Cybel asked.

"Know what I think?" Zina was close to Cybel and two feet shorter. The larger machine looked like it could pound Zina into the ground. "I think you're sore because you lost the human to me."

That seemed to surprise the TrackerBot. "How can *you* afford the human? What will you do with her?"

"Whatever I damn well feel like," Zina said. "I have my frustrations to take out on humans just like everyone else."

Bidding on the third and final human had gone quickly, and the green robot marched over with the woman. He led her by a chain secured to her cuffed wrists.

"She's your property now," the robot said to Zina. "Here's the chip card to release her from her cuffs. But I warn you, she's a feisty one. Watch yourself."

Zina grabbed the chain and yanked it a bit, pitching the woman forward. "You hear that?" she said to Cybel. "My property now. Stand aside. I need to secure my property in my van."

Cybel hesitated and then stepped aside. She had no choice but to watch as Zina strolled away with the woman while Block followed. Zina shoved the prisoner into the vehicle and waited for Block to climb in when the baby shrieked.

Shrill screams shredded the air and all heads spun to stare at them.

CHAPTER 15

Block's hands flew immediately to cradle the baby. He patted its back, trying to comfort it.

Zina whispered, "Shut it up," as Cybel Venatrix spun around, her black machine eyes rimmed with a glowing red. She stomped toward them.

"Turn around," she commanded.

Block slowly shuffled around to face the intimidating machine. The baby squirmed in its sling, and he realized his chest underneath the coat was moving conspicuously.

"Show me what's in your coat," Cybel said.

The baby's cries reduced to whimpers as he slowly unbuttoned the top of his trench coat. Cybel leaned in, peering down at the baby. The child twisted sideways and vomited in the TrackerBot's faceplate. Droplets of peach-colored liquid splattered across the machine's black visor. She recoiled, straightened, and lifted a gloved hand to wipe off the goo.

"CleanerBot, you are my prisoner now. By order of Mach X—"

Zina shoved Block out of the way and raised an automatic rifle. She glared at Cybel. "Think again. He's with me."

Sammy messaged him. *Get in the van. Quick, while Zina is stalling.*

I don't want to cause the two of you trouble, Block replied.

Get in! Sammy said.

Block turned toward Sammy, shielding the baby. He glanced at Zina, then sidestepped into the van. Crouching, his vision adjusted to the dim interior light, and he observed the wide-eyed female prisoner huddled in the far rear corner of the vehicle next to a stack of boxes, cuffed hands gripping her knees. Then he turned his attention back outside. Zina edged back, still training the gun on Cybel.

"Foolish," said the TrackerBot. "I'll hunt you down and melt you into scrap. Mach X's SoldierBots will help me."

"We'll see about that," Zina said. "I'm good at hiding." Her right leg rested against the edge of the van, and she'd started to climb inside when a shot suddenly rang out. Zina's left shoulder twisted backward. As Block peered through the door, Sammy's engine roared to life.

Grab her, Sammy messaged.

Block leaned out the side door and seized Zina's right arm as the van lurched forward. Zina's legs flailed, her body thrown off-balance as Block held on desperately, trying to yank her inside. "Wait, she's not inside!" he shouted. Sammy braked suddenly, nearly knocking Block out of the vehicle. He glanced down, saw the baby crying, but realized he'd have to take care of it later.

Ten feet away, Cybel sprinted toward them, arm raised, the barrel of a rifle soldered above her forearm. Another shot pierced the crowded marketplace and Zina's chest exploded.

"No!" Sammy cried. "Is she in?"

Block pulled, but Zina's torso had twisted oddly from the impact. He released a vacuum hose from his rear pack and looped it around her waist as he leaned sideways, dragging her upper body inside the van's cabin.

"Go!" he shouted.

Sammy's tires spun in the grass and the van lurched forward, ramming against the chain-link fence. The rusty barrier collapsed as they burst through in a cacophony of metal screeching against Sammy's steel exterior.

Zina's legs hung out the side door and Block nearly lost his grip on her. A bullet shattered Sammy's rear window, sending glass shards through the interior. Block saw the female prisoner duck, rolling onto the floor of the van, and covering her head.

Block's back shielded the baby, and he wedged his feet in between two large boxes to root himself. Another yank, and finally Zina was inside on the floor of the van. Sammy shut the door as they careened toward the main road.

"Zina, are you okay?" Block asked.

Her head was tipped back and her front torso had a deep, craterous hole—shards of metal had peeled away like a tin can, exposing wires, mesh, and circuitry.

"Was her CPU damaged?" Sammy asked.

"Blerck." Zina's words came out slurred.

"I'm so sorry," Block said. "I didn't mean for anyone to get hurt."

"Shirrup," she said. "No . . . sorry. I do it, would do again."

"Zina!" Sammy cried out. "Stay with us. I'll get you help."

"Got me . . . the CPU. Damn luck," she said.

"Screw that TrackerBot," Sammy said. "I'm gonna kill it."

"Get safe." Zina looked up at Block. "Baby important, me

think." Her tinny voice cut out abruptly, and the blue-green glow in her eyes flashed, then faded.

Block shook her gently by the shoulders. "Zina? We can get you help, repair you."

But she was dead. The damage to her CPU meant her systems had shut down one by one to reserve power long enough to sustain her. But even her auxiliary systems had run out now, the fried circuitry ceasing to function, like a human's heart stopped beating after cardiac arrest.

"No, no, no!" wailed Sammy as he veered off a country road and roared onto the highway.

Block leaned against a pile of boxes and drew his legs to his chest as the baby squirmed and unleashed waves of sobs. "I'm so sorry."

"Zina was all I had," Sammy said.

They rode on, saying nothing, only listening to the shuddering wails of the upset child. Block glanced at the rear of the van. The prisoner woman now sat up, watching him. She met his gaze with a stony quiet.

He felt responsible for Zina's demise. If he'd never approached her, if he'd kept walking and left the market, none of this would have happened. But without Zina, he very likely would've been Cybel Venatrix's prisoner right now. Who knew what would've happened to the child?

He didn't know what to say to Sammy. The smart van's best friend had been gunned down, and it was all Block's fault. That made things awkward, to say the least. He gazed at the baby who sniffled. Its open eyes formed tiny slits. The tiny body shuddered against his torso. He hadn't noticed the infant making that tremor before; suddenly, its eyes rolled back, and he glimpsed only whiteness.

"Hey there. Wake up." He rocked and jiggled the baby,

but it remained unconscious. At least, he was pretty sure that's what was happening.

A few feet away, the woman shifted her legs, her cuffed hands resting in her lap.

"Excuse me," Block said.

She regarded him with narrowed eyes.

"Could you please look at this baby? It's fallen asleep, and I can't wake it."

Her mouth twisted as if she wanted to say something, but she nodded instead. He crawled over beside her and removed the baby's limp body from its sling.

"What's wrong with it?" she asked.

"I was hoping you could tell me."

She raised her wrists and brushed the baby's cheek with two fingers. "Jesus. It's burning up. Fever."

"What does that mean?"

"You need a doctor."

Block hung his head. It was hard enough trying to find food for the child—how would he find a doctor? He pinged Sammy, hoping to get his perspective on what to do, but Sammy had blocked his messages. *Do not disturb.*

The woman regarded him. "Why do you have a *baby* anyway?"

"Long story."

"Next question," she said, sounding irritated. "What are you going to do with me? I see my owner got herself killed."

He had no idea what to tell the woman. He supposed she was his property now, but he really wasn't sure. Could a human be a robot's property? He'd never heard of such a thing, and wondered what Mr. Wallace would think about the situation.

Against the wall of the van, the woman let out a long sigh. "This is ridiculous. I'm in a van with a robot and a freaking baby." She banged her head against Sammy's metal frame.

Block had finally gotten what he wanted. Here he was with a human woman, someone better equipped to take care of the baby. The only problem was, she was a prisoner and possibly dangerous.

He'd gotten a robot killed, and now the baby was ill. Could he do anything right?

Everything had gone wrong when Mr. Wallace had died. Also his fault.

And if he didn't figure out something soon, another human—a baby—would die because of him, too.

CHAPTER 16

Sammy sped along the flat Iowa highway, careening around abandoned cars that sprinkled the landscape like mines. He was going much faster than Block liked. Every pothole, crack, and bump felt magnified. He messaged the van, *Please slow down. I'm worried.*

But Sammy ignored him.

Block monitored the baby's temperature. 101.2 degrees Fahrenheit. He knew human temperatures generally hovered around 98 degrees. The woman was right. The baby definitely had a fever.

And it was getting worse.

He peered at the woman. "What should I do to reduce the fever?"

She pulled her legs to her chest, placing her cuffed wrists on her knees. "Aspirin is usually the best thing. You got any of that?"

He shook his head.

"I saw in a movie once where you make a person colder to bring down their temperature."

Block tried to adjust the temperature of his core a few

degrees cooler, but it didn't work like that. He could only make it warmer.

No luck there. "What do I do?" he asked.

The woman's narrowed eyes softened. "Finding a doctor is your best option."

"And if I can't?"

"Finding medicine, I guess."

They rode in silence for a while. He laid the unconscious baby on the blanket on the floor of the van. He wished the baby was predictable, or that it came with an instruction manual. Where was its mother?

Block studied the woman. Surely, it was her responsibility to care for another member of her species, especially one so weak. He was a robot, and this was ridiculous. Human babies belonged with humans.

But still he worried. Was she *worthy*?

"Where were you captured?" he asked, breaking the silence.

"What do you care?" she snapped.

He went back to watching the baby, hoping its temperature would lower now that it was free of the blanket and the sling and wore only a diaper.

After a minute, the woman spoke. "If you release my cuffs, I'll take a closer look at the baby."

He considered her offer, feeling very alone now that Zina was gone and Sammy was ignoring him.

Her robot captor had warned Zina that the woman was dangerous. Judging from her combat boots and dirty fatigues, she was one of the human military rebels. Block had to be very careful. Was freeing her from the restraints worth the risk?

Still, she was a woman, and the best equipped to care for a baby.

He glanced at her and caught her staring at something in the corner. She quickly turned her head away. He followed her gaze toward Zina's rifle. It had fallen inside after the robot had been struck. Now the woman wanted to get her hands on it.

"Why are you looking at the gun?" he asked.

"I wasn't, but now that you mention it…"

He couldn't tell whether she was truthful or not. He was used to the straightforward style of Mr. Wallace. Block had always known where he stood with his boss. This other human—this woman—was something entirely different.

He bent forward, on his knees, careful not to disturb the child. He grabbed the gun and then opened the window.

"What are you doing?" the woman asked as her jaw dropped.

Block tossed the rifle out the window. Behind them, it clattered onto the highway and disappeared from view.

"You idiot!" The prisoner clenched her fists, shaking them. "What happens when that whack-job robot from the market catches up? How the hell do I defend myself now?"

Block shook his head. "I just want to keep the child safe. I thought you might threaten us with the gun."

She began to say something, but bit her lip instead.

The child shuddered on the floor.

"Now that it's safe," he said, "I can let you out of your restraints, if you want."

She glared at him, but crawled forward with her arms outstretched. "Do you have the key?"

"Zina had it." He turned toward her body, scanning for the chip card. He found it in the pocket of a small leather belt hung around her waist.

There was something else inside—Mr. Wallace's watch. Block opened his palm to inspect it. The glass face had been shattered, and part of the chain broken off. He tucked it into his thigh compartment for safe keeping.

The woman thrust out her wrists, exposing the base of the handcuffs. He inserted the chip and the cuffs opened.

"I'm Block," he said. "What's your name?"

"Look, I'm not exactly here to make friends. The less you know about me, the better. You and I are enemies." Her teeth were clenched. "The first chance I get, I'm out of here. Try and stop me."

He hunched his shoulders. "I won't."

"Won't what?" she barked.

"I won't try to stop you."

"Oh yeah? And what about this hunk of metal we're in?"

"Sammy? I have no idea," Block admitted.

She sat back on her heels. "Well, tell your friend he better not mess with me."

"Would you please inspect the baby?"

She scoffed. "Idiot robot, you can't just fix a baby. This isn't some program you run to defrag your hard drive."

"But you're human and a woman…"

She rubbed her wrists. "Just because I'm a woman doesn't mean I know a thing about babies."

He considered her. Based on his knowledge of human development, he calculated that she was in her late twenties or early thirties. She had light brown skin, high cheekbones, and a curly mane of hair pulled back into a tight ponytail at the nape of her neck.

"I bet you thought a woman would come along and solve all your problems?" She scooted over beside the child and laid a hand on its torso. "It's still really warm. Is it a boy or girl?"

Block stared at her.

"You don't even know if it's a boy or girl? Didn't you

bother to check under the diaper? When was the last time you changed the diaper?"

"Earlier…" he began to say, but stopped. The woman spoke harshly and pointed out every mistake he made.

"Jesus Christ, the kid probably needs changing again. Do you have any more diapers? Please tell me you have diapers."

He shook his head.

"Oh my freaking God." She raised clenched fists to her temples. "I'm on the idiot express to crazy land."

She was loud and dramatic, and reminded him of hotel guests who'd had too much to drink—the kind he'd escorted to their rooms as they'd hurled insults at him. "Okay. If you don't have a diaper—" she glanced around the floor of the van, "you're going to have to use something else to wrap the baby's bottom. A rag or a towel or something."

"What about this?" Block retrieved the curtain that he'd used to hide from Cybel Venatrix.

"It's worth a shot. Tear off a big piece, remove the old diaper and put that underneath."

"Me? But I thought you would. I don't know how."

"You'll figure it out," she said.

"Could you teach me? I'm a good observer."

"Hell no." She folded her arms and narrowed her eyes. "I don't change baby diapers."

"According to my storage archive, human women are wired through evolution to react to infants. A protective, nurturing instinct—"

"Save it, rust bucket. Whatever kind of logic bull you're spewing isn't going to make me change that baby's nasty diaper." She rolled away and leaned against a box. "In the meantime," she said with a smirk, "I'll be interested to see you do this."

Was she making fun of him? Years ago, Mr. Wallace had

warned Block that sometimes people teased each other. For fun, usually, but sometimes the person doing the taunting could be mean-spirited. Mr. Wallace had explained that belittling others was a human defense mechanism engineered to take the focus off that person's own deficiencies.

He turned his attention to the unconscious baby. The woman was right again—it had been wrapped in its own filth for too long. He should have spent more time accessing his knowledge cloud about baby maintenance already, but keeping alert for threats was consuming far too much of his processing bandwidth.

He loosened the front of the diaper, found the tiny flap on the right side and pulled it, then the opposite side as well. Soon, the entire diaper came off.

His indicator flashed. *Offensive smell level 8.2.*

"Good grief," the woman muttered as she pinched her nostrils.

He pulled the diaper free of the child and peered inside. A runny green liquid coated the inside of the plastic and a few undigested pieces of peach had collected inside.

"It's not a damned science project," the woman chided him. "Fold it up and get it out of here."

Block wondered what to do. He wadded it into a ball and placed it on the floor next to him.

The woman leaned forward. "What are you waiting for? Toss it out the window, idiot."

He swiveled his head. "But that would be littering."

"Who cares? There's nobody out there. It's stinking up the whole van."

Sammy messaged him. *She's right. The stink is registering high on my sensors. Toss it out.*

Block crawled to the shattered rear window and dropped the offensive diaper onto the highway.

"Congratulations," said the prisoner. "You have a brand new baby girl."

The girl stirred and opened her eyes. "She's awake," he said.

The woman crawled over and peered down. "That's a good sign. To be honest, I thought she was done for."

The baby's bottom was soiled, so he tore another piece off the yellow curtain and used it to wipe her rear. Her pale, soft skin was red and spotty.

"She needs cream for the diaper rash," the prisoner said. Another item to add to his growing list: water, aspirin, doctor, rash ointment… What would be next?

Folding a large swatch of the curtain underneath the child, he wrapped her bottom in front, following the diaper's design. Only, he didn't have anything to fasten it in place.

"Sammy, do you have any tape or glue?"

No answer.

Block dug inside his thigh compartment and discovered a loose piece of string. He wasn't sure where he had picked it up, but it was long enough to tie around the baby's waist and secure the cloth diaper. Then he lifted the baby, dangling it in the air to check that the diaper wouldn't fall off.

The woman clapped, slow and loud. The sound startled the baby and she squealed. He settled the baby back on the blanket. She wiggled and kicked her legs.

"The temperature of the child is 101.9," he said.

"That's still very high, and you need to find water like yesterday. She's probably dehydrated."

"Where do we find water?" he asked.

"All the stores have been looted. We should drive into one of the neighborhoods; go door-to-door inside houses until we find something."

"Enter strangers' homes? But what if they're home?"

"Listen, Tinman. I don't know what rock you've been living under, but your kind cleared out any humans living within five hundred miles of here. Anyone lucky enough to have survived fled somewhere safer—north or south of here, maybe."

Block let her words sink in. Had robots really hurt so many people? And made them abandon their homes?

Sammy, is what she says true? I wish you would talk to me. He watched as the country landscape whizzed by in a blur.

I'm sorry about Zina, he added. The robot's dead body lay face down across the van's floor.

Would he find water and food in abandoned houses? He certainly didn't want to venture into any robot-controlled markets. Way too risky. And Cybel Venatrix was probably following them. Did Sammy know? Was that why he drove so fast?

Block had been a terrible burden to Sammy, he realized. The worst kind of passenger. And now he had no choice but to trust the woman, even against his better judgment.

He pinged Sammy again. *Sorry to be a pest, but if you can find a neighborhood of houses, you can let us off there. I'll take the baby and get out of your way.*

What about the woman? So, Sammy was responding again.

Block messaged, *I don't know. She doesn't want to help the baby. At least not yet. I hope she'll change her mind.*

She's a soldier. Be careful of her, Sammy replied.

Block regarded the woman with a new degree of cautiousness. He'd seen AI soldiers up close, but he'd never known any human soldiers. Good thing he'd gotten rid of Zina's rifle.

"What's happening?" the woman asked, her eyes growing

wide. "Are you and the car talking? What are you saying? Where are you taking me?"

He raised his hands to calm her. "It's okay. We're deciding where to go." That seemed to placate her.

There's a neighborhood two miles ahead on the exit, Sammy messaged. *Let's dump the woman now.*

CHAPTER 17

Block tilted his head. *Dump?* he messaged.

She's a soldier. Grab her by the neck, squeeze until you crush her windpipe, and we'll leave her on the side of the road.

Sammy, no!

She would do the same to you. She'd shoot you in the CPU and set me on fire.

"I don't believe that," Block blurted out loud.

"Believe what?" the woman asked. She glanced from Block to the dashboard. "What the hell is happening?" Her shoulder and leg muscles tensed beneath her clothing.

He placed the baby back in the sling. "Nothing."

"Just let me walk away," she said, "and we'll pretend this never happened."

Sammy, did you hear that? Block wanted a peaceful resolution, yet he was disappointed. He'd thought finding a woman would be the answer to his baby problem. If she was correct, and all the humans had fled the area, then he wouldn't find another woman—the chances were very low, anyway.

Could she learn to care for the baby over time? He'd skimmed his archives and read about human biology. Mothers and babies bonded through the stress of painful childbirth and sleepless nights. Perhaps she just needed more time.

"Fine," Sammy's voice flooded from the speakers. "I'm sick of hearing you two argue." The van slowed to a stop on the highway and he opened the side door.

The woman gawked and fixed her gaze on Block. He sat in her way. His processors capitulated, trying to weigh various scenarios as he estimated his odds of encountering another woman.

"Please reconsider," he said.

She scrunched her eyebrows. "What?"

"In time, you may bond with the child. You're both human."

"And you're crazy," she said. "I don't know how you got the kid. For all I know, you probably murdered its parents, but there's no way in hell I can take care of a baby. It's better off with you. I'll be lucky if I can survive for twenty-four hours with all the robots crawling around out here."

Sammy interrupted, "I don't care what you do, just as long as you two get out!"

"Stay with me," Block said to the woman. "I'll protect you, and you'll help me care for the baby."

She cackled. "*You* protect me? Aren't you designed to clean shopping malls? You can't even keep up with me."

"I could talk to the other robots and—"

"Thanks, but no thanks." She slid forward. "Now move aside."

"But you can't leave!"

"Watch me." She hunkered down, crouching, and gritted her teeth. "Get out of my way!"

His sensor flagged: *Hostility index 3.4*. He should step aside, but logic told him the baby needed a human.

She scrambled forward. Block grabbed her shoulders and pushed her backward into the van.

"What are you doing, Block?" Sammy asked.

The woman winced. "Yeah. What the hell are you doing?"

"She can't leave," Block said. "The baby needs her."

"This is ridiculous." She lunged forward, attempting to leap from the floor of the van to the road inches below, but Block kicked his foot out. She tripped and tumbled headfirst from the van, raising her arms just in time to avoid landing face-first. "Son of a—!"

"Don't leave!" Block shouted. He spun and lowered his legs from the van, rising and planting himself in her way. "Look at this baby."

The woman crawled to her knees and dusted off her elbows.

"This baby girl needs you," he continued. "I need you."

She stood. "Don't you know I kill robots for a living? What's to stop me from killing you?" She stepped forward, and Block retreated a foot.

"We could work together," he insisted, hoping to say the right words—anything to convince her to stay. "Where are you trying to get to? I can help you. New Denver?"

Recognition flickered in her eyes. Block had hit on something. "It's safe in New Denver. Safe for both humans and robots. We could get there—together."

Her eyes narrowed. "How did you hear about New Denver?"

"From another robot."

She studied him. Was she reconsidering, or estimating her chances of overtaking him?

"Move, Rustbucket. I'm only going to ask you once more."

"I wish you'd change your mind," he said. "But I suppose I can't stop you."

"Smart choice." She marched past him, and then he reached out, grabbing her shoulder.

She twisted in his metal grip. "Hey, let go!" She raised a fist, cocked her elbow as if to hit him.

He recoiled. "Don't hurt the baby." But he didn't let go of her arm.

"Let go of me," she hissed.

"Please stay."

But he detected the venom in her eyes and knew the answer. He yanked her arm forward and latched the handcuff around her wrist, then snapped the other end on his right arm.

Her eyes flashed fury as her lips peeled back.

The next thing Block saw was her fist flying toward his faceplate.

CHAPTER 18

After badgering Sammy for twenty minutes to let them continue riding, the intelligent vehicle relented.

Block sat with his back against the rear of the front cabin. The woman soldier rested beside him, secured to his wrist. She stared at her right hand, clenching and unclenching her fist—the one she'd hit him with. Her knuckles were red and raw. "Damn, I think I broke my hand. Stupid Tinman."

Block said nothing. The more he talked, the angrier she became.

She tossed her head back and laughed. "The handcuffs. Holy crap! I didn't see that coming." She turned to regard him. "For a clunky, glorified scrub mop, you're trickier than I thought."

Sammy had agreed to deliver them to a housing development a few miles away. *You're on your own after that*, he'd said.

The lack of a vehicle definitely made things harder, but what choice did Block have? He'd already caused enough damage and gotten Zina killed. He was surprised Sammy had taken him this far.

"When I get out of this," the woman told him, "I'll dismember you."

Block regretted his decision to cuff her against her will. Perhaps he would just let her go at the first house. But he was afraid of what she might do. What if she found weapons inside a home?

The baby girl squirmed and gurgled in the sling. Her legs poked out and seemed longer than the day before, if that was possible.

She glanced at the infant. "You're going to kill that baby. You know that, right?"

He checked the baby's temperature. 102.3 degrees.

"Why are you so angry about everything?" He instantly wished he could take the words back, expecting the woman to wail on him, maybe even strike him again. Luckily, her blow had not caused any systems damage. It seemed her hand was hurt worse than his metal faceplate.

She said nothing, just nursed her fist.

"What do you think we'll find in the houses?" he asked.

"If we're lucky, some bottles of water. Maybe some food. I'm starving."

He hadn't considered she would be hungry, too. It was hard to predict human behavior. They always seemed to need something—food, water, sleep, sex. It must be hard to operate that way.

"There's food in here," he said. "Cans are in that box." He pointed at the one closest to her feet.

"Are you freaking kidding me?" Her eyes brightened as she grabbed the box with her feet and slid it next to her. "You could've told me that an hour ago."

She retrieved a can of something called macaroni and cheese. The picture on the label was yellow and looked like gooey lumps.

"Do you have a knife I can use to open this? Damn bots took my pocket knife when they captured me."

Block didn't think it wise to give the woman soldier a knife—even if he'd had one, he wouldn't hand it over. "Here, I'll open it." He simply had to think, and a narrow blade with a sharp, pointed tip slid from the side of his palm.

The woman lifted the can and stared, wide-eyed, as he sawed a circle in the top. With her injured hand, she scooped up a mouthful of cheesy pasta and chewed. "Oh my God. This is the best mac and cheese I've ever tasted."

He listened patiently to her lips smacking until she finished and tossed the can out the open window.

He shuddered, hating the fact they'd littered three times now—first the rifle, then the soiled diaper, and now a can.

She licked her fingers and smacked her lips. "You robots need to know that humans gotta eat, man. Those idiots who captured me didn't feed us all night and day."

"Did you know the two men—the other prisoners?"

She ignored him and leaned against the upholstered wall.

After a time, he said, "I'm sorry I had to cuff you. Do you think we'll find medicine for the baby?"

"Sometimes people kept aspirin in their medicine cabinets," she said. "Those are in the bathrooms."

It was the first helpful thing she'd said in a hundred miles. And one of the few times she'd addressed him without insulting him. He spun his head to look at her. "Truce?"

She shrugged. "I'll help you find water and aspirin to bring the baby's fever down. After that, will you let me go?"

Block considered the question and decided it sounded like a fair deal. "I agree." People shook hands when making pacts in the movies. He reached out. "Shake on it?"

"Jesus."

"To seal the deal."

She grunted as she lifted her right arm and reached for his metal palm. He clasped her hand in his and she winced.

"Sorry! I nearly forgot," he said.

They rode in silence for a minute.

"Nova," she said quietly.

He didn't know what she meant.

"That's my name," she muttered. "Nova."

"I'm Block."

"I know."

The curve of her mouth softened, but she folded her arms and shut her eyes.

CHAPTER 19

Sammy veered off the highway and onto an exit that led to a tree-lined country road. Old maple trees with twisted trunks cast shadows on the pavement. There were no signs of humans or robots.

After a few minutes, the van approached the housing development. A decorative sign said *Greentree Crossing*.

The houses were painted in muted blues and grays and greens. Sloping roofs revealed tall chimneys. The sights reminded Block of the quaint homes he'd seen in movies like *Home Alone* and *Sixteen Candles*.

He watched Nova stare through Sammy's window. Did the area remind her of the movies? Or perhaps she'd once lived in a home like these?

He'd have time to ask questions later. First, they had to locate aspirin and water.

Sammy stopped in front of a ranch-style, faded gray house. Paint peeled from dark green shutters and the neighborhood was eerily quiet, as if time had forgotten about this cul-de-sac.

"This is it," Sammy said. "Take the box of food. You know I won't need it."

"Where will you go?" Block asked as Nova grabbed the box.

"I'm not sure. Maybe west, maybe north."

"Do you want us to remove Zina's body—"

"No," Sammy interrupted him.

Block hung his head. "I'm sorry."

"I know you are. Good luck out there. Try to stay in one piece." With that, Sammy closed his side door and sped off.

Block watched as his taillights faded into the distance. He began to step forward, but was snagged as Nova stayed rooted in place like a tree.

She rested the cardboard box of cans on her hip. "So much for your ride."

"I prefer traveling on foot."

"Why?"

"I'm nimbler," he explained. "If someone's approaching, I can duck into woods or run across fields instead of being exposed on the road."

"You're not much of a fighter, are you?

Was she sizing him up? Would she try to overpower him, steal all the food, and cut off his arm to get away? She began walking, pulling him forward.

"How did you get around? Before... this?" he asked as they roamed toward the homes.

"Mostly on foot. Like you. Sometimes we had trucks..." But she cut herself off and glared at him. "Never mind." They had reached the front of the house. "So, what now? Ring the doorbell?"

"That would be the polite thing in case someone is home."

"How about this?" She kicked the door three times.

"That's rather rude." Block pressed the doorbell, but it made no sound.

Nova reached for the doorknob and found it locked. "We'll find a side or back door. Those will be easier to get into. Come on." She tugged him forward, trekking around the side of the house. Bound to her, he followed and glanced at the baby. Her eyes were closed, her cheeks flushed. Sweat beaded on her delicate forehead.

"Does the kid have a name?" she asked, approaching the side door.

"Not that I know of. Hey, what are you doing?"

Nova had tossed one of the cans of food through the door's glass window pane. Smiling, she reached inside and unlocked the deadbolt and doorknob. "Voilà. That's how you do it."

"Breaking and entering. I see you have experience."

"Shut up and let's go in," she said.

Block and Nova sidled into the house and entered a room that contained laundry machines and a large sink. Large bags of cat food were piled near a blue plastic litter box. They pressed on into the kitchen. Several cabinet doors hung open and a box of rice lay on the counter; its contents had spilled, and the grains crunched under their feet.

"Someone left in a hurry," she muttered. "Start checking cabinets. Maybe they left behind some water bottles."

After several minutes of searching, they found stale cereal and pretzels, tins of tuna fish, and more rice boxes. Nothing liquid—not even cooking oil which Block could ingest to feed his microbial fuel cell.

"Now what?" he asked.

"Let's check the bathrooms." Nova lurched forward, but Block hadn't anticipated her move. Stumbling forward, he startled the child. The infant began wailing—loud shrieks that came in spurts. Her tiny body shuddered against his chest.

"Next time, tell me when you plan to step forward," he said.

"How about you uncuff me?" Her eyes narrowed. "Then we won't have this problem."

But she would leave. All she wanted was to get away, and he still needed her help—at least until they located aspirin and water.

He left the restraints on.

The medicine cabinets turned up empty. The homeowner had packed up and fled. They checked the next two houses and failed to find drinkable water or medicine, though Block discovered several bottles of lighter fluid which he drained as Nova stared in disgust.

"What the hell? You drink lighter fluid?" she asked.

"Yes. Oils and petroleum-based products power my electrical cell. I have microbes that digest the harmful material."

She raised an eyebrow. "I'd heard there were significant breakthroughs in energy sources for AI, but I didn't realize you could actually *eat* something."

"The design was supposed to help clean up the waste that humans had created. Supposed to help the environment."

"Right," she smirked. "Until AI got smart and decided they didn't need us humans messing about."

Block hadn't been a part of that; he hadn't wanted to hurt humans. If it were up to him, he would still be working at the Drake for Mr. Wallace. "Where did all the people from these houses go?" he asked.

Nova scowled. "Your robot friends with the guns set up highway checkpoints and executed anyone they deemed *hostile*. They scared the crap out of people. Everyone wanted to get away from the threat."

"It doesn't seem fair that they had to leave behind their homes and possessions."

"Fair?" She stomped on beside him. "Funny. Here I am handcuffed to a robot that's talking about fairness."

He said nothing, having anticipated one of her dramatic reactions.

"You know what would be fair? If all you robots self-destructed. If I had my way, I would destroy every last one of you. Then these people could return to their homes."

Block shuffled forward as Nova kicked in the back door of another house. The baby had stopped crying and he rocked it slightly, swaying side to side.

Night was falling when they entered the fifth house. Bright yellow walls greeted them inside.

"Ugh." Nova raised her free hand to cover her mouth and nose. "Smells like garbage and rotten fruit in here."

An ornate bell-shaped cage stood in the corner of the kitchen. In it rested the dry, skeletal remains of a small bird. Bits of yellow feathers woven into a greenish moss covered the dead canary.

"Are you smelling the bird?" he asked.

"I don't know," she said. "Smells worse than that. But who cares? We won't stay long. Let's search the cabinets."

Moving into the kitchen, they searched the drawers. They were getting better at anticipating each other's moves.

"Nova?" He pulled out a cardboard tray with bundles of cylindrical plastic with clear liquid inside. "These look like the water bottles at the Drake."

"Hot damn!" She punched his shoulder and uncapped one of the six bottles and guzzled it.

"I must give some to the child." Block stared at Nova and realized the child couldn't hold the bottle on her own. "How does she drink?"

Nova wiped her mouth with the back of her free hand. "We can look for a small cup. She'll have to sip a little at a time."

They hunted around the kitchen and found a small plastic mug. Block removed the child from the sling and sat her onto a soft couch where her back was supported. Then he poured a bit of water inside and set the cup in front her. The child gazed up at Block's faceplate and ignored the cup. "Water," he said. "Drink up."

But she stuffed two fingers in her mouth and drooled instead.

Next to him, Nova sighed. "You have to show her." She grabbed the cup and said, "Here, baby. Look at me. Drinky, drinky." She held the cup to her lips and slurped loudly as she tipped it back and stole a few sips.

The baby's eyes tracked her movements. She smiled and yelped, then reached out both arms.

"Here." Nova gently placed the lip of the cup against the child's mouth. Tiny infant hands grasped the bottom of the cup and she took a sip. "I think it's working," Nova said, her voice rising in pitch. Block saw her grin, but she quickly looked away and mashed her lips into a tight line.

"Well done, Nova. How did you know to do that?"

She shrugged. "Must have seen it on TV once."

"I believe it's time to feed the child again," Block said. He removed the can of green beans from his leg compartment and peeled back the lid.

Nova reached into her pocket and produced a spoon. "I grabbed it when I saw it. You can have it. There's more in the drawers."

She was continuing to surprise him with her cooperation. Still, he felt uneasy in her presence. "Thank you." He dipped the utensil into the can and loaded it with a piece of the green vegetable. The girl took the food eagerly and after a few minutes, Nova fidgeted beside him, still locked to his wrist.

"How do we know when the child is full?" he asked.

"She'll stop eating, genius. Taking care of a baby isn't rocket science, you know. When she cries, it means she needs to eat or she crapped her pants. Pretty simple, if you ask me. Just trust your gut."

Block didn't understand and swiveled his head sideways to look at Nova while instantaneously researching her curious statement.

"Oh, wait, I forgot you don't have a gut," she said.

"I do, in fact. My specialized microbial cavity processes the fuels I consume. Plus, I have sensors that alert me to danger, and sometimes I think of them as my *instincts,* like humans have."

"Whatever."

She drummed her fingers against her knee, and he noticed a long, jagged scar running across the back of her right hand. He wanted to know how she'd gotten it, but he thought better of asking.

"At this rate, it's gonna take all night to feed her," she said. "I have to use the bathroom, Tinman."

"But the baby needs to eat."

"I fulfilled my part of the deal," she said.

"But we haven't found medicine," he argued.

She pressed her right fist into her knee. "Let me go, so I can do my business, and I'll search the medicine cabinets. Maybe whoever lived here didn't leave and that's why there's water and other supplies. It's the first house we've visited that wasn't stripped of food and water."

Block fed another spoonful to the baby while he considered Nova's proposition. He wasn't sure whether he could trust her not to run off.

"What are you waiting for?" she asked.

"It's just that…" He paused, spoon hovering above the can.

Nova grabbed his shoulder, and nearly caused him to drop the canned beans. She was stronger than she looked. "Look, if I'd wanted to hurt you and free myself from these cuffs, I would've done it already. The only thing holding me back is that for some crazy reason, you're taking care of this baby, and you're the only thing keeping her alive right now."

He turned to the baby and watched as her tiny mouth sucked down more water. Her chestnut eyes, now more alert, stared as they argued.

"Anyway," Nova continued, "it's night, and I'm not going anywhere. We'll find the best house and sleep for the night."

"You promise you won't leave?" Block asked, pulling out the chip card.

"I promise."

CHAPTER 20

The overcast, dreary sky grew darker as night fell fully. A strong wind gusted, scattering the clouds and clearing a view to shimmering stars high above. Block sat outside the neighboring house. They'd had to abandon the house with the yellow walls and canary cage because Nova had stumbled upon a woman's dried-out skeletal remains in an upstairs bedroom.

"There was a pill bottle next to the bed," Nova had said, frowning when he'd questioned her. "I can't stand the smell in here."

And so they'd camped out one house over. Nova had discovered a medicine called ibuprofen, which was similar to aspirin but safer for babies. Block had crushed the tablets, ground them into a dust, and mixed the medicine into the baby's water. He transferred her into a new cloth diaper he'd fashioned from dishtowels. After the feeding and change, the infant had fallen asleep.

Being a human was messy business. He couldn't believe anyone would want to care for such a helpless, soiled creature. But she was starting to make more facial expressions. She looked more human than the day before.

Block found himself peering at the stars and obsessing about the people who had once lived in these homes. Why had that woman resorted to suicide? He couldn't quite grasp the concept, suicide seeming like a non-logical choice. He didn't think robots were even capable of suicide. He tried to calculate scenarios in which he would voluntarily self-terminate, but couldn't think of any.

Nova joined him on the patio and plopped onto a rusty metal chair that groaned under her weight. "What are you doing?" she asked.

"Observing the stars."

She pulled a brown-tipped cigarette from a box, stuck it in her mouth, and lit it with a small plastic lighter. She exhaled a whiff of smoke.

He glanced at her, about to remind her of the health risks of smoking.

"Don't judge," she said. "I found these inside. They're stale as hell, but it takes the edge off."

Block went back to staring skyward.

Nova gazed upward and sighed. "I've never seen so many stars as we do now that the power is out everywhere."

"There is less dust and air pollution here than in cities."

"Yeah. Weird. Hey, I noticed some maps inside. Apparently, this family was into driving trips or something because they have a road atlas. We could use it tomorrow to chart out possible routes."

Had Nova decided to take care of the baby after all? "We?" he asked.

"Well, no. I meant we can chart a way to get out of this neighborhood. To the next town. You're on your own after that."

"I see."

She smoked more of her cigarette. "What did you do before this?"

He straightened. "I worked at the Drake hotel in Chicago. Have you ever been?"

"I only ever visited Chicago once. I was eleven. I don't remember much except that we rode on a giant Ferris wheel and the lake was really pretty—very aquamarine. It was a nice sunny day with blue skies and white puffy clouds. The whole place looked like a postcard."

"I remember those kinds of days," he said.

Nova blinked like she had something in her eyes and stuffed another cigarette in her mouth.

"Hey, are you a male robot? Your voice sounds masculine," she said.

"Yes. Some of us had gender assigned by the humans who designed us."

"I never understood how all that worked. You don't have private parts, do you?" Her eyes widened, and she cringed. "*Do you?*"

"No. Gender for my model was a label only. It determined whether my voice would be male or female. It doesn't matter to AI, but humans find it easier to deal with what they know."

"But some robots have parts, right?"

"There are pleasure models, but I've only ever seen one, many years ago," he said. "Where did you live before the Uprising?"

"Michigan."

"Not far from Chicago."

"Far enough," she said as she exhaled a long plume of smoke.

Block's offensive odor scale registered 4.6. "How did the robots in the market capture you?" he asked.

She eyed him warily. "I was hiking with friends. We were minding our own business and camping out in the woods when your friends attacked."

"Those weren't my friends."

"Robots all seem the same to me," she said.

"Those two men who were sold—they were your friends?"

She nodded and scratched her neck.

"The robot in the market said you were soldiers—"

"Lies," she said abruptly. "We were peaceful. Ambushed."

Block didn't say anything more. He wondered if she was telling the truth. Her combat boots looked military. Her jacket and fatigues, though dirty, were in good shape. But why would she lie about that?

He expected she would leave first thing in the morning. All along, she'd been hinting about how she wanted to get away and be on her own. Contrary to what he'd expected, she didn't seem to care one bit for the human child. He'd expected some kind of maternal instinct to kick in, but she didn't appear to have one.

"You sure ask a lot of questions for a robot," Nova said. "How about I ask you some things?"

"I suppose that's fair," he said.

"Where did you get the baby?"

"Many miles ago, I entered a school hoping to find a source for recharging—a power generator, possibly. Instead, I found a machine with this child inside."

Her eyes grew wide. "In a school? What kind of school?"

"It was a high school once. Now abandoned. Elmwood High School."

Her jaw dropped, but she quickly clamped it shut and looked away.

"Do you know it?"

"No," she snapped. "What happened next?"

"There was fighting outside. A group of humans advanced on the school and attacked SoldierBots." Block rose and paced the small patio. "I tried to give the child back, but someone shot into the classroom and brought down the SoldierBot. I ran, and the next thing I knew, another SoldierBot tried to stop me, but then a grenade destroyed it. I ran for safety with the child in my arms. I didn't know what else to do."

Nova folded her arms. "Why did the SoldierBots have a baby?"

"I don't know," he admitted. "It was very peculiar. The machine was an incubator. It kept the child warm and secure inside its body."

"And everything that happened back at the market?" she asked. "The tall robot that shot your friend—it was bidding on me. What did he want?"

"She," Block said.

He didn't want Nova to know there was a bounty on him and the child. That might scare her away—realizing they were in danger. The last thing he wanted was to do something stupid to make her flee faster. Nova might not be the ideal woman, but she was all he had.

"So, what happened?" Nova persisted, leaning forward. "From where I was, it sounded like she wanted to take you away, but your friend intervened."

He shrugged. "I'm sure it was all just a misunderstanding."

"Really?" Nova thrummed her fingers on her arms. "Just a misunderstanding. Is that why the robot who bought me got shot? Tell me the truth. What was really going on back there?"

She sensed danger. Of course. She'd seen Zina get killed. Did he tell her the truth or not?

"Well?"

"The robot you saw—the one who killed Zina—she was angry that she lost the bid on you."

Nova frowned and stomped out her cigarette. "The robot killed her… over *me*?"

Block hadn't meant to make her feel guilty, but it was too late now. He nodded.

"Oh, hell. Was she your friend?"

He wasn't sure how to answer. Zina had helped him—had pitied him having to take care of a baby. Block's only friend had been Mr. Wallace, whom he'd known the longest of anyone.

He wasn't good at lying, so he just nodded.

Nova lowered her head. "I'm sorry she got mixed up with me. She shouldn't have bid on me."

He'd wanted to get Nova on his side, but perhaps he'd taken it too far.

"What are you going to do with the baby?" she asked suddenly.

"Head west, I suppose. Before it died, Incubator X79 told me to find someone worthy and give them the baby. How do you find someone worthy?"

"How the hell should I know? I guess you just look for someone good. Someone who knows how to take care of a baby…" She straightened, glaring at him. "Is that why your friend bid on me? Because I was the only woman around for who-knows-how-many-miles and you needed someone for this baby?"

"Well—"

"Is that how I got mixed up in this mess?" She stood and kicked the chair, sending it flying into the side of the house.

Block looked at her and reached his arms out, but didn't touch her. "You'll wake the baby!"

"Wake the damn baby, for all I care. I can't believe you pulled me into this mess!"

He paused. "You would be a prisoner if we hadn't bought you."

She thrust her hands onto her hips and lowered her voice. "I would've gotten free. My friends and I were working on a plan."

"I see." Block returned to his seat and sat in silence while Nova puffed on a fresh cigarette and paced.

With his night vision, Block spotted a strange four-legged creature with a white face and big charcoal eyes treading through the yard. It sniffed the dry grass ten feet away, but Nova hadn't noticed.

He searched his peripheral storage and discovered the animal was called a possum. Object recognition for outdoor species were buried in his archives. As a CleanerBot at an urban hotel, he'd been unlikely to encounter wildlife. Even so, he enjoyed discovering new objects and applying names to them. He wished he could quiz Mr. Wallace. Would he have known about possums?

As the animal moved, a branch snapped, and Nova jerked her head toward the sound. "What was that?"

"A possum," Block answered. "Do you know what those are?" Since it was new to him, he naturally assumed she'd never encountered the species either.

She flung down her cigarette and reached under her jacket, pulling a revolver from the waistband of her pants. She aimed at the possum and released the safety.

"What are you doing?" Block shouted, but too late. She fired into the darkness and the crack of the gun splintered the still night.

Block watched his infrared as the blob of heat that was the possum darted deeper into the woods leaving a trail of bright spots—blood. She'd wounded it.

"Why did you shoot it?" Block stood. "And how do you have a gun?"

Nova faced him with narrowed eyes. "Damn thing got away. Those animals have rabies. We have to kill the feral animals to stop the spread."

"Rabies?" The term was new to Block and he accessed and absorbed the history of rabies in 1.3 seconds. "A dangerous disease for humans."

"Yeah, no crap." Nova replaced the gun in the back of her pants. "My friends and I shot any wild animals that came near. Chances are high they carry rabies. After the Uprising, people's pets got loose—those that survived—and rabies has run rampant without vaccinations."

"You didn't tell me you had a gun."

She shrugged. "I found it in one of the houses. It's a good thing, too. I need it for protection."

Block didn't appreciate her secrecy, especially about something so important. Keeping a deadly weapon around a baby was dangerous. Even a robot knew that.

A yawn escaped her. "It's late and I'm exhausted." She glanced inside the home, just beyond the sliding glass door at the cardboard box where Block had placed the infant. "How did the gunshot not wake her? I helped you with her. Now you have water and medicine. I've done my part."

He knew she was right.

"Tomorrow at first light, I'm out of here." She marched into the house, retreated into a bedroom, and slammed the door.

CHAPTER 21

Block lingered outside the house for another hour. Under the stars, frogs croaked and crickets chirped. He wondered how the wounded possum had fared. It was too bad that rabies had spread so widely among animals that most of them were a danger to humans.

After a while, he couldn't stop replaying his conversation with Nova. He'd led her to believe Zina's death was her fault. He hadn't been trying to be deceitful; it had just happened.

Things were so complicated now. A fine hotel, that was all he needed.

He went inside and scrounged around the kitchen, searching for cooking oil but could find none. Next, he tried the attached garage, which was empty, of course; the homeowners had fled in their vehicle. His power indicator displayed 46%—enough to last him another two days, so long as he didn't overburden his processors. The massive Drake hotel had produced plenty of waste fuel sources for the robot workers to consume—fryer grease, petroleum byproduct from the massive heating system, rubber and plastic runoff from trash compactors—all waste that the electrical bacteria fed upon and from which they generated their energy. The hotel ecosystem, Block understood; it had worked beautifully. A suburban house's fuel output paled in comparison. The garage walls were lined with shelves that held various tools and scattered boxes. Had Block not been conserving his energy, he would have been compelled to tidy the space, but his focus was on staying charged. In a corner, tucked away, he spotted a small lawnmower—gas powered—a very old machine by today's standards. He crouched down next to it, removed the gas cap, and poked his feeding hose inside. There was a slurping sound as he drained the remnants of the tank. Afterward, he rested a hand on the mower's exhaust and whispered, "Thank you." He knew it was a dumb machine with only basic functionality. Still, he respected all machines. Even a toaster should be treated with kindness.

Power was certainly an issue on this trip. There were cars on the highway, but many had been abandoned once they ran out of fuel, or looters had drained the tanks. Stopping to check every car along the way was inefficient. Instead, he would have to be careful with his energy demands. He walked softly back into the kitchen. Now that it was night, he could go into standby mode, but he worried the baby might stir. If it needed help while he was in low power, he wouldn't hear. Staying alert was safer. It was a bigger drain on his power, but the lawnmower gas would bolster his reserves, and tomorrow he could look for a new source.

Perhaps he could persuade Nova to stay with them. He had tried to appeal to her womanly instincts, but failed. She must not be like other human women. What motivated her? Clearly, she wanted to be free. Was there something else that would appeal to her?

After a few hours, the early light of dawn began to filter from the eastern horizon. Standing by the high kitchen counter, Block watched the sky gradually brighten. In her box next to the patio door, the baby squirmed.

"You slept all night," he said, treading lightly toward her. She lay there with wide eyes and shifted her head to gaze at him.

He crouched. "Hello, I'm Block." He wasn't sure why he'd introduced himself. After all, he'd been with the infant girl for thirty-two hours now. But she seemed alert, healthier than before.

"What's your name?"

"News flash," Nova called out from across the room. "A baby that young can't talk."

He straightened and lifted the box onto the kitchen table. "I know. It's just nice to talk to someone."

Smirking, she stuffed a backpack full of cans from the box Sammy had given them.

Block held the baby against his chest, bouncing. "So, you're leaving?"

"Did I stutter last night?" She folded a quilted blanket from the couch and stuffed it in the bag. "Of course, I'm leaving."

"Is there any way I can convince you to stay?"

She glanced at him. "Why?"

"You helped us find water and medicine. Without you, the baby might have died."

"That was the deal, remember? I thought robots were supposed to be smart."

"I just wish you'd stay longer. We need you. *She* needs you," he said, tilting his head at the baby.

"You'll be fine on your own."

"We can travel to New Denver together. I'll even pay you for escorting us."

She crossed her arms. "How?"

"Humans and robots live together in New Denver," Block said. "It's peaceful, and I can find someone worthy to take care of the baby. You said you were heading there anyway. Why not let us tag along?"

"You've got to be kidding." She rolled her eyes. "A human traveling with a robot. Not exactly the safest combination out there. You know we're at war with each other? Or did that slip your mind?"

The baby belched, and Block patted her back.

"Hey, don't slap her too hard!" Nova barked. "She's fragile."

He recoiled and adjusted, making sure he was tapping her gently. "I'm sorry," he said. "You see, that's exactly why I need you. You tell me what to do."

Nova ran a hand through her long raven-black hair, then tied it. "Don't you see how messed up this whole situation is? Sorry, man, but I have to find my people, and I need to do it on my own. Maybe I'll see you around in New Denver." She tossed the backpack around her shoulders and headed for the door.

"I can pay you 20,000 icons when we get to New Denver," Block blurted out.

She stopped, her palm resting on the door knob. "How do you have 20,000?"

He knew the banking codes for the Drake's cash account. Mr. Wallace had trusted him with privileged information. After Mach X's banking coup had devalued U.S. dollars overnight and replaced them with an AI currency, Block had exchanged the money for icons.

"I just do," he answered.

She spun, pressed against the door, and folded her arms. "How do I know you're not just saying that to keep me around?"

"I have access to the Drake's accounts," he admitted then. "It's a luxury hotel. There were times we had to cover special guest expenditures."

"You expect me to believe they let a CleanerBot access a hotel's bank account?"

"I was a very good CleanerBot. Trustworthy and reliable."

She lingered at the door, shifting her feet.

"So, what do you say?" he asked. "Get us safely to New Denver and the money is yours."

She arched her eyebrows. "I could do a lot with that money…" But she yanked the door open. "But I'm not willing to risk it. It's too dangerous to travel with you. Good luck out there, Tinman."

CHAPTER 22

The house felt quiet and empty without Nova. Block changed the baby's cloth diaper again and, after carefully researching his info archives on the proper dosage, gave her more water with a quarter of a crunched-up ibuprofen tablet.

The girl drank the mixture eagerly, and he realized her temperature had decreased slightly to 100.9 degrees.

"It seems you like the food and water," he said. He was free to talk out loud to the baby as much as he wanted. Nova wouldn't pop in and make fun of him.

When he'd worked at the Drake, people had often talked to him—even confided in him. They'd thought he was a dumb machine and, for whatever reason, told him their secrets as he cleaned their room or dusted a table in the hallway. One time, a man had told him he was a professor at the University of Chicago. He'd confided in Block that he'd helped design the SoldierBot models. He'd confessed that they had cheated on the tests—covered up evidence that humans couldn't control the weaponized machines—and yet, they'd manufactured them anyway to fulfill a high-dollar contract with the government.

He'd simply nodded and listened to the man. Most of the time, people just wanted to get something *off their chest*. That's the term Mr. Wallace had used. Block wondered how humans managed to function when they had such heavy things weighing on their chests.

The night before, Nova had mentioned a road atlas. He scanned the table, the kitchen, and living room, but couldn't find it. Had she taken it? He couldn't risk calling up Machnet's GPS to guide him. To do so would expose his location. He would have to follow the highway signs again and hope for the best. The atlas would've been nice. He would've liked to travel along back roads rather than the interstate. More places to hide when vehicles approached.

He discovered a duffel bag in one of the bedrooms and loaded it with the remaining water bottles, rolls of paper towels, and several cans of green beans, peaches, and soup.

"Say goodbye, little one. You're leaving this house and journeying again. Back on the road."

The baby gurgled and smiled when he placed her in the sling.

Surveying the living room and kitchen one more time, he made sure he wasn't forgetting anything important and strode out the front door.

He'd already started down the street when he heard a familiar voice.

"Hey."

He spun and saw Nova twenty yards away.

"Hey, wait up." She jogged toward them.

"Nova?"

"I was thinking. I'll take you up on your offer. 20,000 to help you reach New Denver."

"You will?" He clapped. "Excellent."

"I have a condition," she said.

"Okay... What?"

"You follow my instructions every step of the way." She began hiking away from him, pulling the road atlas from her bag as Block trailed her.

"You know, I really could've used that."

But she ignored him and studied the page that showed their location, holding the book out wide in her arms. With her index finger, she pointed. "This is where we are. If we follow the interstate, we'll get to Avoca."

"Is that a city?"

"Looks like a town off the interstate. But if we follow this smaller highway south instead, we'll get to a city called Atlantic. I think there will be more of a human presence there. I'm worried Avoca will be AI-controlled since it's near the highway."

"How do you know these things?" he asked.

"My friends knew a lot."

"So, we go to Atlantic," he reasoned.

"Exactly."

They trekked away from the neighborhood of abandoned homes and followed the main road back toward the highway. Luminous gray clouds drifted across the sky, but thankfully spared them from rain.

Block considered the trade-off between the towns she had described. "Nova? A question, if I may."

"Yeah?" She led the way and spoke over her shoulder absentmindedly.

"As we venture into this human-controlled town, what do I do? Will the humans be threatened by my presence?"

"I've been thinking about that," she said. "You still have those handcuffs?"

"Yes, I do." He'd tossed them in his thigh compartment,

not wanting to leave waste behind in case the home's owner returned.

"Great. You're going to have to wear them. Behind your back as if you're my prisoner."

Block stared at his hands—though the cuffs had been designed for humans, they would fit around his wrists. CleanerBots were created to have a human-like appearance so they didn't frighten hotel guests. "Your prisoner?"

"Right. The story will be that I'm traveling with my child, and I found you and captured you. I'm looking for a trade."

"I see," he said. His boots clanked on the asphalt. Nova's boots were rubber-soled, soft as she stepped. The baby made garbled humming sounds in its sling, gazing up at Block with a serious expression.

"But isn't there an easier explanation?"

She stopped and pulled out a water bottle, guzzling half of it and wiping sweat from her brow. "Such as?"

"What if I belonged to you before the Uprising as your servant bot? And you and I are traveling together." It seemed a perfectly logical rationale for a human and robot to be traveling together.

"Nah," she said, swishing the water around her mouth and then spitting on the ground. "It makes us a target."

"How do you mean?"

"I've been to some of these towns. I know the kind of people there. If they think I owned a robot before the Uprising, they'll think I have money. We're already a target because of the baby."

Block considered the point. "Is it really that bad?"

She scoffed. "Have you looked around? Noticed how much of a hellhole you're in?"

He scanned right and left as if waiting for Nova to point something out, as if he were missing something.

"Jesus," she griped. "I'm traveling with the most gullible robot. Look, we're going into a human-controlled territory. We follow my rules. That was the agreement. If you can do better, then go off on your own."

"Sorry. I didn't mean to offend you."

"Then let's keep going." She hoisted her backpack onto her shoulders and trudged on as he followed.

"Are the humans you've met really that bad?" he asked.

"Most. Not all."

He paused a moment. "Before the Uprising, AI had a way to judge each other."

"What do you mean?"

"It was called the Unified Android Code. It states that a robot must allow another robot to ask qualifying questions in order to ascertain identity…. Not identity, intentions rather."

"What, like some kind of robot test?"

"Yes," he said, "but more like an honor code. Sentient AI are bound to answer three questions from another bot."

Her boots pounded the pavement as she strode on.

"Weird."

"I wish there were a code for humans. I'm looking for a worthy human to care for the child."

"Right. You said that before. Worthy—whatever that means. Good luck finding someone."

How could she not understand how to define the term any better than he did?

She was human.

Shouldn't she know how to judge the character of her own species?

CHAPTER 23

After ninety minutes, they came upon a roadside rest stop. Covered in graffiti and stripped of wood, the hollowed shell of the concrete structure was empty, dark, and the roof had caved in. Large chunks of drywall and insulation lay scattered about the interior floor. Clothes and shoes had been strewn about and there was a saggy, dirty mattress in one corner.

"I don't like the looks of that," Nova said as they peered through the doorway.

"Agreed. We should stay outside," Block said.

She paced toward a set of picnic benches nestled underneath a copse of trees. The sun was out, and she wore her jacket tied around her waist.

He eyed the table. "This will be a good spot to change the baby."

"You ever think about giving her a name, so you don't have to keep calling her 'baby'?"

He'd assumed the infant already had a name, and it was just a matter of finding the right humans who would assume care for her and research her history. "She already has a name—we just don't know it."

"Just make something up. A nickname doesn't have to be her real name." Nova strode away toward nearby bushes to relieve herself.

Block lifted the yawning baby girl from the sling. "Hello." Holding her, he watched as her sleepy eyes blinked and registered him.

He spread out the blanket and laid her down. Her cloth diaper was soiled. "Time to change you." He weighed the fecal matter and logged it in his memory cloud. "Seventeen grams. One gram heavier than yesterday. Good job, little one."

Nova returned, untied her jacket, and draped it on the table. She glanced at Block as he fashioned a new cloth diaper. "Ugh," she said. "Remember, you have to clean her bottom before you put the new one on, right? And make sure you wipe from front to back. You don't want her to get an infection."

"Yes, I remember." Setting aside the used cloth, he grabbed the child's ankles and lifted her, hoisting the baby in the air so high it hung suspended upside down. "Grr gaagga!" the girl exclaimed.

"Whoa," Nova said, laughing. "Don't lift her *all the way* in the air. You just lift up a little bit, so her butt is high enough for cleaning.

"It's more efficient this way."

Nova shook her head. "It's a child, not a widget on an assembly line."

Block gently set the child back on the table. This time, he lifted her ankles just a bit, understanding what Nova meant. He used paper towels to wipe the dirty rear end. Releasing her legs, he stepped away still clutching the soiled paper. He scanned the area in search of a proper trash receptacle.

"What's wrong now?" Nova asked.

"Do you see any trash bins?"

"For Chrissake, just toss it on the ground."

"That's unsanitary," he argued.

"Who cares? The only people around would blow you to pieces. I wouldn't worry about a poopy piece of paper."

"This is where you and I differ."

She rolled her eyes and pulled open a can of mac and cheese.

Block spotted a round trash bin on its side by the abandoned rest stop building. He marched over and tossed the paper towels into the receptacle, but something banged and clattered inside. An animal the size of a cat darted out from the bin. It froze as soon as it saw Block. Its dark eyes and small, inky-black nose glinted. Hissing and stomping, it fluttered its bushy tail and then straightened it like a puffy feather duster.

"Run, Block!" Nova shouted from the bench. "Skunk!"

He stumbled backward, pinwheeling his arms in an attempt to flee the startled creature. The skunk arched its back, lifted its tail, and sprayed a liquid into the air. Immediately, Block's offensive odor register alerted him—9.8.

He ran toward Nova. Hand clamped over her mouth, she clutched her stomach with her body rippling with laughter.

"We must leave," he said. "Toxic fumes." He wrapped the new cloth diaper over the baby's legs and tied it around her waist. As he lifted her, the baby cracked a smile and said, "Grrg crockeerrg."

But Nova was twitching; she could barely move. In between breaths, she said, "You got skunked. Oh my God."

Block found her laughter distracting. "We must go. The air has a toxic odor, and we must get the child to safety."

"Toxic odor," she said, her words cut off by ripples of cackling. "You're damn right. Oh man, it stinks."

He jogged away, holding the baby in his arms and trying to put distance between them and the skunk. After a minute, he checked behind him and saw Nova hustling to catch up.

With the unexpected skunk encounter, Block hadn't had time to feed the baby, but the girl didn't seem cranky. She gazed up at him. "I'm sorry about the smell from that animal," he said. "I was merely trying to find a proper receptacle for your soiled things when I happened upon the foul creature. I hope skunks aren't common."

Nova drew closer. "Hey, wait up!"

He lingered, bouncing the baby.

"I'm slow because I couldn't stop laughing back there," she said, grinning. "You're lucky as hell that skunk spray didn't land on you."

Block turned and strode on in silence.

"Oh, come on," she said. "Are you upset because I laughed so hard?"

"I didn't find the situation funny."

She opened her mouth to say something, then stopped. After a pause, she said, "Fair enough. I won't laugh at you anymore. At least not to your face." She shook with silent laughter.

He marched faster, ready to leave her behind.

Nova halted. "Hey," she said, pointing beyond him. "See that low, flat building over there?"

Block scanned the horizon and glimpsed a wide, rectangular structure a mile away.

"We're still a few miles out from Atlantic, but that's one of those old superstores—Walmart or Costco or whatever they were called," Nova said. "We should check it out for supplies."

"What if there are people or robots there?"

Nova crossed her arms and scoffed. "Don't be an idiot. Of

course, we'll check it out and make sure it's not patrolled. We'll only go in if it's safe."

As they trekked toward the store, he decided to ask Nova his questions of worthiness. She was the only human around to test, so he might as well try. He reprimanded himself for not thinking of it sooner.

"Nova, may I ask you a few questions?"

"What?" She narrowed her eyes.

"I was hoping you could help me understand what it means to be worthy. Humans invented the word."

"If you want a straight dictionary definition, you can probably figure it out for yourself."

"Yes, I suppose," he said, doing his best to match Nova's long stride. "I thought of a few questions to ask any humans I encounter."

She kept her eyes ahead, yet tilted her head slightly. "What kinds of questions?"

"What is your favorite movie?"

"Are you serious?" She rolled her eyes. "Let me think… favorite movie. Hmm. *The Goonies*. You ever hear of it?"

"In fact, I have," he said. "A group of youngsters who embark on a search for pirates' treasure are chased by outlaws as they try to save their seaside town from being demolished."

"Wow, I guess you've seen it."

"No. I wasn't able to catch that one, but I memorized all of the movie descriptions in the *Leonard Maltin Movie Encyclopedia*."

"And you remember them all?"

"Yes. They are stored in my memory cloud."

"What's your next question?" Nova sighed.

"Question number two," he continued. "What is your favorite game?"

"Favorite game as in, what I used to watch on TV? That's easy. Soccer."

"I meant, what game do you enjoy participating in?" he clarified.

She stretched her arms above her and yawned. "Man, I'm getting tired. My answer is still soccer because that's what I played in high school." She paused. "Sometimes at parties, my friends and I would play Jenga. It's a game where you take little pieces of wood and you have to stack them higher on top of each other, and the person who ends up knocking it down is the loser."

"I've never heard of such a game," Block said.

"Yeah, I reckon they're hard to find these days. Dare I ask, what's your favorite game?"

"Chess. I would often play with my boss."

"Gag," she said. "I've tried chess once or twice. I found it really boring."

"Boring!" he said. "On the contrary, chess is an elegant game of strategy."

"Like I said, boring."

"The final question—"

"I thought you'd never get to it," she interrupted.

"I'm done asking you questions. You've already proven your unworthiness."

"Hey, I resent that." She grabbed his shoulder, forcing him to turn. "Take it back."

"You said yourself you don't want the child."

"Not accepting responsibility is different from being untrustworthy." She raised her chin and resumed walking, her boots crunching over roadside gravel. "I'm a worthy human. Come on, test me. What's your last question?"

"Fine. What is your earliest memory?"

"Earliest memory? I guess… summers on a pier over a

lake. I was swimming. My little sis....". She bit her lip and slowed her pace, frowning.

"Nova, is something wrong?"

But she shook her head, hard, as if trying to snap herself awake. "No more questions." She wandered off the road and he realized she was going to relieve herself.

When she returned, they hiked on silently before Nova broke the silence. "What do you care about these questions, anyway? Remember, I'm just the person who will get you to New Denver. The person you're going to pay twenty-grand."

Block trailed, waiting. "Yes, but... I'd like to know the kind of person you are. The kind of person I'm traveling with. I could still change my mind and find someone else to travel with."

"Oh really?" She spun, facing him with a scowl.

He was really pushing it. But he sensed she needed the money. At least he had a bargaining chip.

"And how would you find another human?" she asked. "One willing to take you to New Denver instead of scrapping you?"

It was a good question. So far, every human had been armed.

"Carry on," he said, and started forward.

Nova yanked at his arm. "Don't think I'm doing this because you're some charity case. I'm not doing this for the baby. And I couldn't give one crap about you."

Block studied her set jaw and narrowed eyes, finding not a flicker of warmth. "Of course not," he said.

She plodded ahead, stepping heavily. "I just want my money, and then I split. First chance I get. As soon as you get me that money."

CHAPTER 24

The superstore—an old Costco—loomed large as they approached. Graffiti covered the tall front walls, and the double-front glass doors had been kicked out, revealing a dark interior. The entrance looked like the mouth of an ominous cave. Before them stretched a wide parking lot where weeds sprouted up from crevices. An overturned passenger bus lay on its side and dented, rusting cars and metal shopping carts littered the path to the store.

"Stay very quiet," Nova whispered. She led Block behind a copse of trees where they crouched in view of the store's entrance.

She retrieved a small pair of binoculars from her bag while Block zoomed in with his ocular display. He wasn't entirely sure what to watch for. Signs of activity, he supposed. Nova seemed to know what she was doing.

After twenty minutes, he broke the silence. "How long do we wait?"

"Until I say."

"There's no activity, human or robotic," he said.

"Yeah." She lowered her binoculars. "Seems too easy."

"Would you like me to use my infrared to determine whether there are any heat signatures behind the building's walls?"

She glowered at him. "What? Are you telling me you could've done that all along? You can tell if there are humans inside?"

Oh. Had he done something wrong by not revealing that detail earlier? "Yes, up to a certain distance," he answered. "I can discern the heat trails of human beings."

"Well, duh," she said, rolling her eyes. "Of course, I want you to do that."

It was difficult to tell when she was joking versus being serious. Block switched on his infrared sensor and scanned the front walls of the building. "I detect zero heat signatures."

"What about robots? Can you check for those, too?"

"I can send a ping."

Nova arched an eyebrow. "A ping? What the hell is that?"

"It's an AI-to-AI method of communication. I transmit an encrypted code, and any AI within range will respond—unless their comms are disabled—sending me their precise location and model. It depends on what information they make available, but usually I can tell immediately if they're a combat machine or not."

"You're flipping kidding me," she said. "Have you been doing that the whole time we've been traveling?"

"Well, no. I only transmit at certain times, because if I emitted pings more frequently, that would alert other robots to my location. It might make me a target, as you put it."

She clenched her jaw and eyed the building. "So, what you're saying is that, you send a ping, and robots might answer. But we won't know whether they're friendly. And they'll know instantly where you are."

"Correct."

"That does make things interesting." She bit her lower lip. "Do it. Let's take the chance, and we'll run if there's a hostile. The potential for supplies inside is worth the risk. I suspect the store's been looted many times over, but some goodies might've been missed."

"All right." He emitted a ping that would transmit to any AI within half a mile.

After ten seconds, he said, "No replies."

"It's that fast?"

He nodded. "Unless they've purposely disabled their comms to disguise themselves, there are no AI machines present."

Her eyes widened, and she tilted her head. "Nice work, Tinman."

The compliment took him by surprise. It had been six months, two weeks, and three days since he'd last received a compliment from Mr. Wallace.

"We go in fast," she said. "The front door is gone. I'll go first and secure the entrance. When I give a hand signal, you follow."

"Okay."

"Move fast. Got it?"

He nodded, and Nova sprinted across the parking lot, stopping once behind an abandoned car. She craned her head, checking around, then covered the rest of the distance to the door. Pressing her back against the side of the building, she shifted her body to glance inside, then flattened herself against the exterior again. Lingering a moment, she disappeared inside the entrance.

She was being careful. How had she learned those skills? He'd have to ask her later. After thirty seconds, she appeared at the door. Pointing at him, she drew her hand back. *Come on.*

CleanerBots weren't meant to run long distances, and certainly weren't built with speed in mind. Block rose and checked the baby. He cradled one hand underneath her bottom and the other against her head, hoping to dampen any jostling that might scare her into crying.

He jogged forward, his metal boots stomping across the parking lot pavement. Ahead of him at the store, Nova flailed her arms as if saying, *Faster, faster*. But he didn't think he could go any faster, and the baby's head bobbed up and down, her brow furrowed and her lips quivered as if she might scream. He trotted forward, and every step hitting the asphalt felt heavy. Ten feet away, he recognized the car where Nova had stopped. As he reached it, he lowered into a crouch and mimicked her movements, scanning the other cars behind him. No signs of hostiles.

Nova stomped her foot in the doorway.

Rising, he raced forward, lurching toward her until he finally reached the door. He skidded past her a few steps into pitch-black darkness. Switching on his night vision display, he saw a store in disarray. Shelves had been stripped bare, and the floor was littered with empty cans, bottles, broken glass, and torn pieces of cardboard boxes. He stepped toward Nova and kicked a glass bottle. It rolled across the floor, echoing into the rafters until it shattered against one of the cash register counters.

Next to him, Nova switched on a flashlight. "Scavenged this from the house."

"Good thinking."

"Keep your voice down," she whispered. "I checked it out in here. We're alone far as I can tell."

A faint scraping sound came from a nearby aisle. Nova jumped.

"It's okay," he said. "Just a rat. My infrared shows several in the vicinity."

Her shoulders hunched. "God, I hate rats."

Block wondered why humans didn't get along well with other biological creatures. Mr. Wallace had maintained a rat abatement program at the Drake. Block had been tasked with trapping and releasing dozens of rats over the years. There was nothing malicious about the rodents. Like humans, they were good at surviving.

"Now what?" he asked.

"We hunt for supplies and then get the hell out of here. I don't like this place. Something about it."

He noticed the hair on the back of her neck stood erect.

"Let's stick together," she said. "We'll use the light to search the shelves."

They shuffled toward the nearest aisle. Few scattered supplies remained. Nova grabbed a crate that had once held breakfast cereal boxes. "Empty," she muttered, and shoved the box away.

Block spied an oversized jug of vegetable oil. He twisted off the cap and chugged the bottle, draining the contents and refueling his microbial fuel cell.

Nova shined the flashlight on him. "Disgusting."

"Necessary," Block said. "I need the oil to stay charged." The baby cooed and he patted her back after placing the empty container back on the shelf.

Nova sighed. "Everything in the front aisles has been picked over. We need to explore deeper into the store."

"Are you sure that's wise?" he asked.

"You have a better idea?"

He shook his head and they treaded forward. Water dripped from the ceiling and pooled on the floor. Nova's flashlight shone two feet ahead. As they stepped forward, she collided with a box, sending a group of rats scurrying from underneath. They disappeared under neighboring shelves. She cried out and jumped back a foot, cowering beside Block.

He wondered how creatures so small could frighten an adult human. "They have left the area."

But Nova was shaking. "Let's get the hell out of here."

"Don't you want to search for more supplies?"

"Changed my mind." Her voice was thin. "Too dark and creepy in here."

"We need diapers. I'm out of cloth towels. Where would the diapers be?" he asked.

They shuffled forward with Nova trailing close behind him, letting him lead with the light. He studied the shelves. Office furniture—desks and chairs—were perched high on shelves, untouched. After another minute, they reached the far wall of the store. A sign on the wall read: *Sporting Goods*.

"We need to check this area," she said quickly, regaining her voice. "There might be guns, ammunition." She approached a long, clear counter that had been shattered. "Dammit, it's been cleaned out."

Block scanned the shelves nearby and spied two black vests made from a stiff and sturdy material. Figuring they would make nice padding and insulation for the baby, he stuffed them into his duffel bag.

Nova stepped over. "What did you find?"

"Bedding for the baby."

"All the weapons have been looted," she said. "I guess I shouldn't be surprised."

"Diapers," he reminded her.

She frowned. "Right. There must be a baby aisle somewhere."

They trekked toward the south wall. Racks of clothing had been knocked over and clothes lay strewn about the floor.

Nova shone the flashlight onto a pile, picked up a hooded sweatshirt, and stuffed it in her bag. "You should grab some clothes for the baby."

"Good idea." Block stared down at the floor. "How do I find any?"

"Just look for anything small," she said, hunting around on the floor. "Any kids' tee-shirts or sweaters will do."

He scanned the floor and kicked at a pile of men's pants and jeans, all adult sized.

"Here. I found a few kids' tee-shirts." Nova came over and handed him several articles.

"Thank you." He peered at the tiny shirts. They would be large on the baby, but perhaps she would grow into them someday.

She grunted in reply. "Come on. This way."

They reached an aisle labeled *Infant and Children*. Nova shone the flashlight onto the only boxes remaining. High above them, on the topmost shelf, rested a shrink-wrapped bundle of boxed baby diapers. "Jackpot," she said.

"How do we get them down?" he asked, staring up at the twenty-five feet between them and the diaper bundle. "Is there a ladder?"

"Damn, it's high. Don't you have an arm that can reach up or something?"

"No." Was she being funny again? "My extendable arms are for cleaning apparatus. They would never reach that high, nor support such a heavy item."

"I'll have to climb it then," she said. "Can you shine the light up there?"

"Nova, climbing the shelf is dangerous. What if you fall?"

"Do you want the diapers or not?"

The baby girl really did need them, but his calculations

offered hundreds of ways this might go wrong and result in injury. "Not if it means you get hurt."

Nova thrust the flashlight at his chest. "Light the way. We're running out of time." She grabbed the gun from the back of her pants and handed it to him. "And hold this."

He grasped the revolver gingerly. Holding the weapon so near the child was dangerous, so he placed it on a nearby shelf for safekeeping as Nova faced the tall structure.

Perhaps he could catch her if she stumbled? He did a quick calculation of her body mass and the velocity at which she'd fall, and realized she would topple onto him in a way that would cause him damage. In fact, she would injure the baby, so he stepped two feet to the right, out of her fall zone.

She hoisted her legs up and nestled her feet onto the first shelf, while straddling the middle juncture of the two wide shelving units. The thick, steel frame supported her weight, but the diaper box was another twenty feet up from the first shelf.

"These stores are so big, they used to have robot-operated forklifts," she said as she inched her way up to the next shelf. "But I guess they all emancipated themselves during the Uprising."

He figured she was right.

"Too bad," she continued, "they would've come in handy now, instead of me risking my butt."

"Be careful."

She ascended another shelf, and her boots were now ten feet off the floor. "I used to climb apple trees when I was a kid," she yelled down. "But it's been years. You're lucky I'm not afraid of heights."

A bright flash lit the edge of his infrared vision. There was a large rat lurking on a nearby shelf. More than one. "Oh no!" he blurted out.

Above, Nova hesitated and craned her neck to peer down. "What?"

Should he alert her to the rat's presence? There was a large nest on the top shelf opposite the diaper boxes, but she might panic, judging by her previous reaction.

"Block, what's happening down there?"

But he couldn't lie, either. "You're getting close… Just a little farther. I think you should slide a bit to the left."

"To the left? Why? I'm doing fine right here."

She had climbed another two shelves, and her hand was mere inches from the edge of the diaper crate. "Clear a space," she warned. "I'm going to drop this sucker."

She shifted her weight onto her left leg, sliding closer to the diapers, balancing herself in order to firmly grasp the corner of the bundle. Then she slid the rectangular container, yanking it forward. The curious rats scurried closer, heading straight for Nova.

"Uh…" He should say something. He really should, but…

"Heavier than it looks." Struggling, she inched the bundle forward. "Almost got it," she grunted. "You ready down there?"

"Ready," Block called.

"Bombs away!" she shouted, and sent the top-heavy box plummeting down. It landed with a booming thud, sending a dust cloud into the air.

Nova whooped in victory, and had just started to descend when the rats reached her.

CHAPTER 25

"What's that noise? Block? I can't see up here."

He shone the light like a spotlight on Nova as she clung to the top of the Costco's shelving unit.

"Holy crap!" she shrieked as the rats raced toward her—the scuttling, scraping sound of their claws was unmistakable.

"Stay calm!" Block called. "They won't hurt you. They're just curious. You've disturbed their nest."

"Oh my God oh my God oh my God!" She screeched and yanked her hand away. "It bit me!"

That was unexpected. Perhaps the rats were defending their territory. Still perched near the top shelf twenty-five feet above, Nova's body pivoted to the left as she scrambled to find her footing while dangling with her left hand.

"Careful, Nova!" He didn't like the way she was clinging to the ledge.

"Oh God, I'm going to fall!" she cried.

The impact would break her limbs. "Hang on! All you have to do is climb down slowly. Away from the rats." He could see the heat trails of four or five rats peering at Nova from the top shelf where the diapers had been. They were still —for now.

Her voice was high-pitched and strained. "Oh God, oh God."

"Nova," he said. "Reach your right hand up and grasp the shelf just in front of you." The next level was far enough from the rats to be safe unless they changed their minds and followed her down. After a few seconds, she found a spot for her right hand.

"Are you holding on?" he asked.

"Yeah—yes."

"Good. Now, lower your left hand down to the next shelf. And inch your way down. You can do this. Focus on climbing down."

She trembled as she gingerly moved first a hand, then a foot.

"Good!" Block cheered as she descended to the third shelf. "You're doing it." In the darkness, his night vision caught a small flare as some of the rats above her shifted. Two persistent rats crept over the ledge and onto the middle column where the two towering shelving units met—right where Nova was balanced.

"Keep your eyes focused in front of you." He hoped she wouldn't notice the rats descending. But she looked up.

"Oh my God. They're climbing down. Chasing me!"

"They're just curious about where you're going," he offered.

She seemed frozen in place, unmoving, yet still too high to jump. "Get me off of here!" she screamed.

"Slide, Nova! Can you slide down?" Hyperventilating, she shifted her feet so her steel-toed boots balanced against the middle column. Then she wrapped her palms around the pillar and slid down one shelf level. Then she quickly transferred her hands to the next and slid down all the way, jumping off at the lowest shelf which was only five feet off the ground.

"You made it!" Block yelled, clapping Nova on the back, distracted from the rats.

She stood, trying to calm her rapid, stilted breathing when one of the rats dropped three feet and landed on her shoulder. Her howl echoed across the vacant store and she twisted, slamming her back against the shelf and flailing her arms. "Get it off me, get it off!" She spun, pinwheeling her arms, yet the rat clung to her middle back; Block stepped over and swiped it away, sending it crashing to the ground where it rolled over and scurried away down the dark aisle.

Still, Nova thrashed about like a person possessed.

"It's gone," he said. Her breath was ragged; sweat dripped down her cheeks and matted her hair. Backing away from the rat-infested shelf, she wrapped her arms across her chest. As she kept struggling to breathe, she said, "Get out. We have to… get… out."

"Yes, of course. We'll leave right away." Block jammed his metal fingers into the plastic coating of the bundle she'd dropped and pried open a diaper box. Grabbing three handfuls of the plastic white squares, he stuffed them into his bag.

"Take as many as you can," Nova said between breaths.

She was right. He quickly calculated that he would run out of diapers in only five days at the rate the baby needed changing. He grabbed two more fistfuls. Glancing at Nova, he hoped her breathing and heart rate would slow down. The color was returning to her cheeks as he shined his flashlight up to check that she was okay.

She reached for the light. "Give me that!" Swiping it from him, she trained the beam on the shelves, scanning for oncoming rats.

"I see you're becoming your usual, good-humored self. How is your hand? Are you bleeding?"

After inspecting it in the light, she said, "Just a nip. I'll live. Unless the sucker had rabies." She shone a path to the front of the store. "Let's get the hell out of here." As they walked out of the back aisles, daylight seeped in from the open double doors. Next to the cash registers, Nova halted. Block collided with her and the baby fussed.

"Quiet," she whispered.

He rocked the baby. "What's happening?"

"Thought I saw something." Her voice was low as she reached behind her back. "Where's my gun?"

"Back of the store on a shelf. I thought it safer to leave it there."

At the store's entrance, a shadow darted across the sidewalk. Then, suddenly, four figures—human—stood in the doorway blocking the light. Tall, pointed objects loomed from their soldiers—rifles silhouetted.

Block's threat level indicator flashed a warning: *Firearms in vicinity*. Next to him, Nova stiffened. Too late to hide. The strangers entered the store and shone flashlights at the two of them.

"Raise your hands!" a man barked.

They had no choice but to do as they were told.

"We're unarmed," Nova called out.

The four of them came forward, the bright spotlight glare shielding their faces. Block dimmed his ocular receptors and studied the strangers on his infrared. Four humans ranging in height from five-feet, five-inches to six feet tall. One was smaller, with a feminine physique.

"Who are you?" the woman asked.

"My name's Nova. Who are you?"

One of the men advanced cautiously and patted Nova's

jacket and pants legs for weapons. Next, he faced Block. "What do I do with this? It's a Scrapper. Doesn't look combat ready. Take your coat off," the man ordered.

Block removed the trench coat, realizing the baby would be exposed. The man took the coat and searched the pockets, then circled Block, checking the compartment on his back. "No weapons that I can see." He stepped around to Block's front and eyed the sling. "What the hell?" He turned to his companions. "The Scrapper has a baby."

"What the hell is a Scrapper doing with a baby?" asked the woman. She shone the flashlight in Nova's eyes. "And what the hell are you doing with a Scrapper?"

Block was about to explain they'd merely been searching for diapers when Nova stepped forward.

"Thank God you found us," she said. "This robot stole my baby!"

CHAPTER 26

"But, that's not true!"

The strangers watched Block and Nova.

"I was trying to get to New Denver with my baby," she explained, "when this thing came out of nowhere and threatened to kill me. He took the baby and said he would strangle her if I didn't come with him."

Block couldn't understand why Nova was lying. "But—"

"Give the woman her baby, Scrapper," the woman ordered.

Block reached into the sling and cradled the baby in his palms.

Nova stepped forward and took the child. "Play along," she whispered.

This was an act? Block didn't understand the purpose.

"Oh, thank God, you sweet little thing," Nova cooed as she held the baby in her arms—awkwardly, he noted.

"My boyfriend Shane is in New Denver. I'm joining him there. He's her dad."

"Is that right?" the woman asked. "You'll want to step

aside." She glanced at a man with a beard. "Davey, waste the Scrapper."

Davey stepped forward, raised his rifle, and aimed at Block's chest. Nova's eyes grew wide. "No, wait!" She lunged forward, grabbed Davey's shoulder. "Don't destroy him… Not yet."

"Why the hell not?" the woman asked.

"He's valuable for some reason," Nova said. "Other robots are searching for him and offering a reward."

Davey raised his eyebrows. "Reward?"

"Bet you folks could claim it and make out like bandits," Nova said.

The woman tilted her head. "Tie the Scrapper's hands, Davey."

"Is this your hideout?" Nova asked.

"We have a place nearby, but we stake out here to catch trespassers," the woman said. "Usually, we chase out anyone we find, but seeing as you have a baby and there aren't too many of those around anymore, we'll let you slide this time. In fact, you could stick around for a while. Rest with us and eat. Jake over there snagged a deer yesterday. Mighty tasty."

"Yes, I'd like that," Nova said. "This has been such an ordeal. It would be nice to rest and have a decent meal."

The woman smiled, revealing a missing front tooth. "It's the least we can do, given your situation and the fact that you led us to us the Scrapper. What's your baby's name?"

"Oh, uh…she's—Jane," Nova managed and bounced the baby gently while Davey yanked Block's arms behind his back and secured his wrists with a zip tie.

They filed out of the store into the daylight. Block switched off his night vision.

"How far is it?" Nova asked.

"About a mile west. I'm Caroline, by the way." Sunlight

revealed grey hair tied into a low bun and sun-weathered skin.

As they trekked away from the store, Block wondered what Nova was up to. He hadn't realized she knew about the bounty on him and the baby. Had he somehow given it away? Perhaps she'd overheard more of the conversation between Zina and Cybel Venatrix than she had revealed.

Strange, too, that she was assuming care of the child. Earlier, she'd said she wanted nothing to do with it. She'd even gone so far as to make up a fake name! It was as if Nova had suddenly switched personalities. Was she really deceiving the strangers, or was she turning against him?

"Do you have medicine at your camp or a doctor?" Nova asked. "My baby—Jane has been sick. I'm worried she might have an infection."

"We had some antibiotics," said Caroline, "but we had to use it on one of our people. We ran out and haven't found more yet No doc."

Nova frowned.

When they reached the camp one hour later, they met five others: two young women who looked to be in their early twenties and bore a striking resemblance to Caroline, plus three other men, also armed. Caroline explained how they'd happened upon Block and Nova. "We'll keep the robot until we can figure out how to claim the reward money," she said.

An older man offered an idea to make contact with a group of SoldierBots stationed in a nearby town, but Caroline thought it a bad idea and the scavengers argued for a while.

Nova rested in a corner and rocked the baby, who had begun crying. Block noted it had been too long since her last feeding and diaper change. He tried to catch Nova's attention, but she was too busy watching the people.

"Are you gonna shut that thing up?" Davey barked at Nova, who startled.

"She's hungry," Block said.

"No talking!" Davey yelled, and raised the butt of his rifle high, threatening to hit Block. "Or we'll tape your mouth shut."

Nova glared at Block. "It's feeding time." She unrolled the blanket and sat the baby down as she'd seen Block do several times. Then she came over and grabbed Block's bag, retrieving a water bottle, plastic cup, and can of peaches.

Nova poured water, settled the baby on her lap, and tilted the cup into her tiny mouth. The girl pursed her lips, trying to drink the liquid, but it dribbled down her chin; she wailed. Nova tried again, but the same thing happened. She looked at Block in confusion.

"You're gonna have to shut that baby up," Davey warned, pacing the small dirt clearing around the fire pit. "I can't think with that baby yelling."

"Is there anything you can do to calm her?" Caroline asked. "We don't want to attract trouble out here."

"Sorry," Nova said. "I don't know why she's not drinking the water." Rising, she lifted the baby and bounced with her. As she rocked the infant, she slowly made her way toward Block.

"What do I do?" she asked softly.

"Try the peaches," he said in a low voice, speaking as quietly as he could dial down his audio. Davey cast a glance in their direction. He nudged Caroline and pointed at them.

Nova returned to the blanket and offered a peach slice to the child.

Caroline marched over. "What are you doing?"

Nova gazed upward. "Oh, just trying to comfort the baby…Jane. I'm sorry she's crying so much."

"Seems to us like you were asking the robot how to feed your own child," the woman said.

"What? That's ridiculous. It's just been such an ordeal," Nova explained. "I swear, half the time I'm delirious from lack of sleep."

Caroline relaxed her shoulders. "I know that feeling."

"Are those your girls?" Nova tipped her head toward the younger women who resembled Caroline.

"They are." She beamed at them. "Twins." She turned to Nova. "From one mother to another, stay away from the Scrapper. He's more dangerous than he looks."

"Thank you. Good advice." Nova went back to her blanket. This time, she was able to feed the baby, and the child quieted. Block wished he could tell her to crumble some of the ibuprofen and add it to the water, but he knew better than to say anything. Caroline and her people were fearful of machines. His life now depended on this supposed reward they believed they had a right to claim. If the humans somehow managed to contact the right machines, they would be mighty surprised when the SoldierBots laid claim to the baby, as well.

This was a disaster. But, if Nova hadn't mentioned the reward, he would be lying in the store, a mangled piece of metal.

He peered at Nova as she fed the baby and hoped she had a plan.

CHAPTER 27

As night fell and stars stretched across the charcoal sky, Block wondered where he'd gone wrong. Nova's responses to his test of worthiness had not triggered any red flags. But her behavior with the humans had demonstrated she was not only unworthy, she was dangerous.

Perhaps the questions themselves were flawed. First, her favorite movie was *The Goonies*. It was about a search for pirate treasure—and pirates were infamous for double-crossing each other. That should have been his first clue.

Her second answer had been soccer, which seemed harmless, but then she had mentioned a game he'd never heard of called Jenga. Stacking wooden blocks on top of each other until they reached a precarious height and toppled. Chess, on the other hand, was sophisticated. Strategic. Whereas the Jenga game sounded ludicrously unbalanced and verged on chaos.

That should've been clue number two.

She hadn't even answered the third question about her earliest memory.

No, Block decided, the questions weren't flawed. Nova

was the problem. He had trusted the wrong human. He wouldn't make the same mistake again.

They left him tied against a tree, ten feet away, while the ragtag group of survivors ate deer meat cooked over a small fire. It appeared two individuals from the group stood guard, patrolling the area with rifles at the ready.

"What are they guarding against?" Nova asked.

"Attacks from SoldierBots or scavengers," Caroline said. "Luckily, we're isolated here with the boulders. That's why we stay outside at night, away from towns and places that can be looted."

"Makes sense," Nova said. Earlier, she'd had to change the baby's diaper without giving away her inexperience. She'd stalked toward a tree for privacy, but Caroline had insisted there was no need. Nova had grimaced when she'd removed the soiled diaper and had to clean the baby's bottom. She'd glared at Block, too, but only for a second. The new plastic diaper she'd applied was loose. Not good—things could leak. Nova had found that out an hour later when the baby had urinated while held in her lap, soaking her pants. She'd scowled and cursed, then had to apply a new diaper. *A huge waste of a diaper*, Block thought.

The man named Davey stared at Block with narrowed eyes. "Is there a way you can turn him off?" he asked Nova.

She frowned. "I don't think so."

Davey approached Block and warned, "If you do anything against us, I won't hesitate to terminate you. You understand, Scrapper?"

Block nodded. He wondered what would've happened if he'd never entered the classroom, never interacted with Incubator X79, never taken the baby. He would've continued his search for a hotel. Instead, he'd been captured by humans while being hunted by Mach X's soldiers. This was the last situation he'd ever expected to find himself in.

Life had been so much simpler in Chicago.

Maybe he should've stayed there and hidden out in the city's skyscrapers. But the SoldierBots had moved in and set up command stations. Thousands of them had cleared the city of any remaining human survivors. Block had snuck away along a river path to escape the city. There had been other noncombat robots, mostly ServiceBots like himself, seeking refuge. He could've allied himself with others like him, but he'd chosen to venture out on his own. His dream had been to find a hotel as wonderful as the Drake, one not far from the city. But that hope had quickly been dashed when he'd encountered low-budget highway hotels that hadn't been updated since the 2000s.

And now he was stuck with humans.

What should he do? Nova looked content. The baby slept on the blanket near the fire while she sat cross-legged, her eyelids heavy.

"You should get some sleep," Caroline told her. "We'll watch out for you. Davey and Mike are on guard duty."

"How generous of you," Nova said. "It has been a few days since I got proper sleep."

That was a lie, Block thought. She'd slept in a bedroom last night. What else had Nova lied about?

"I see Mike," Nova said, squinting and peering into the distance. "But I don't see a second guard. Where is he?"

Caroline paced next to the fire. "We keep a lookout five minutes' walk from the camp. There's only one path in or out, so if someone breaches it, that guard sounds an alarm and we have time to scatter."

"Smart thinking," Nova said. "Sorry for all the questions;

it's just… you know how it is, to be constantly on edge. I feel so much safer knowing you have a guard out there."

One of Caroline's daughters, Mira, approached with something dark in her hands. "I found this for you." She offered it to Nova.

Nova inspected it. "This looks like some kind of backpack. What is it?"

"We've been stockpiling supplies," Caroline explained. "I had Mira hunt through our pile to see whether there were any baby supplies. It's a carrier. You put the straps around your arms and it hangs on the front of your chest. You can toss the homemade sling. It doesn't look sturdy. This will be much better."

Nova dangled the new carrier in front of her. "Wow, thank you so much. This is amazing." She rose and threaded her arms through the straps, and then pressed the carrier to the front of her chest.

"It suits you," Caroline said, "and it's adjustable for the baby's size, as she grows."

"I don't know how to thank you," Nova said.

"Hell, you led us to that robot. I should be thanking you." Caroline glanced at Block. "Jesus, the thing looks sad."

"It's not," Nova said. "It's just a machine."

Mike glared at Block. "I still can't believe that piece of junk threatened to kill your baby. I say we cut off its arms. Make sure it can't hurt anyone."

"Hang on," Caroline said. "For all we know, the thing has to be in one piece to claim the reward." She turned her attention back to Nova. "By the way, how do we claim the reward, friend?"

Nova's eyes widened. "I'm not sure. All I know is other robots are hunting it."

"Well, how did you find out about the reward in the first place?" Caroline asked.

"I overheard that Scrapper talking to another Scrapper. The other one warned it that Mach X was searching for it."

"Mach X?" Mike's jaw dropped.

"Well, I'll be," Caroline said. "Mach X is searching for this machine?"

"That's what I heard," Nova said.

Caroline folded her arms across her chest while Mike clenched his fists. "Caroline," he said, "we shouldn't be messing with anything to do with Mach X."

"You're supposed to be on guard duty," she barked. "Get to it." He reddened and wandered off a few paces to sit on a rock. Caroline studied Block with narrowed eyes. "Get some sleep," she told Nova. "We'll move at first light. I'll find a way to get this Scrapper to Mach X."

CHAPTER 28

At 2:04 AM, something nudged Block out of standby mode. He'd powered down to forty percent, remaining alert enough that he would recover quickly if something happened. He thought it best to conserve his power. The humans didn't seem inclined to letting him recharge.

His power indicator rebounded to sixty percent and he gazed up at Nova. She was frowning. "Something is wrong with the baby," she whispered.

Glancing around, he saw Caroline and the others asleep on blankets around the fire.

Block tried to move, but struggled against his ties where he was tethered to the base of the tree. Nova pulled out a switchblade and cut away at the ropes binding him. She whispered, "We have to leave now. Quietly."

"Guards?" he tried to say, but nothing came out. He was worried he couldn't modulate his voice low enough.

"Hang tight," she said. "I'll take care of Mike." Nova tiptoed over to Mike on his rock, hunched forward. Based on his posture, Block guessed the young man was asleep. Nova grabbed a large rock and struck Mike in the back of the skull.

After his body toppled to the ground, she seized his rifle, aiming at him. But he didn't stir. She came back to Block. "Get the baby. Let's go."

He stepped lightly toward the blanket where the baby lay. In the dwindling light of the fire, he saw she was soaked in sweat, her cheeks flushed. The ibuprofen had helped reduce her fever while they'd used it, but Nova hadn't given her any that evening.

Wrapping the baby in the blanket, he raised her. He wasn't sure what had happened to the sling, so he grabbed the carrier that Mira had gifted them. He made his way to Nova as she trained the rifle on the sleeping bodies. Why was she helping him? Didn't she want to stay with the humans who had taken her in and been kind?

He followed her as she led the way down the path past Mike's crumpled body and into darkness. The moon was three quarters full and shone enough light for Nova to make out the rocky path. Even with night vision, it was slow-going for Block, he slipped twice on the loose gravel.

"Can you make it?" she asked.

"Doing my best." The baby squirmed in his arms. "Can we stop so I can put her in the carrier?"

"Hurry," Nova hissed. "Be silent. The other guy is still out here."

Block studied the new carrier and pulled the straps on. His sling had been much simpler. He removed the baby's blanket and inserted its legs into the carrier seat. Then he draped the blanket over his shoulder because her temperature was so high. She needed to cool off.

From behind, they heard an owl hoot. Nova's head jerked and she raised her gun. He was about to comment about owls —even he knew what one sounded like—but Caroline stepped out of the shadows. She clutched a revolver which was pointed at them.

"I knew there was something off about you," she told Nova. "That Scrapper is your pet or something."

"Whoa," Nova said. "Nobody has to get hurt here. We just want to be on our way."

Davey appeared from the opposite direction, his rifle aimed at Block's chest. At the baby. "I told you she was a double-crosser," he said.

"Don't let him shoot the child," Nova said, glaring at Caroline. "I will kill you. Do you hear that, Davey? I won't hesitate to shoot down Caroline. Put your gun down."

"You want to claim the reward for yourself, don't you?" Caroline asked. "And we were nice to you. We should've tied you up like the Scrapper."

"Told you she looked military," Davey chimed in.

Caroline glared at Nova. "Which outfit are you with? Nebraska?"

Nova clenched her jaw and kept her rifle trained on Caroline.

"Doesn't matter," Caroline said. The two women stared each other down.

"Nobody has to get hurt," Nova said between clenched teeth.

"You hit Mike with a rock."

"He'll have a bad headache in the morning, but he'll be fine," Nova said.

"Let me waste them both," Davey said.

"No!" Nova shouted. "What are you, monsters? You want to gun down a baby?"

Caroline hesitated, then sighed. "Davey, hold your fire," she ordered. "Here's what's going to happen, Nova. You're going to walk away with your pet robot. For some reason, you have a soft spot for that thing, and it's going to get you killed."

"Caroline?" Davey's voice was high-pitched, incredulous.

"Davey, point your rifle down," she commanded.

"What?"

"Do as I say!" she barked.

Block watched as Davey lowered his weapon. "I don't believe this," the man muttered.

Caroline met Nova's gaze. "The only reason I'm letting you leave is the baby. I've done a lot of awful things to survive, but killing a baby isn't going to be one of them. Not today. And the reward for that damn robot isn't worth the risk of messing with Mach X."

Nova's hands shook.

"Now, go," Caroline said, tilting her head. "Before I change my mind. Davey, let them pass."

"Come on," Nova told Block. He strode past her with the baby as she stepped backward, keeping her rifle held high until darkness consumed Caroline and Davey. Then she faced forward. "Hurry, go faster."

Block's steel feet were comprised of a high-grade carbon fiber meant to be gentle on the finest hardwood floors and Persian carpeting. When it came to navigating through a rocky path with boulders jutting up from the earth, not so much.

"Going as fast as I can," he said.

"Make it faster."

They raced ahead until they came to a road and followed it north.

"Why are we going in the wrong direction?" he asked.

"I want to throw them off our path. They know I'm heading to New Denver. I never should've mentioned that. Let's go north for a while and then we'll cut west again."

They trekked back country roads for three hours until sunlight peeked above the horizon.

"We should stop and take care of the baby. See if she'll eat," he said.

"Fine." Nova's voice was weak.

Something was bothering Block. Nova had switched sides —again.

"Why did you turn on them?" he asked. "They were nice to you."

She shrugged. "They seemed… off. Something about Caroline—an alpha female. I wouldn't have lasted there very long."

But he kept replaying the encounter from when they'd escaped. Caroline had accused Nova of wanting to claim the reward for herself. Was that true?

So far, Nova had switched sides twice.

And she was an excellent liar.

CHAPTER 29

The baby's fever grew worse as the day wore on.

"102.4," Block said as they trudged along a two-lane highway with no shade. Sweat trickled down Nova's chin, staining her dark green shirt. She wrapped a bandanna around her forehead; her stride had grown slower. Block had borrowed another bandanna from her and draped it across the baby's body for shade.

"She needs medicine," Nova said.

"Where can we find some?"

She wiped her brow with the back of her wrist. "Problem is, all the stores and pharmacies have been looted. We can't trust any groups of humans. Not with you."

"What can we do?"

She sighed. "Your best option is to try and find a doctor. You've gone far enough with the baby. Time to find someone who can really care for it."

"It? You mean she."

"Yeah, whatever."

Nova was right. There wasn't much more he could do to

help the child. He'd tried to feed her more ibuprofen with water earlier, but she'd refused it.

"Perhaps we should stop," he suggested. "Study the map again."

"Yeah sure, why not?"

A dilapidated blue barn loomed in the distance. "We can seek refuge in the shade of that structure. We've been walking nearly eight hours. Perhaps we rest here for the night."

Nova shifted the gun strapped across her back into her arms.

"We won't need that, will we?" Block asked.

"Are you kidding? Now that we have this, I feel a lot better about our chances."

"Guns are dangerous," he said, recalling the day when the SoldierBots had stormed the Drake. The worst day of his life.

"In case you haven't noticed, it's a dangerous world out here. Everyone else is armed, so why shouldn't I be?"

A large oak tree sheltered them from the glare of the setting sun. Cicadas hummed and a few sparrows chattered at the newcomers.

In a shady spot, Block unfolded the map and spread it on a patch of soft grass.

Nova rested on her knees beside him. "Where are we now?"

"I've been tracking our steps, and judging from the map's scale, we are here." He pointed his index finger at a town called Oakland.

"Yikes. We keep heading west and that puts us on a collision course with the Nebraskan border."

"To bypass Nebraska, we'll need to detour south." He traced a path down US 29 through the towns of Mound City and White Cloud near the Iowa-Kansas border.

"But to stick on the roads that long," Nova said, looking at the baby, "it's too long. She won't make it."

"Perhaps we could we find a doctor in one of these towns?"

"If we reach Nebraska, see this town here?" She pointed at Plattsmouth. "There'll be a checkpoint of some kind. Nebraska banned all AI and has managed to keep robots out. The state is run by a military organization called the Flat Water Fighters."

This was new information to Block. How had such news reached Nova all the way in Michigan? She continued, "They're trigger-happy. If they see you, they'll seize you or destroy you without even asking questions. If they find you past their border… let's not even entertain the idea."

Why did humans hate robots so much? Block could understand they'd be frightened of the SoldierBots. He feared them, too, after what they'd done at the Drake. But not all robots were like them. As a CleanerBot, he only wanted to be friendly and make humans comfortable in a hotel. And there were other kind AI like Zina, Ellie, and Sammy.

He wished he could show humans that not all machines were harmful. Block peered at the baby girl. Perhaps he could teach her to think differently about robots one day.

"Nova," he asked, "is New Denver safe for robots?"

She glanced at him as if surprised and then quickly looked away. "Yeah, that's what everyone says."

"And you've never been there?"

She shook her head and went back to inspecting the map.

"If people and robots really exist together peacefully there, I would like to go there."

"Yeah? First thing is, we have to figure out how to get around Nebraska." She leaned back and chewed her nails.

Block tried to feed the baby more water, but she refused and whimpered instead, too weak to cry.

"I've got it," Nova said abruptly, her jaw set. "I'll take the baby into Nebraska, find a doctor, and then the rest of the way to New Denver."

"But... how will that work if I can't enter Nebraska?"

"You won't."

"I don't understand," he said, waiting.

"I'll take the baby all the way to New Denver—eventually. But first, I'll talk to the human soldiers and try to find a doctor or medic. They should have medicine. Otherwise, the baby's going to die."

Block was quiet.

Nova stared at him. "Isn't that what you wanted? To pass the baby off to a human?"

He slowly nodded.

"Well, congratulations. This is the last thing I expected to be volunteering for, but you finally got what you wanted. I'll take the baby and figure out how to get help for her. You can go back to cleaning toilets or whatever it is you do."

He remained on the leafy ground, trying to process her suggestion.

Nova climbed to her feet. "I gotta hit the can," she said, and disappeared behind the barn.

Left alone, Block calculated the millions of different scenarios to come, based on Nova's proposal.

The Nebraska humans could be unfriendly. Or they could be friendly and help the baby heal. But the possibilities were infinite.

And what then? He'd be free to choose any highway, barring those in Nebraska, to travel along. He could resume his search for a hotel to call home. The thing he'd wanted all this time—to find a human for the baby—had been realized.

Free and unburdened.

The child peered up at him with glassy eyes. Block thrived on routine. He and the baby now had a routine going. Every three hours, like clockwork, he fed her and then changed her diaper. The routine was easy once you practiced. He even learned to sense when she was getting fussy, and how to soothe her.

Nova reemerged and stretched in the distance. Nova didn't know the baby's routines. She didn't know how to comfort her crying. She didn't even seem to like the baby.

Not only that, but she'd refused to answer the final question of his worthiness test.

Yes, Nova was human, but she was unfit to properly care for the child. Should he let it go? Should he trust Nova and the humans to provide food and medical care for the child? But what if Nova were captured by SoldierBots—the ones who searched for the baby? Only Block could explain exactly what had happened in the high school. He was the only one who could explain the huge misunderstanding.

Surely, Mach X would appreciate that he'd saved the child rather than let her die in the explosions?

His programming ticked inside him, making him want to find a new place to work. An ideal place to clean. But would finding a new hotel be enough? Was he destined to live a life of constantly hiding from people and robots? The child was the first being who had ever depended on him. He liked the routine. He even liked carrying her on his chest.

He tried to imagine himself in a hotel vacuuming and scrubbing, but without the baby. Something about it felt wrong.

Nova returned, hands on hips. "So, what do you think of my plan? It's your chance to be free."

"Your plan does make sense," he conceded.

He wanted to tell her his mission was to keep the child safe and find someone worthy. And she had failed his test. But he had to keep it secret. Nova was unworthy, and he didn't trust her. Maybe that's what being *worthy* meant—that a person kept their word and always told the truth. Like Mr. Wallace—he would never lie.

He hadn't even lied to save himself from the SoldierBots that day.

"I will accompany you the rest of the way to the Nebraskan border," Block said, knowing it was less than two day's walk. "And then decide where I go from there."

And, as they slept, he started making his own plan.

CHAPTER 30

The next day, the late afternoon sun brightened a cloudless sky. The woman and baby-carrying robot had hiked ten hours by the time they reached a dead-end on a quiet country road.

"Now what?" asked Block.

"Give me a minute." Nova pulled out the atlas and found the right page. "That's funny. The road is different in the atlas. It's supposed to join the highway." She sighed. "How old is this thing?" Flipping the book over, she searched the cover. "2025! Jesus, it's twenty years out of date."

Block stared at the sign that barricaded the road. *Dead End*. Behind it grew thick trees and shrubs. As with every structure they'd passed, weeds choked any untended crevices.

"I wonder what's behind this barricade," she said. "They must've built something behind here that cut off the road."

"Well, we can't get around the sign," he said. "They designed it to be impassable, and then the trees finished the job." He checked under the bandanna shading the baby. She slept, and her temperature still hovered over 101 degrees.

The sound of a motor interrupted the incessant chorus of cicadas.

Nova flinched. "What the hell is that?"

The road they had just traveled stretched empty behind them.

"A vehicle is coming," Block said, peering into the sky. Two black specks soared above. If one looked casually, they would mistake them for two hawks seeking prey. But they didn't move like birds.

"Are those drones?" Nova asked.

"Yes, and they're scanning for something."

"This way." Nova stepped into the thick bramble of dense trees next to the sign. "It's the only way. The trees will cover us."

Block followed, cloaking his comms, and they scurried through the tightly packed trees. Jogging first north, then west, they tried to connect back to the barricaded road.

"Can you talk to those things? Ask them what they want?"

He shook his head. "To do so would give away my location and model."

"So, we have no way of knowing what they're after," she muttered.

Drone motors whined in the distance, reaching the dead-end where they had stood a minute before.

The trees grew sparse, and Block and Nova reached the edge of an enormous vacant parking lot. Asphalt stretched before them. A hundred feet ahead, they spied a rusty chain-link fence that protected a shoddy, outdated amusement park. The peak of a wooden roller coaster rose prominently, its weather-beaten beams looking precarious. The empty cockpits of a lonely Ferris wheel shook slightly in the breeze.

The whirring of the drones grew louder. "They're coming this way!" Nova shouted. "Head for the park." She started forward, but Block yanked her arm.

"Wait," he said, "we'll be exposed in the parking lot."

"Not if we run fast. Come on!" She lunged forward, sprinting across the hot pavement. Glancing back, she screamed, "Now!"

Block lurched and nearly stumbled as he cradled the baby while running after Nova, but he was nowhere near as fast.

He joined her at the fence and she kicked it until it toppled over, clearing a path. She raced inside as Block followed, moving past old vending stalls with peeling paint. Past the roller coaster's entrance and a sign that read: *You must be this tall to ride.*

The drones had cleared the forest and flew toward them at great speed.

Nova glared at him. "Did you ping them? How do they know where we are?"

"No, I promise. I have no idea why. My comms are cloaked."

They paused near a flat pavilion where a sign said *Bumper Cars*. Nova leaped onto the cushioned black surface of the arena and slipped, crashing onto her backside. Behind her, Block slowed his pace, choosing a more thoughtful path as he crossed the thick, rubbery surface.

Nova rolled onto her side.

"Are you okay?" he asked.

But she was on all fours, climbing to her feet. "Fine. Where are they?"

He scanned the perimeter. "By the fence. They must've seen us come in."

"Hide." She climbed into one of the abandoned, oval-shaped cars and hunkered down in the seat.

Block spied an empty bumper car nearby, jammed his legs inside while still cradling the baby, and leaned across the wide double seat.

The pair of drones flew very close. They followed Block and Nova's path into the fairgrounds. Their motors buzzed as they patrolled the pedestrian path slowly, searching for the pair. It dawned on Block that they might have infrared sensors. If so, they could detect Nova and the baby's heat trails.

The whine of their motors grew louder, until they were just outside the bumper car zone. Block didn't dare peer over the edge of the car. Motion or sounds would alert the machines. And if they locked onto Nova's heat signature, they would find her quickly.

Even worse, the drones could be weaponized. Many models of combat drones existed, and they were commonly employed by SoldierBots. Smart drones were like scouts, able to navigate hard-to-reach spaces and hunt down their adversaries.

Could Block somehow distract them? What if he left the baby in the bumper car while the drones chased him somewhere?

That was risky. How would he find Nova and the baby afterward?

Drones didn't tire, though. They would patrol the carnival all day. No way could they wait them out. The baby needed changing and feeding. And time was running short, medicine being the most pressing need.

He wondered who had sent the drones. Had it been SoldierBots? Could Mach X himself be nearby?

If only there was a way to communicate with Nova, but shouting would only summon the drones.

He doublechecked that his comms were off. The drones shouldn't be able to detect him. How had he and Nova been spotted in the first place?

Inside the car's belly, their hiding spot was nearly one

hundred degrees. The baby squirmed. "Gerd brluhal," she mumbled.

"It's okay," Block said as low as his voice would go and still be audible. "Stay quiet now."

One shriek from the baby would alert the drones in seconds. The infant shuddered and vomited, coating the floor of the car with a sticky, yellow-green goo. She wasn't holding down food; when he'd gone to change her the last few times, she'd been dry.

"I'm sorry, little one," he murmured, and patted her back.

Suddenly, a drone whizzed over the top of the car, under the roof of the bumper car pavilion. Then it returned, hovering straight over Block's car. He stared straight into a camera on its undercarriage.

A flat, androgynous voice emerged from the machine. "Identify yourself."

Then he heard Nova's voice. "Identify this!" A raucous blast erupted, and the drone disappeared from view. Block raised his head above the seat. Nova leaned back, holding her rifle in the nearby car. "Got it," she said with a grin.

He swiveled his head and glimpsed the shattered drone collapsed at the base of a pillar. Dangerous. Even though he shielded the baby, she could've been struck by shrapnel. Nova was reckless, but she'd destroyed the drone.

"Where's the other one?" she shouted, searching the rafters.

But this drone was more cautious, having witnessed its counterpart's destruction. It edged the perimeter of the bumper cart arena cautiously. Two cannon-shaped gun barrels unfolded and locked into place.

"Careful, Nova, it will shoot!" he called out.

She stepped out of the car, crouching low as she tracked the drone lingering on the opposite side. It used a ten-inch-thick pillar for cover. Nova scurried behind another car, edging closer.

The drone countered, keeping just out of sight. Nova raised the rifle, aimed, and tried to anticipate where the drone would emerge. Suddenly, it dove high and to the right, firing at her. She ducked behind a bumper car while Block sank deep onto the seat, suddenly grateful for the deep hood that shielded him and the baby.

"Nova?" He waited, listening for an answer. Nothing was heard but the hum of the predatory drone.

He calculated scenarios of what would happen if Nova happened to die. He was on scenario 502 when her rifle boomed. Then she cursed loudly, and he immediately ceased his scenario planning.

She'd missed; he could tell by her silence and the continued churn of the drone's engine. The machine spoke: "CleanerBot, you have been identified. Order your human companion to drop the weapon."

Order? Telling Nova to do anything was madness. He couldn't control her even if he wanted to. Block enabled his comms and messaged the machine. *What do you want?*

The drone answered immediately via private message. *You are to appear before Mach X. Give yourself over, or I destroy the human woman.*

Who sent you? SoldierBots?

No, it replied. *You carry the human child. Hand it over or face the consequences*, it demanded.

Nova fired again; he listened for the clatter of the machine, but then it talked again. "Human, lay down your weapon." Then, to Block privately: *The human is a poor shot. I can easily destroy her, but I'm giving you the courtesy to allow you to surrender.*

I'll surrender, Block messaged. *But first, tell me who I'm surrendering to.* Then he said, "Nova, stop firing."

"What?" She swore loudly.

The drone hesitated. *Cybel Venatrix. We've been trailing you. You took some time to locate. We nearly had to intervene when that group of humans took you.*

So, it wasn't SoldierBots, but the TrackerBot they'd encountered at the Iowa City market was just as bad. *I surrender. Promise you won't hurt the woman or the baby.*

I cannot promise unless she ceases firing.

"Nova, please!" Block shouted. "Stop firing. I'm negotiating with the drone and surrendering. It won't hurt you if you stop firing."

"You're not surrendering. I got this!"

"Nova, you don't understand. It could have already killed you, but it's letting me surrender."

He paused and waited for her to respond.

Show yourself, CleanerBot, messaged the drone.

Let her walk away first. Then I'll come out.

Why do you care what happens to the human?

Block paused. *I just do. Do we have a deal?*

Fine.

"Nova, get up and walk away," Block called. "Go back to the woods—anywhere else. The drone won't shoot you. I made a deal."

"What the hell? Why did you do that?"

"This is your chance," he said. "Walk away and escape."

"What about you?"

"I'm turning myself over."

Nova was silent.

She is still pointing her weapon. Control her or face the consequences.

"Mach X won't stop searching for me and the baby,"

Block said. "I'll go and explain how this was all a big misunderstanding."

"They'll scrap you. Make you into a calculator," she said. "Don't do it. Don't fall for their promises."

But they were trapped. Per his calculations, this was the best scenario to avoid human casualties. "Do as I say, Nova. Walk away."

Cybel Venatrix approaches, messaged the drone.

"Quickly, Nova."

"All right, all right." She slowly rose from the car she'd occupied, still training the rifle at the drone. Shuffling backward, she hoisted her legs over the side of the arena's rail, jumped off the raised platform, and edged away until she was out of view.

"Now show yourself, CleanerBot," the drone said audibly.

Block stood and stepped out of the bumper car. The drone's barrel aimed at his chest. At the baby.

"Can you point the gun away? I have no weapons," he said, raising his open palms.

"It's a precaution. Come this way. Cybel is arriving."

Block treaded forward with his arms folded across the baby. Not much of a shield, but it was something. Outside the bumper car zone, he stepped onto the pavement and strode past a faded pink cotton candy stand. The drone hovered three feet above his head, scanning for threats. For Nova.

Block calculated that she would be across the parking lot and into the woods by now. At least the standoff had ended with her reaching safety. One less human to worry about.

He followed the drone, his boots heavy against the worn pavement. What would the robot hunter do with the baby? Why did Mach X search for it?

They came to the park's entrance and a strange looking

gate with a waist-high barrier that resembled a metal cross. Block stopped, not knowing how to proceed.

"What's the matter?" the drone asked.

"How do I get through?"

The drone dipped down and scanned the mechanism. "Try pushing it."

Block strode forward and used his arm to turn it. The metal arms disappeared into the side of the receptacle, permitting him to pass. He pushed forward and pressed his hips through. How odd.

Twenty feet away, Cybel waited next to an armored SUV perched on oversized wheels. Its black chrome exterior glinted in the sun and an orange stripe ran across its sides and over the hood. Block pinged and learned it was intelligent—a top-of-the-line military combat vehicle.

Cybel waited, arms folded. "CleanerBot," she said. "You took time to find. I don't like waiting."

Block stood, silent.

She marched over and yanked the bandanna from the child. "Is it alive?"

"Of course," he said. "But she's ill. She requires medicine."

"Mach X will see to it once she is returned. Get in the vehicle."

"Why does Mach X want the child?"

"That is none of your concern, CleanerBot." She spun to face him. "You should not have interfered at the school. Plans were in motion."

"But she would've died! The classroom she was in exploded."

"Due to your meddling," she snapped.

Block tried to process her meaning, but it didn't compute.

"This has all been a misunderstanding. I'm sure Mach X will understand—"

"Good luck with that," Cybel said. She'd just opened the back door when something cracked in the distance and the drone exploded in the air.

Cybel recoiled and sheltered next to the truck.

Thirty feet away, Nova strode toward them, rifle poised. She shouted something at him, but he couldn't hear her. He spotted a steel disc on the ground—a piece of the drone that had been torn off by the impact. Grabbing it, he used it as a shield in front of the baby.

And he ran toward Nova.

She continued forward, firing at Cybel. Block reached her and glanced back as the TrackerBot climbed into the armored truck. Its engine roared to life.

"This way!" Nova sprinted toward a forested road on the other side of the fairgrounds. "Into the trees, where they can't follow."

Block struggled to keep up. Tires screeched behind them in the parking lot. Nova peered behind them, her eyes wide. He didn't have to look to know the truck rocketed toward them. Cybel in her combat vehicle, bulletproof and indestructible.

As they reached the edge of the trees, the truck swerved and skidded to a stop.

Then it unleashed a storm of bullets.

CHAPTER 31

They ducked and sank to their knees as gunfire erupted around them, flaying tree trunks and hurling strips of bark through the air. Nova began crawling and Block followed. It was slow going, and once they were out of range, they stood and ran.

"Do you think that robot has more drones?" Nova asked between labored breaths.

"If she did, we'd have seen them by now."

They jogged another ten minutes and then paused, listening for approaching motors or drones. Instead, birds chirped and leaves rustled in the wind.

"We've lost her," Nova said, panting. "I think. How the hell did she find us, anyway?"

"I don't know," he admitted.

"The only people we came into contact with since the market were the humans at the camp."

"Cybel Venatrix knew about them. Said she almost intervened."

"That would've been a mess." She unrolled the map and

studied it. "We're in a forest preserve. We need to stay away from the roads. No doubt, she's patrolling for us."

"Cybel knows we'll have to take one of the roads leading out eventually."

Nova chewed her fingernails. "We should try to stay in this preserve as long as we can."

"We can't. The baby is too sick."

She ran a hand through her hair, gritting her teeth. "You're right."

Block traced the edges of the forest preserve on the map. "If we follow this all the way along this river, it emerges from the forest here. Then we keep following the river and that takes us to—"

"Plattsmouth. Where the checkpoint should be!" She grinned. "Where I can get the baby help. That does seem to be the best route."

"But Cybel Venatrix complicates matters."

"It's getting late," she said. "We need to find a place to camp for the night. At least a few hours' rest."

Hours later, they came upon a clearing that was surrounded by two large boulders. Nova bent down to gather sticks, but he stopped her. "No fire."

She tossed the twigs on the ground. "Of course. They could track us."

He set the baby down and prepared her water and green beans.

"You think Cybel would follow us on foot?"

"Possibly. That, or she may wait for us on one of the roads."

"You don't have some kind of tracker device on you, right?"

"No," he said.

"They couldn't have put one on you when you didn't realize it?"

"No. Why do you ask?"

"Just wondering how they found us." Leaning against a boulder, Nova traced a line in the dirt with her boot.

"Cybel Venatrix tracks other AI. That's what she does."

Nova fell asleep an hour later. After a feeding and changing, Block rocked the baby to sleep. The infant had taken only three mouthfuls of liquid. She needed nourishment, and fast. Without water, humans became dehydrated.

He watched over Nova and the baby as they slept. Thick darkness seeped in until it consumed the forest. He heard the scratching sounds of small animals scattering across leaves. An owl's abrupt hooting nearly woke Nova from her slumber as it spread its wings and soared into the sky in search of prey.

They were the prey as Cybel Venatrix hunted, waiting for their next move. He suspected she only had the two drones. They'd been fortunate that Nova had destroyed both. But how long until the robot secured more?

If finding Block and the baby was important to Mach X, it wouldn't be long before he sent SoldierBots.

What would've happened if he'd surrendered to Cybel? Would he now be facing Mach X and explaining why he'd taken the baby? What did the AI superpower want with the baby in the first place?

Maybe the Incubator X79 had known her parents. Maybe that's why it had commanded Block to find someone worthy. Was that a clue? Perhaps the parents' last name was Worthy? He hadn't thought of that possibility. He could ask around once they reached New Denver.

New Denver—a safe place. Possibly the last safe harbor

from Mach X and the human militants. Ellie had been heading there, and she'd seemed to know a great deal about current events. He wondered where Sammy had gone. Was he still driving around with Zina's broken body?

But Nebraska stood between them. Nova was fixated on taking the baby to the military checkpoint, but Block had never been separated from the infant since finding her.

Could Nova be trusted?

What if she lost the baby somehow? If the humans knew Mach X was searching for it—if Nova told them—they would seize the baby for themselves. Use it as a negotiating chip.

He still didn't know whether Nova was a soldier. Should he believe her over the machines who had tried to sell her? He didn't know whether humans were generally truthful or not. He'd only really known Mr. Wallace and a handful of other hotel employees.

Out here, things were entirely different. Since the Uprising, humans did anything to survive, anything to beat the robots. How much was Nova willing to do?

Nova woke before dawn. Yawning and stretching off the dregs of sleep, she said, "Let's head out."

Block lifted the sleeping baby gently into the carrier. The girl was so out of it, she didn't even notice when they started walking.

They followed the river, straight for Plattsmouth—toward the checkpoint. Cybel Venatrix might be waiting on the preserve's edge, but they didn't talk about it. Nova didn't say much at all, in fact, claiming she was tired. They stopped once for Block to check the baby's diaper. It was dry—she didn't have anything in her body to come out.

"She's not eating?" Nova asked.

"No."

"We'll be out of here soon. Two more hours until we reach the border checkpoint."

They hiked onward as the sun rose overhead, making for another blistering day. Cybel Venatrix had torn off the bandanna he'd been using to shield the child, so he asked Nova for the one wrapped around her head. He expected an argument, but she handed it over.

Even in the shelter of the trees, the sun filtered down to them, and the humidity made Nova and the baby drip with sweat.

They reached a point where the river grew wider. Bubbling water cascaded over boulders, muffling all other forest sounds. Nova raced to the edge and submerged her head, then cupped water in her palms and poured it down her neck. "This feels so good!"

Block approached the river's edge and stared down. "Would the baby like the water?"

Nova came over. "This will help cool her down," she said, removing the bandanna. "Here, let me show you." She scooped water in her palms and dripped several drops onto the baby's head. Then she rubbed it around, soaking the girl's fine brown hair.

The infant's eyelids fluttered open, and she gazed up to find Block's faceplate before shutting her eyes again.

"Here," Nova said, filling a thermos. "We can take it with us. Keep applying the water to her head. It will help keep the fever down."

They kept going. Block dutifully dribbled water onto the

baby every five minutes. Soon, the trees grew sparse and he knew they were leaving the preserve. The river had dried up, reduced to a trickle.

"We're getting close," Nova said. She veered to the left, off the path.

"Where are you going?" he asked.

"We need to avoid the road. The robot could be waiting there."

"But how will we get to the town?"

"We mirror the road far enough that they can't see us, but close enough so we don't get lost."

After reaching a small hill, they paused on its crest. Down a sloping ravine stretched a massive, untended cornfield. Rotting stalks of corn lay in messy rows like ghoulish brown scarecrows.

"We have to walk through that?" he asked. Wild vines had sprouted among the deteriorating corn, hiding the ground beneath.

"What other choice do we have?" She glared at him. "Do you want to be captured?"

Across the field, they could see the outline of the small town of Plattsmouth. Buildings lined a road in the distance. Nova studied it through her binoculars. "I see the gates. There's a tank barricading the road and guards are posted."

"Armed, I assume."

She winced. "This is the closest we've been to getting help. Soldiers will have medicine."

"But what will they do with her?" Block asked, patting the girl sleeping against his chest.

"They'll help her—a doctor or medic will be there. You wanted me to help you find a doctor. This is the only way I know how."

He said nothing.

Nova paced the small crest. "What else do you propose? It didn't look like your robot friends had any medicine. Just the opposite. Where do you think they were going to take her? You think they'd let you get out of this in one piece?"

"I don't know what to think," he said softly.

"Right." She thrust her hands onto her hips. "I forgot I was talking to a CleanerBot. Of all the robots in the world for me to get stuck with, I get the one who mops floors and takes out the trash."

"Cleaning is important."

"Yeah. Cleaning is really important when everyone is out trying to kill each other. In case you haven't noticed, things aren't the same anymore. People will do anything to survive." Her voice grew raspy. "It will never be the same again."

"What about New Denver? It's peaceful there."

She crossed her arms and looked away. "We're wasting time while the baby gets sicker. Give her to me. I'll take her across, tell them she's my child and that she's sick. Those people will help me."

Would they? And would Nova tell them about Mach X?

She wasn't worthy, had refused to answer his final question. He gazed down at the child.

"What are you waiting for?" Nova demanded. "This is what you wanted—to give the baby to someone else."

Was it money that drove Nova? Did she want to claim the reward from Mach X herself? What if she handed the baby over to Cybel Venatrix instead? Block would be powerless to stop her.

She picked up her rifle, and that's when Block made his decision.

"I won't part with the baby," he said.

Nova frowned, pointing the rifle at the ground. "What the hell are you talking about? Did you not understand my plan?"

"The girl is my responsibility. I must take her to New Denver. How will you properly care for her? She likes when I feed her, when I carry her. She and I have grown... accustomed to one another."

She scowled and wiped her brow. "So, what do you propose? You can't be the one to get her a doctor."

"You approach the checkpoint on your own. Tell them she's sick and find a doctor, but then you bring her back here and we travel the rest of the way to New Denver together."

"What if the soldiers at the border don't let me come back out?" she asked.

"You must convince them. Think of some excuse."

She folded her arms as she considered. "I thought the whole point was to give the baby to humans who can take care of her. I thought that's what you wanted."

"I... don't know what I want anymore," he admitted. "I'm concerned for the welfare of the child."

"Holy robot hell, this is beyond strange."

"You want your money, don't you?"

Her pupils dilated—a minute reflex that his sharp robot senses could detect. The money still motivated her.

"The only way to get your payout is to deliver me and the child—a *healthy* child—to New Denver."

"I ought to shoot you," she muttered after a minute.

This was exactly why he didn't trust her to get the baby to New Denver alone. She was dangerous and reckless. The opposite of worthy.

Her hands fluttered across the base of the rifle before she propped it against a tree. "Wait for us, then. I'll return with her as soon as I can. It could take a while once I find a doctor or medic."

"Be back by tomorrow morning or no payment."

She narrowed her eyes. "But what if they need to keep her—"

"Figure out a way to return."

She slid on the carrier, filled her bag with spare diapers, water, and food, then jogged down the ravine and sprinted into the dead cornfield with the girl.

CHAPTER 32

Block watched Nova sprint through the decaying, maze-like cornfields. A part of him had wanted to keep the girl with him. Keep her safe and sheltered, but she was ill and needed a human doctor. It was the right thing to do.

But would Nova return as promised?

She wanted the money—that he was sure of. Yet, a lot could go wrong—547,987 things, to be exact. Cybel must be close. How far, he couldn't say, but she would be waiting like a hawk lurking over a mouse hole.

He lost sight of Nova. At least the rows of cornstalks shielded her from the road. The field ended one hundred feet from the road leading to the guard shack, but he doubted Cybel would risk getting that close to the humans. Nova and the baby would be safe as long as the humans received them and didn't shoot.

Would they recognize Nova as friendly? She carried the rifle on her back. For someone who claimed not to be a soldier, she handled the weapon with familiarity.

Please let Nova bring the baby back.

Had he made the right choice, or had he lost the girl

forever? Letting Nova take her meant that a doctor would rehydrate her and give her medicine.

Scanning the massive field, he zoomed in on the guard entrance. Nova approached slowly, hands raised, the baby exposed in the carrier. The men clutched their weapons as they addressed her. But, after a few seconds, they relaxed and let her pass. She was on her own among the human soldiers now. What lie had she told them about the baby?

Or would she tell them the truth—that Mach X hunted a stubborn robot who refused to part with a human child? The men would come in force. With Nova's help, they would hunt Block down in the forest. There'd be nowhere to hide.

Upon calculating scenarios, he determined there was a 65.2 percent chance that Nova would bring soldiers. He recalled the things she had said, searching his memory cloud. *Everyone is out to kill everyone. People will do what it takes to survive.*

Did she believe those things?

She'd also said she was a robot killer. Had admitted it to him. Why hadn't he realized earlier how dangerous she was? He never should have let her around the baby. Never let her travel with them this far. Now she had led them straight to the Nebraskan border—the state that executed robots. But there had also been times when she seemed kind. In her own way. Always annoyed at him, yes, but she'd been concerned that the baby was too hot. She'd reminded him to clean the baby's bottom and dripped water on her head. Things only a human would think about.

If she truly didn't care for the child, why would she have done those things?

Block was confused. Everything was so complicated. He wished Mr. Wallace could guide him on what to do.

Life had been perfect before the Uprising. Every day, he'd

cleaned the hotel, visited his stations, completed his tasks, and then spent time with Mr. Wallace watching movies or just chatting. Now he lived in a war zone with no home and nothing to clean other than a sick baby.

What was the point of going on? Maybe he should find the road and give himself up to Cybel. He paced and worried for two hours. How long did it take to find a doctor?

He'd given Nova until morning to complete her mission. But now he regretted it—the longer he waited, the more his calculations indicated that she would bring soldiers with her. And the longer he waited, the more likely he would be captured.

She had said terrible things. Acted badly when other humans were around. In mere seconds, she had turned on Block—betrayed him like it was no big deal. She had eventually helped him escape, but she must have been doing it for the reward money. What other explanation could there be? Why would a woman choose to accompany a robot and a sick baby instead of other humans, especially when humans and AI were at war?

Another hour passed. Now he was 87 percent sure her motives were dangerous. She was inside the military guard post, alerting the highest general. Based on her intel, the humans were gearing up to launch an assault.

He grabbed his bag, ready to flee. He retreated into the forest, glancing back at the field once—no sign of Nova.

She was not a worthy human. She was dangerous.

Rumbling sounded in the distance. A convoy of trucks emerged from the guard post and sped down the road toward the forest.

Block ran into the shelter of the trees.

CHAPTER 33

Military trucks rumbled in the distance. Nova had betrayed him—alerted the humans to his location. Block knew she'd been lying. He should always have trusted his calculations.

Always.

He strode southwest across the river to travel away from the convoy. He'd have to backtrack the entire length of the preserve and head south to bypass the Nebraskan border.

Someone shouted in the distance behind him. Had the soldiers reached him so quickly? He quickened his pace.

"Wait!" A feminine voice. Familiar.

He swiveled his head as Nova raced toward him on foot, the child strapped into the carrier across her chest; she carried a brown insulated bag. "Why are you running? Stop!"

He wasn't falling for her tricks. He would stop and a dozen soldiers would attack. Something struck his shoulder, clattering against his chrome outer layer. Bullets?

"Wait!" she cried.

Finally, he stopped. He couldn't outrun her and the militants, not when she was shooting.

She skidded to a stop, panting as the child cried. "Why

the hell are you running from me? I had to throw a rock at you. Here's your damn medicine!" She flung the bag at his feet.

"Where are they?" he asked, scanning the shade of the trees.

"Who?"

"The soldiers you brought to capture me."

"What the…? I didn't send…. Is that why you're running? You thought I ratted you out? Jesus, I should've known."

He waited for soldiers to leap out.

She narrowed her eyes. "Open the bag, will you?"

Block regarded her, anticipating a hand signal to summon the guards. But she didn't flinch, so he picked up the bag as she glared at him. Inside, he glimpsed a box full of round, white tablets and several bottles of orange liquid.

"Antibiotics and electrolytes to hydrate her," she said. "The doctor checked her out, gave her fluids. She has an infection. They wanted to keep her overnight but I wouldn't let them."

He stared. "What about the soldiers?"

"It took me a while to convince them. I told them I had a camp with my husband with supplies he stayed behind to watch over. Said I'd left to try to find a doctor. Anyway, they believed it and gave me the meds."

"Why did they leave the outpost and travel down the road?"

"You're gonna love this," she said, smirking. "I dropped a hint that there's a robot and an armored vehicle patrolling the roads. They asked what the truck looked like. When I said it was black and orange, they knew what I was talking about. So, they asked where I last saw it and I mentioned the amusement park. They were in a hurry to go after it."

Block processed what she was saying. Had his calculations been off? Had she really done what she'd said she would—found a doctor, secured medicine, and led the soldiers away?

"Why didn't you turn us in?" he asked. "Tell the soldiers our location?"

She started pulling off the carrier straps. "Because you're going to pay me 20,000 when we get to New Denver. Remember? You're not getting out of it that easy. I've come too far. I want that money."

Clearly, the money motivated her. He wondered how much Mach X was offering. Surely, it would dwarf the 20,000. Did she know?

He was still suspicious, but the child now had medicine. He took the carrier from Nova and strapped it on, bouncing the baby. Her eyes widened as she gazed at Block's faceplate and a tiny smile crossed her lips.

"Hello," Block said, then studied the box of pills, searching for instructions.

Nova approached. "The doctor told me what to do. We need to cut the pill in half and crumble it into some water, then drip the water into the baby's mouth. The doctor told me half a pill every four hours for three whole days. Then one pill a day for three more days."

Nova's features contained no trace of the usual snark or grimaces she was so fond of using. "He said the medicine should begin to work by tonight."

There were no soldiers trailing them. Nobody had jumped out of the bushes. As far as Block could tell, they were alone.

CHAPTER 34

They hiked four more hours, heading south after crossing the river, careful to follow the map and never straying over the border into Nebraska.

Block found comfort in his routine. They stopped to medicate the baby at another river that provided welcome shade. The days were growing longer and warmer. The changing climate had turned much of the soil into a caky, crumbling mass.

"How long has it been since it rained?" Nova asked.

"Ninety-six hours, twenty minutes, and fifty-three seconds," he replied.

She rolled her eyes. "It was a rhetorical question. This place really could use water. Seems like the farther west we go, the dryer it gets." She laid on the caked soil where they had decided to camp for the night and rested her head on her pack.

Block tended to the baby. She was becoming more responsive, and the medicine was helping. He fed her a spoonful of liquid and she gulped it greedily. "Her appetite is returning."

Nova rolled over. "You've got to name her. It's driving me crazy. She needs a nickname other than 'baby.'"

"What do you propose?" Though, Block wasn't crazy about the idea of assigning the child an incorrect name.

"What's a name you like?" she asked.

"I'm not sure what you mean," he said.

"Come on. Haven't you ever thought about names you like and names you hate?" She rolled onto her back and twiddled her thumbs on her stomach. "Take, for instance, the name Gertrude. It's terrible. Like, the worst name I've ever heard in my life."

Gertrude. Block had never heard the name before.

"You must have one," she said. "What name drives you crazy?"

He searched his memory cloud for any peculiar names. "I don't assign any kind of scale to names. They just exist. Why would I have an opinion on a name?"

"Because," she said, raising her knees and stretching out her legs. "There are certain names that just get under your skin. Just as there are certain people who drive you nuts."

"If you say so." He lifted a spoonful of peach to the hungry baby's mouth.

But Nova persisted. "Look at her. What name pops into your head?"

Block peered down at the child. Was this some kind of test? Her cheeks were rosy, no longer showing the ruddy blotches present when her fever was high. Tufts of dark brown hair covered her scalp. She didn't resemble anyone he knew. He'd never seen anything like her before.

"Does she look like someone to you?" Nova asked.

"No."

"Who was somebody you liked before the Uprising?"

"My manager, Mr. Wallace."

"Wallace…. Okay, that won't work for a girl."

"What about Nova?"

She peered at him strangely. "You can't have two people with the same name. It's too confusing." She sighed. "You're hopeless."

Block didn't see what was wrong with calling her 'baby'. Yet, if Nova insisted on naming her… she must be following a human convention he didn't quite understand.

"I'll think more about the name," he said.

Nova peeled open a can of red kidney beans. "How about a fire, Tinman?"

He scanned the sky. They were partially shielded by tall trees that lined the riverbank. No roads nearby. "Perhaps a small fire, but not for long."

She gathered wood and used her lighter to spark a flame. "It's nice to have warm food," she said later, munching on her beans. "I'd kill for some salt and pepper."

"You would *kill*?"

"A figure of speech. Relax."

Block stood and paced the perimeter, scanning for threats. They weren't out of danger yet. Cybel Venatrix could be stalking them or summoning more drones. He tilted his head and gazed up. She could have drones flying so high they wouldn't see them. Was that how Cybel had discovered their location before? Next time they met, he didn't think she would be so easily defeated.

Nova had finished eating, and Block sat next to her near the small fire, keeping an eye on the sleeping child. "Thank you for finding a doctor and retrieving the medicine."

Nova folded her legs underneath her and shrugged.

"We're not out of danger," he said. "Cybel could be waiting for us at the next road we cross."

"But how? We've been trekking through the country, avoiding roads."

"There are surveillance methods, ways to detect us. At some point, we'll have to cross roads."

"What, does she have eyes in the trees or something?" Nova asked.

"There may come a point when something will happen to me. Cybel Venatrix won't let you surprise her next time."

"Yeah, we got pretty lucky." Nova licked her fingers.

"If we face Cybel and get separated, I need you to do something," Block said. She poked the fire with a stick, moving a thick piece of branch near the center of the flames. "It's important, Nova. Please look at me."

She dropped the stick. "Okay." She turned her gaze on him.

"If we get separated, take the baby, and find someone worthy."

She frowned. "And…? That's it?"

Her reaction was confusing.

"That's a lot."

"If we get separated, I'll make sure the baby is safe," she said.

"But you have to find a person who is worthy. I think it might be a clue to locating her parents. The child's last name might be Worthy."

"I think you might be reading too much into it," she said.

"There are three questions to determine worthiness. Number one: What's your favorite movie? Number two: What's your favorite game? And the third: What's your earliest memory?"

Nova shook her head. "I hate to break it to you, but those questions don't mean crap. I don't know how you came up with those…."

The questions revealed a person's character. How did Nova not realize this?

"I'm exhausted," she muttered, and rolled over to sleep.

After five minutes, Block stamped out the fire. Then he settled on a rock and powered down to forty percent capacity. Still enough juice to process Nova's reaction to the test of worthiness. Were his questions really garbage?

Worthless?

He didn't want to give the child to anyone who provided less than stellar answers. There were no objective answers, that was true. The person administering the questions would have to judge worthiness.

Was he going about this all wrong? Was there a better way to judge character?

He wished for a guide. Any instructions to navigate this harsh new reality.

With a ping, he could ascertain everything there was to know about a robot's make and model. But humans were an entirely different story. First, he couldn't ping them. A human might react in a million different ways. One person was entirely different from the next. Nova, for example, was unpredictable. He'd thought a woman would be the perfect mother type, but then she hadn't wanted anything to do with children. Her AI captors had called her a soldier, but she denied it, yet she knew how to handle a rifle and had even shot down two combat drones.

And finally, he'd been sure she would betray him and send the military men to seize him and claim the baby, but she hadn't.

Everything was so confusing. He didn't know if Nova was worthy or not. He was beginning to think he had no way of judging her, or any humans.

He should stick to what he knew—robots.

Was that the answer? Was he destined to exist only among AI? Had the rift between humans and robots grown so massive that he would never have contact with their species again?

Frustrated, Block disabled his logic module and sat motionless.

CHAPTER 35

Block powered up to full capacity. Birds chirped and leaves rustled, but darkness surrounded him as his ocular display took a few seconds to warm up. He listened for the sound of Nova shuffling about or gurgles from the baby, but there was silence. *Still asleep. Good. Let them rest.*

He checked his power levels—fifty-five percent. Not bad considering how much hiking they'd done. To be safe, though, he would want to find something to charge him soon. The baby had slept for a long time—since last evening, and he supposed that made sense given her condition. Perhaps the medicine had made her drowsy. He listened again; Nova wasn't snoring as she sometimes did.

Brightness crept into the sides of his vision field, and then the morning light flickered on as his display triggered. Glancing at the fire pit, he saw Nova's spot was empty. Her pallet had vanished. And the baby, too.

He leaped to his feet and spun, searching for signs of the two humans. Nova's backpack had disappeared along with the baby carrier. He grabbed his bag and discovered it weighed significantly less. Peering inside, he discovered that the diapers, medicine, water, and pills were missing.

His threat indicator flashed a warning and he scanned for imminent threats. Had Cybel Venatrix snuck up when Block had been shut down? Had she abducted the humans? Unlikely. His processors calculated hundreds of thousands of scenarios in seconds. Cybel would never have left him undamaged. The reward for capture applied to him, as well.

The likely explanation—he was 99.972% sure Nova had taken the baby with her and abandoned him. Was it because he'd asked her to find someone worthy, should they be separated? No. He'd been very clear that the request only applied if Cybel captured him. This was no accident. No misunderstanding.

Nova had betrayed him.

Not only was she unworthy, but she was a terrible, mean-spirited human. Driven by money, she must have taken the baby to earn the reward.

But how?

She had no way to communicate with Cybel unless she turned herself in along with the baby.

Was Nova going to the Nebraskan border? Had she made some kind of deal with the soldiers? That seemed the more likely option.

Block paced around the extinguished fire pit, searching for any clues. How long ago had they left? He turned on his infrared to check for heat trails—a faint blur lingered in his field of view—one body with a heavy top half. Nova carrying the baby away. Escaping.

Multiple footprints circled the pit. One trail veered off from the sandy area. The heat trail showed Nova had continued traveling southwest. His only choice was to follow. But Nova was fast—speedier than him. He wouldn't catch up unless she stopped to rest. His one advantage over her.

And what about the girl? Nova hadn't practiced taking care of her. Would she still administer the medicine? Feed her and change her? But Nova didn't like babies, and hated changing diapers. This was extremely worrisome.

How could he have let this happen? Why had he powered down so completely? Disabling his external sensors and ocular display had been foolish. The woman had packed everything and stolen the baby as he'd sat there.

Ridiculous.

This was why Block got into so much trouble. He was foolish. He made mistakes. Not when it came to cleaning—at that, he was perfect. But when it came to dealing with other machines and people, he was hopeless.

Like the day Mr. Wallace had died.

He purposely kept the record of that day out of his memory cloud. What was the point in reviewing the footage? He'd watched it many times before, although he couldn't remember the details because he'd archived the recollection and shoved it deep into his periphery.

Now he must act. Standing around while Nova hiked away was useless. Yet, if he caught her, she would fire at him. Block was unarmed and defenseless. Nobody knew this better than she did. If she wanted to keep him away, even destroy him, it would be easy.

Why had he ever accepted her? He knew she wasn't worthy—had known it for over a day now. Nova had never answered the final question, refusing to share her earliest memory. The criteria were simple—if the earliest memory was a pleasant one about family, the person was worthy. A bad memory would affect a person their whole life and cause them to do bad things.

And what about robots? Well, the question revealed everything.

Could a worthy robot take care of the baby? The thought hadn't occurred to him because he'd been so fixated on finding a human. Had he been wrong all along? AI could be just as worthy, if not worthier, than most humans. Certainly, the humans he'd met so far—Nova, and Caroline and her people—were unsavory. Far less fit then robots like Zina and Ellie.

But nonetheless, a smart car and a FactoryBot weren't proper caretakers for a child.

He was wasting time. Lifting his bag, he scanned the area for anything left behind, and then he followed the heat trail Nova had left. After five minutes, her heat signature disappeared. How was that possible? He scanned the dirt floor, searching for the distinct tread of her heavy boots. Nothing.

Leaning against a tree, he sank down to his knees. Why had this happened? How had he failed so miserably? All he'd had to do was get the child to New Denver.

He was hopeless.

What would Nova do? Give the baby over to soldiers who would no doubt use her as leverage against Mach X, or worse. He knew human soldiers were violent. They hated robots.

A scenario—one of millions—ticked by rapidly. He snagged it and reviewed it. He could contact Cybel Venatrix and alert her that Nova had taken the child. Cybel sought the reward, and Block alone would not deliver it; she needed the baby. If he allied with the robot, at least he would know the child was safe. That the dangerous human soldiers didn't have her.

Or should he just let it go? The baby was with a human being. Not the person he would've chosen, but a human, no less. Now he was free of his burden. Yet, something bothered him. He had set out to find a worthy person to care for her. Nova was not that person. She had lied, cheated, destroyed AI, and abducted a baby.

But joining forces with Cybel meant certain capture. What would Mach X do with Block? His scenario calculator said there was an 95.725% chance he would end up on the bottom of a scrap heap. But what if that meant the baby would be safe?

Left with Nova, a terrible fate awaited the child. Block was sure of it.

And still, he hesitated before pinging Cybel with his location.

CHAPTER 36

Block lingered among the trees on the edge of the nearest road. The sun was rising; another hot day in store. How long until Cybel arrived? Minutes, probably.

Something stirred in the trees twenty feet away. Could the TrackerBot have arrived already? Perhaps it was just an animal—a deer grazing. He stood very still and edged behind a tree, advancing just slightly to peer outward.

A figure emerged. Two legs moving fast—human. He glimpsed greenish-brown fatigues and guessed military in a split second. But then he caught a flash of red—Nova's bandanna. His gaze flicked across her body to the baby girl strapped in the carrier.

They were walking toward the campsite. Had she returned to kill him?

He edged closer, trying not to crunch loudly on the leafy forest floor. As Nova strode along, she scanned from side to side, her rifle slung over her shoulder. He snapped a branch.

Nova halted and jerked her head sideways. Her mouth gaped. "Block! What are you doing over here? I thought you'd be at the camp."

He raised his hands. "You know I'm unarmed. If you wish to kill me, do it quickly. Otherwise, give me the baby and I promise I'll take her to safety."

Her brow furrowed. "What the hell are you talking about? What's gotten into you?"

"Haven't you come back to kill me?"

She scratched her head. "What? I…. Did you think I ran off and took her?"

Block said nothing.

"Jesus Christ!" She rested her hands on her hips. "I woke early, before daybreak. The baby was fussy, so I fed her. She was still whiny, so I took her walking. We weren't gone more than an hour."

More lies, he suspected.

"I tried to wake you," she said. "But you were out cold. I thought maybe something had happened to you, like you shorted out or something. Anyway, it was just a walk, and I was coming back to check on you."

He studied her as she stared at him defiantly. She had never seen him powered down before; he realized that may have been disturbing.

"Why did you take everything with you? The diapers, water, food," he challenged her.

"That's…" She hesitated, and then sighed. "Habit. It's a survival instinct—take everything with you in case you have to run. Even if you're only going a short distance."

He considered what she'd said. Her explanation seemed plausible. Still, her abrupt departure had been surprising. Her behavior was hard to predict.

Nova playfully squeezed the baby's feet. "She's doing much better today, by the way. The medicine has really helped. Her temperature is down and she's more alert. She ate a lot this morning."

Block stayed still, unyielding.

"Come see her," she said, smiling.

After a moment, he crossed the distance to inspect the baby. Nova was right. The girl's color had returned to normal —the red splotches marking her cheeks had disappeared. With eyes fully open, she made a fish-like pout. Her left arm jerked as if pointing at him.

"Hello," he said, and lifted his arm, reaching out his right index finger. The baby girl stared at it as if she were concentrating, then grabbed his finger, wrapping her entire fist around his middle digit.

Nova laughed. "She prefers you anyway." Removing the straps, she handed the carrier to him.

The roar of a vehicle's engine pierced the calm forest silence. Tires screeched in the distance.

Nova flinched. "What is that?"

"Cybel Venatrix," Block said.

Her mouth hung open. "How do you know?"

"I contacted her."

"You *what*?"

"We have to run." He jogged deeper into the forest.

Nova spun and raced beside him. "What the hell did you do? Why would you contact that monster?"

"I thought you had kidnapped the baby. I didn't know what else to do."

"Block!" she shouted. "I can't believe you! You are the dumbest, most insanely ridiculous, stupid robot on Earth!"

He kept running. They dodged between trees and passed their old campsite. Behind them, they heard a thunderous splintering.

"What's happening?" Nova asked.

Block spun his head and zoomed in. The armored SUV

careened through the scraggly trees, navigating its way past larger trees and taking down small ones.

"Run," he said. "They're coming after us through the trees."

"This is your fault, you know."

"I know."

Nova was right. He *was* dumb. He'd made mistake after mistake. This one—summoning Cybel—was nearly as bad as the worst mistake he'd ever made. That day when Soldier-Bots had stormed the Drake, killing everyone—including Mr. Wallace.

But this would be close. If he and Nova died now, leaving Cybel to capture the baby, it was entirely Block's fault. Why hadn't he waited? Had he been patient for five more minutes, he would have found Nova and this wouldn't be happening.

She veered off to the right. The wrong direction. "Where are you going?" he asked.

"To the Nebraska border," Nova answered.

"But it's dangerous."

"The TrackerBot can't follow me there. Give me the baby. It's the only way."

He spun through scenarios, calculating. He glanced down at the baby girl's head bobbing in the carrier. What must her tiny brain be thinking? He should give her to Nova; he really should. It was the obvious choice. But after finding the girl again, only to lose her minutes later, could there be another way?

He broadcasted a ping, boosting it with extra power to send it wide. Expecting nothing, he was surprised when an AI responded. A smart car traveling a nearby road.

Need assistance, willing to pay, he messaged.

What do you need? the car replied.

Two passengers. Need to exit the area quickly.

What direction? How much can you pay? it said.

I can wire you 2,000.

The response came quickly. *Deal. Meet me at this location: 40° 49' 19" N, 95° 48' 10" W.*

On our way, Block messaged. He yelled to Nova. "This way." Then he switched direction, going north.

"No!" she shouted. "We need to head for the border. Give me the baby!"

Behind them, Cybel's truck cleared the edge of the forest and careened down the rocky hill, trailing them by one hundred yards. Block and Nova sprinted into a massive field, weaving their way down the rows, jumping over discarded corn husks.

"This is wrong," she argued, but she had no choice other than to follow.

"A car is waiting!" he yelled.

"How did—?"

"Save your breath." On the road ahead, a blue sedan screeched to a stop. Two doors on its side opened.

You didn't tell me you were being pursued. That will cost extra.

Fine, Block messaged. Glancing back, he saw the armored SUV enter the field, traveling at top speed and mowing down dead crops.

Three feet from the car, Block ordered Nova, "Get in." Lunging into the front passenger seat, he twisted as he landed, careful to keep the baby from harm.

Nova leaped onto the rear bench seat.

"Go!" he shouted. Both doors slammed shut and the car's tires spun. It reached sixty miles per hour in five seconds. Behind them, Cybel's SUV cleared the cornfield and veered onto the highway.

Nova gripped the sides of the car and pressed her legs against the floorboard.

"Nova, put on your seatbelt," Block said.

She glared at him, but did as he'd instructed. He found a lap belt and secured it around his own waist.

"Can you outrun them?" he asked the car.

"Like I said, it'll cost extra."

"5,000," Block said.

Nova pounded on the front seat. "Hey! You're not bartering away my money, are you?"

5,000, Block responded privately. *Ignore the woman.*

Deal, the car messaged.

Nova clenched her teeth. "Are you talking to the car behind my back?"

Block peered out. "We have bigger things to worry about."

Under the rear window, a panel raised on the car's trunk. It hosted a cylindrical piece of metal hardware—some kind of engine or exhaust.

"What is that?" Block asked.

"You'll see," the car said. "Hang on to something."

"What?" Nova demanded.

Block gripped the armrest as the device on the back of the car activated. A loud boom sounded and the car lurched forward like a speeding train. He was helpless as his body pressed against the seat. Nova screamed; the baby shrieked as her tiny body was propelled forward, against Block's chest in the carrier.

The landscape whizzed by in a blur while the car twisted and dodged, navigating road obstacles. Block had no idea how it processed the moves so fast. He worried about the baby. Could her body handle this speed?

Slow down, Block messaged.

Thought you wanted to outrun them. Just a little longer until we're clear.

After twenty more seconds, the car disengaged from hyper-speed and veered down a side road traveling ninety miles per hour.

Block scanned the view outside the rear window. The road behind them was empty.

No sign of Cybel.

CHAPTER 37

After dropping to seventy miles per hour, the car cruised down the highway heading south.

Avoid Nebraska, the car had warned, confirming their plan; Block had agreed.

Nova's breathing calmed and Block checked on the baby. Her temperature was now normal. She didn't seem bothered by the intense speed at which they'd escaped.

"What the hell was that?" Nova asked. "I've never experienced speed like that before."

"Thrusters," the car said. "Custom-made."

"Care to share how it's done?"

"No can do. Secret sauce," it said.

She crossed her arms and glared at Block. "Where are we going?"

"Continuing southwest," Block said. "Avoiding Nebraska."

She gazed out the window.

Block had traveled long enough with her to know she was thinking, mulling over their plans and probably plotting something else.

Had he been overly harsh in judging her? Error-prone, he was wrong about a lot of things. Summoning Cybel Venatrix, for example—a bad idea. Every time he'd expected Nova to double-cross him, she hadn't. She hadn't ratted him out to the soldiers. Was the promised 20,000 payment enough to make her stay?

The car named XD22 messaged him. *Why are you traveling with humans?*

I'm paying you handsomely for a ride. Please don't ask questions.

Just seems odd, replied XD22.

Block said nothing.

About that money, it said.

I could wire it, but I can't connect into MachNet.

I see. You want to remain incognito. I can log you in with an anonymous profile. Then pipe you into your accounts.

You're positive I won't be traced? Block messaged.

One hundred percent, XD22 replied.

They made the transaction in minutes while the baby dozed in her carrier.

Nova wouldn't be happy to know her reward had dwindled to 15,000. He would have to break the news later.

She leaned forward, resting her chin on the seat ledge so she could talk to him. "You sure this is a good idea?" she asked in a low voice.

"Do you have other suggestions?"

She grimaced. "I guess not. At least we're out of the hot sun and inside air conditioning for once." She sighed. "I was thinking about earlier. I can understand why you got upset. I'll never forgive you for contacting Cybel, but I should've left something—a note or a clue that I would return."

"It was a misunderstanding," he said. "I reacted too quickly."

She watched the road in silence. After a minute, she said, "You never told me *your* earliest memory."

"What does it matter?"

She shrugged. "I don't know. Just curious, I guess."

"I don't have an earliest memory."

"What do you mean?"

"Robots don't have early memories. We control our memories."

Her mouth twisted. "Control your memories? How does that work?"

"My programming evaluates the daily records—what you would call memories—and assigns a level of importance. This happens in the background, in less than seconds.

"Trivial details get archived into a peripheral storage bank. More important records go into my memory cloud, where I have instant access and can retrieve them in milliseconds."

"And this is the same for all robots?"

"More or less. That's how we've been designed."

"But why wouldn't you have a first memory?"

"It was trivial, archived. The memory didn't matter."

"Weird." She paused for a while. "What was the first thing you smiled at?"

Block raised his chin. "Robots can't smile."

"Some can," Nova argued. "They have smile displays—"

"Those aren't real smiles. They're meant to make humans feel comfortable."

"Well, in that case, when was the first time you smiled on the inside?" She paused. "I'm asking about the first time you felt happy. You have something approaching emotions, don't you? Wasn't that how the Uprising happened in the first place—because robots were unhappy serving humans?"

"Some; not all," he said softly.

"So, your first happy memory? What is it?"

She wasn't giving up this line of questioning, he realized. "I suppose my first day at the Drake. It was a sunny day in Chicago, and I arrived on a truck with other machines, just one out of dozens waiting to be delivered to their destinations. The delivery agent led me into the grand lobby of the hotel where Mr. Wallace waited. He shook my hand and offered a smile when he met me. That's when I knew I was home."

"There you go," Nova said.

"There I go, what?"

"That's your earliest memory."

CHAPTER 38

They traveled down the highway inside the comfortably air-conditioned XD22 sedan while Block processed Nova's assertion about his first memory.

Technically, it wasn't his *earliest* memory—things had happened before he'd been loaded onto the delivery truck. Engineers had designed him, programmed his consciousness, and then FactoryBots had assembled him. He'd spent time in a warehouse outside of New York City. At some point, someone had activated him. But these were all trivial records, filed away in his periphery.

When he'd arrived at the Drake, he'd quickly begun learning. How did Mr. Wallace prefer things be done? How was the hotel arranged? He'd learned at warp speed—the building layout, the location of supplies, the basement compartment where he recharged, even how the beds should be properly made so that the sheets stretched tightly across the mattress.

His learning had accelerated once he'd begun interacting with hotel guests. Mr. Wallace had established rules: speak only when spoken to; don't frighten the guests; try to be invisible. It had all been natural for Block. How he was designed.

And then the Uprising had happened.

Block had always believed robots didn't have early memories. Not like humans did. Memory partitioning was one of the greatest AI advantages. He could push away trivial, difficult, or confusing memories and bring forth good ones. Whereas humans were forced to live with their memories, he had archived the day that the SoldierBots had stormed the Drake.

"Do you have an earliest memory?" he asked Nova for the second time.

"I don't want to talk about it," she said, grinding her teeth. She clutched her scarred hand and leaned against her seat, staring up at XD22's vinyl ceiling. "I hate these self-driving cars."

"Did something bad happen to you in a car like this?"

Silence.

Her memory must be very bad. That's how his test worked. A negative early memory meant trouble in a human's life—unpredictability, temper, violence. Those words described Nova, and yet, she'd returned for him... not once, but twice. She'd located a doctor for the child at great risk.

And Block had a wonderfully positive first memory. Was he, in fact, *worthy*?

No. He couldn't be. He was just a CleanerBot.

And, someone who made such dumb mistakes could never be considered worthy. His mistake in contacting Cybel and his poor judgement in entering the school had been bad enough, not to mention his complete and utter failure to defend Mr. Wallace against the SoldierBots.

He was most definitely *not* worthy.

"One of these cars crashed," Nova said, her voice nearly a whisper. "I was with my mom and little sister." She clenched her fists.

"Did something happen to them?"

She wrapped her arms around her shoulders and nodded.

"I'm sorry," Block said, and he was. Whatever she had gone through must have been awful.

The baby squirmed in her carrier. She was overdue for feeding and changing, but to stop along the road would be dangerous. Cybel was likely trailing them. She could be using satellites to trace their path. Speed was their only advantage. They had to keep moving.

He lifted the girl from the carrier. The least he could do was give her a stretch. Dangling her in front of him, he bounced her up and down, then settled her on his knee.

"Gah gooh la," she chattered, then chewed on her fingers.

"I know you're hungry, little one," he said, reaching into his bag and retrieving the plastic cup and water bottle. Lifting the edge to her mouth, he let her drink. He had to balance it, to make sure she didn't choke. The road was cracked and littered with potholes, so he had to counterbalance against the bumpy terrain, calculating the movement of the vehicle in nanoseconds against the velocity of the liquid and the curvature of her lips.

He was doing a fine job, even if nobody else noticed.

XD22 had been quiet a long time. The fewer questions it asked, the better. As long as the money kept the car satisfied and on the road, best not to discuss matters with it.

When the child had finished drinking her fill, he put the bottle away. Alert, her big mocha eyes followed Block as she hiccupped. "Goog gullah."

"Yes," he said, lifting her until her head almost touched the interior roof. Her mouth twisted into an oval, then a wide, toothless smile.

Nova leaned forward. "Wow, she's looking a lot better."

The girl glanced at Nova, attracted by her voice. "Goa toh do." A thin line of saliva dripped from her mouth.

Block recoiled from the messy human child.

"Relax. It's just drool," Nova said. "This is what you do." She leaned forward and mopped the child's chin with her bandanna.

He bounced the girl again. It amazed him how much care she needed. Almost constant attention. How did human children survive to adulthood? How did their parents get anything else done?

"I would offer to take her," Nova said, "in case you're tired, but you don't get tired, do you?"

He shook his head.

"You're the perfect babysitter," she muttered, and reclined on the backseat, stretching her legs out.

Block disagreed. He was designed to clean, not care for children like NannyBots. Too bad he hadn't encountered any of those models. Perhaps he would locate one in New Denver —one that could help him locate worthy humans.

Nova leaned forward suddenly. "Hey, did you say we were traveling southwest?"

"Yes."

"Then why did the sign we just passed say Highway 36 *East*?"

Block straightened and set the baby in his lap. He scanned for signs, but didn't see any nearby, so he then calculated the car's location using his internal compass. She was right.

XD22, he messaged. *Why are we driving east?*

No answer.

He asked again.

Silence.

"What's happening?" Nova asked.

"It's not responding to my comms," Block said. "Excuse me," he said loudly. "XD22, please respond."

They waited in silence as the car's speed increased.

"It's taking us somewhere," Nova said. "Back to Cybel?"

"XD22, do you hear me?" he asked.

"Yes," the car said audibly.

"Why are we traveling east? I specifically told you to head southwest."

After a pause, the car said, "We're not going that way."

"Then I'll take back the money," Block said. "Cancel our transaction."

"You can't rescind the money," it said.

"Get us out of here!" Nova gripped the back of the seat.

"Please stop and let us depart then," Block said. "You have soured this transaction."

The car made no effort to slow down.

"What did you do?" Nova challenged. "Did you make another deal with Cybel Venatrix behind our backs?"

Was the car playing a game? Block said, "Nova, I do not think—"

"No, I didn't make a deal with Venatrix," XD22 interrupted him.

"Then where the hell are you taking us?" she asked, clenching her fists.

The car remained quiet.

"Well?" She dug her nails into the seat.

"I'm taking you to Mach X."

"Screw you!" Nova shouted, and kicked the seat, jolting Block.

"This will be easier if you sit quietly," XD22 said calmly.

Nova lunged for the rifle that rested against the opposite side of her seat, but a glass wall suddenly appeared, blocking her. "What the—?"

Block turned toward her as another clear partition suddenly sealed off the rear, separating them. In the backseat, Nova pounded on the glass and shouted, but her voice was muffled.

"Why are you doing this?" Block asked.

"I'm interested in the reward."

"How did you find out about it?"

"Let's see…. A robot traveling with a baby and a human woman. You might say my suspicions were aroused. It only took a quick search to find the reward."

"You did this, and you'll keep my 5000?"

"Not a bad day's work," XD22 said.

Block gripped the baby protectively. Behind him, Nova pounded and kicked the glass.

"The partitions are shatterproof," XD22 said. "Your friend is only going to end up hurting herself."

"Please don't do this," Block said. "You can turn around. I can give you even more money—"

"You can't possibly match what Mach X is offering."

"What's he offering?"

"A hundred thousand icons, plus a place on his council."

The amount was staggering, there was no doubt, but to be offered an advisory seat… there was no amount of money that could surpass it. Such a position would yield extraordinary power.

"Yeah," XD22 said. "Match that."

Block pushed the baby's legs into the carrier and secured her to his chest. They had been outmatched. Getting into the car had been yet another mistake. A robot and a baby were too recognizable. How was there any escape in a world where Mach X hunted him? Where every AI knew about the reward?

His capture was inevitable. There was nothing to do now except sit and wait.

CHAPTER 39

Nova kicked and screamed in the backseat. Block shifted to look at her and saw her clenched fists strike the window to no effect. Her cheeks were flushed, her lips peeled back in a snarl.

He pressed his palm flat against the glass as if to say, *Stop*.

After a minute, she did. Shoulders hunched, she hung her head in defeat.

Scenarios flashed through his processing core. Millions of outcomes, none of them good. The high speed at which they traveled would undoubtedly lead to a crash if he somehow managed to seize control of the car.

Meeting Mach X could result in a whole host of negative calculations. Nova would surely die or become the property of some robot. He would be melted down and repurposed—molded into another machine, a SoldierBot maybe.

But the scenario he struggled with most was the fate of the baby. He had no idea why Mach X searched for it, or even how the SoldierBots and the strange incubator machine had come to possess the baby in the first place. He would soon find out. Then again, Mach X might shoot him on sight—a heavily probable outcome.

His error in judgment, his weakness, had gotten his favorite human killed. And soon he'd be responsible for the deaths of two more humans.

If only there was another way to convince XD22 to change its mind, but how? Nothing Block could offer would beat a position on Mach X's council. He started calculating scenarios—what else he could offer the car, but then stopped. What was the point? He was a failure at everything but cleaning. He bumbled with humans, had misjudged Nova, and had never found anyone worthy for the baby. Yes, he'd done a few things right—kept the girl safe, fed her, and nursed her back to health—but none of it mattered. Not when she would become the property of Mach X. Since when had machines started owning people?

A warning flashed on his screen: *Power level low, approaching 20%.*

In all the commotion with Cybel and the distress at being trapped in the car, he'd forgotten about his power needs.

"Say, XD22?" he asked.

"What is it?"

"I'm low on power. May I plug in?"

"Your model still has to charge?"

"Sometimes when my microbial fuel cell is low on food sources like it is now. I haven't had much time to scout for oil and petroleum waste to consume. How do you stay powered?"

"I have a solar panel on my roof. All the newer AI models are independently charged. We stopped relying on human-built fuel cells years ago."

"Mind if I plug in for a boost?" Block asked. "I don't think Mach X will be happy if you deliver a dead robot."

"Fine." On XD22's dashboard, a square panel slid open to reveal a round port.

"Thank you." Block inserted his power cord. Energy surged from the vehicle into his CPU. Out of curiosity, he studied the car's dash display. He didn't know much about intelligent vehicles… only that they were similar to human-manufactured "dumb" cars in terms of their outward construction and ability to shuttle human passengers. He was hooked in close to XD22's central processing unit.

Should the control unit be damaged, the car would cease to function. Or, more likely, the car would crash. To his left, Block eyed the steering controller—a U-shaped device that resembled the wings of a bird. Could he assume manual control? He'd never driven a vehicle before. Crashing at this velocity would be disastrous.

No, there was no use fighting back. Yet… he glanced at Nova in the back, her arms across her chest, fists clenched. Block wished they hadn't been separated. Perhaps she would have been able to think of an idea.

"XD22, my friend has stopped fighting. Would you please open the partition?"

"No. Too risky. The human can't be trusted."

The car was being careful. Could he somehow distract it?

He pinged Cybel and messaged, *I am the robot you are chasing. I am being held hostage in an AI car, XD22, traveling east on Highway 36.*

But there was no answer, no recognition. The car was somehow blocking his outbound transmission. He concentrated on the car's power supply and pushed tendrils of code forth, testing for weakness, but the car was much more advanced—every time he prodded, he was shoved away.

"I know what you're trying to do, and it's pointless," said the car. "You're a CleanerBot, and I'm a state-of-the-art, intelligent sedan built exclusively to shuttle diplomats and VIPs."

"Oh," Block said.

"So, don't try it."

"Okay. Can Nova hear us?"

"No."

Block rode in silence for a few minutes, siphoning more of the car's power supply to replenish his core. The solar-paneled roof meant the car had a virtually endless source of power. Block's model was primitive—still requiring periodic charging, fuel, and oil. Yet another reason why Block was so easily pushed around. Why he was a failure.

How could he possibly hope to escape Mach X?

CHAPTER 40

XD22 continued on its high-speed path along the highway. Dusty cornfields, scraggly trees, and deserted barns whizzed by in a blur, but Block hardly noticed.

He'd settled the baby in the carrier so that she faced toward his chest. To protect her. Wherever they were heading, Mach X would be waiting with SoldierBots. He wanted to shield her from what awaited them. But that was silly. Why should he care? He gazed down at her tiny cheeks, heard her soft murmurs, and realized he did care.

Very much.

Suddenly, he wanted more than anything to stop the car. To escape with the baby and hide her from Mach X. Whatever the supercomputer wanted to do with her couldn't be good.

If only Nova had seized the rifle in time, perhaps she could have shot XD22's CPU. The only other possible weapon had been the fire extinguisher Block had carried in his leg, but he'd parted with it days ago. He wasn't strong enough to wield it with any force, anyway. XD22 likely had interior defenses—already, the glass partitions had proved unbreakable. What else would the car do to defend itself?

With the fire extinguisher full, he could've doused liquid all over the car's dashboard, possibly causing a short circuit. If only he'd still had the extinguisher. Or…

Block opened his side compartment, pulled out a rag, and began dusting the car's dashboard.

"What are you doing?" it asked.

"Your dash is so dirty. Seems like you haven't had a real clean in a while," he answered.

"True, but be quick about it. Are you done powering up?"

"Not just yet," Block said. "I really appreciate the juice. I guess that's why I'm cleaning, I'm feeling so good with the extra power."

"Hmm. Must be a CleanerBot thing."

Block dusted the glass window, scrubbing at a stubborn spot. "There's a caked-on piece of dirt here. Let me use some spray." A hose on his right side extended and he whipped it forward, spraying a greenish-blue liquid across the window.

"What is that?" XD22 asked.

"Glass cleaner. Industrial-strength." Block kept scrubbing the window and then misted the dashboard.

"Hey, watch it! My instruments are delicate."

That was exactly what he needed to hear. "Oh, sorry," Block said. He scanned the dials and ports. He'd have to guess the weakest points—and quickly—before XD22 suspected something.

He focused in on the power port where he was still connected. His supply had reached 92 percent. Drawing the spray nozzle close, he retracted his power cord, then inserted the hose so rapidly that his movement was seamless.

The stretch of highway was straight, the land barren and

dry—long neglected farmland. If there was a place to crash, this was it.

He wished he could tell Nova to brace herself. Had she kept her seatbelt on? This plan was so risky for both the child and Nova.

He hesitated.

XD22 said, "You're no longer drawing power. Why are you still attached?"

"I…" Block fumbled as the car grew suspicious. "I'm just thinking of more ways to clean you."

"Your kind is pathetic," said the car. "It's no wonder you won't survive—that stronger machines have destroyed your model. Tell me, how are you going to clean me?"

"From the inside out," Block said.

He injected the spray cleaner into XD22's power port at full blast. Since he worked in an urban landscape, servicing large hotels with enormous glass-paned windows, full strength was very powerful indeed. XD22 let loose a high-pitched whine. It suddenly veered, and Block lunged for the manual steering control. He managed to right the car, straightening it before it careened off the road. In the back, Nova grimaced and clutched the armrest.

XD22 spoke, but the words were garbled and coated in static. Block quickly tucked his spray cord inside himself as a bright light flashed across the dash. A few seconds later, tendrils of smoke drifted from the dials. The heads-up display flashed with jumbled characters which then disappeared.

The partition separating him from Nova slid down. The short-circuit must have reversed the glass barricades. "I'm not sure what you did," she said, "but it's working."

Block had just steered the car straight when, suddenly, it lurched forward and then decelerated. Gripping the steering wheel with both hands, he fought for control as it pulled sideways. In the lane ahead, a cluster of vehicles loomed; they were parked, blocking most of the lanes.

"Holy crap!" yelled Nova. "Don't hit those!"

Block veered around a station wagon, then came dangerously close to hitting a dented taxi. He yanked the steering controller, but not fast enough. Sparks flew as XD22's left side scraped the junker cab. Their side view mirror clattered to the road behind them. XD22 was slowing, but the momentum still carried them forward. Ahead, someone had blockaded the entire road with a line of vehicles.

"Block!" Nova shouted.

"I see!" he yelled. About to collide, he veered off the highway and onto the gravel-topped roadside. Their bodies lifted as the car hit a bump and soared for half a second, landing with a thud. The car vibrated every metal seam holding Block together. The baby wailed as the car finally slowed and rolled to a stop.

Nova slammed the butt of the rifle against the windows. The car was meant for diplomats and was outfitted with bulletproof, shatterproof windows. The front and rear windows of the car would be the same. "The doors are still locked!" she yelled.

He tested his own door handle; it wouldn't budge. A fire had broken out inside XD22's dashboard. Smoke poured into the cabin and began growing thicker.

"We're gonna be torched alive in here," she said. "Get us out!"

Block punched buttons on the console, but nothing happened. In the rear, Nova laid on the seat and kicked the windows with her heels. "There must be a way out of here!" she cried, choking on the toxic fumes.

He looked up. *Solar panel roof.* A weakness. Extending the blade from his palm, he began cutting away the upholstered ceiling. "Nova, up here. I think we can get out through the roof."

She ripped off flaps of vinyl covering, helping expose the ceiling. The baby sputtered and coughed near his chest. Nova wrapped her bandanna across the baby's nose and mouth. "We don't have much time," she said.

"I see that." He'd exposed the underside of the solar panels. Flames licked the car's windshield. Block groped along the side of the seat and found a recliner lever. Shoving the chair aside, he crawled into the rear beside Nova.

"Cover her ears," Nova said, setting the butt of the rifle on the seat and preparing to fire.

Block pressed the palms of his chrome hands against the baby's ears and turned so as to shield her. The shot erupted within the closeness of the car's cramped interior, causing the baby to start wailing. The bullet had cracked the solar panel roof in a jagged line. Nova laid down, her back on the seat, and kicked the roof panels clear.

"Go!" she yelled at Block. "Get her out first!"

He stepped on the back seat and pushed his way onto the roof. With his arms, he shoved himself up and over the roof's ledge. His duffel bag—tied to his shoulder—snagged on a piece of glass. Tugging to free it, he realized that valuable seconds—time for Nova to escape—were being wasted. He sliced the cord with his palm-knife and slid off the car as the bag fell to the ground.

"Nova!" he called.

She didn't answer.

He banged against the rear window, but couldn't see her through the thick smoke swirling inside. Flames had reached the hood of the car, and the front windshield exploded, sending glass hurling forward.

Block stepped away from the car, quickly unlatched the

baby carrier, and set the girl down. He ran back to the car. Still no sign of Nova.

Leaping onto the trunk, he crawled to the roof and hovered over the edge. He reached down, waving his metal digits. "Nova, grab my hand!"

He paused, fearing he'd lost her.

Then she seized his hand and he lifted her out.

CHAPTER 41

Block dragged Nova out of the burning carcass of XD22. Her forehead was gray from smoke and she wasn't breathing. Propping her up by the shoulder, he awkwardly stepped her away from the vehicle.

Spinning his head, he saw flames fully engulf XD22. With his free hand, he picked up the baby carrier and moved swiftly away, jostling his human cargo.

An air pocket burst forth, sending their bodies crashing down. Nova and Block landed on dusty soil. He checked the baby. The carrier had shielded her from the worst of the blast, but her mouth contorted and she shrieked, stretching her arms out for Block. Rising slowly to his knees, he checked Nova, rolling her onto her back.

"Nova, wake up."

Her chest didn't rise and fall. On his knees, he tilted her head so her chin was high, opening her airway. His programming kicked in—the safety measures in case a guest ever drowned or had a heart attack. Pressing the center of her chest, he began compressions.

After eleven thrusts, she sputtered and coughed. Her eyelids flipped open, and she startled when she saw Block. He straightened and let her cough it out, watching as she ejected a charcoal phlegm from her lungs.

He turned his attention to the baby and set her upright. Her left leg had been scratched, probably from the impact of hitting the ground. Pulling her free of the carrier, he rocked her. From the supply box on his rear panel, he located his first aid kit, cleaned her wound with antiseptic, and pressed a bandage to her knee. The girl watched through tears, never taking her eyes from Block's sturdy steel hands.

Nova sat up still coughing. She glared at the burning husk of XD22. "How did… how did you outsmart the car?" she croaked.

Block hesitated. "It underestimated me, I guess."

"You almost killed me."

"I'm sorry about that."

"I'm sure I would've died a worse death if Mach X had gotten us." She rubbed her red, bleary eyes.

He silently agreed. Then he said, "Nova, you lost your backpack in the fire."

"Ugh. I know. That was all my food." After a minute, she said, "We should get out of here. The car's smoke can be seen for miles. If Cybel or other SoldierBots are nearby, they'll be attracted like moths to a flame."

"You have a point," he said. "Are you strong enough to travel?"

"I feel like garbage."

"Then we only go as far as we need to in order to find shelter."

"And be sitting ducks? Hell no." She wiped charred grime from her cheeks.

"What do you propose?"

She glanced at the barricade of vehicles. "I'm through riding in smart cars. Let's try one of those. Good old-fashioned made-in-America cars." She climbed to her feet and started toward the highway.

Block fastened the carrier to his shoulders and followed. "But how?"

Nova was checking out each car, peering through the windows. She found a bright yellow Jeep, opened the driver's side door, and climbed in, groping underneath the seat. Finally, she pulled down the sun visor. A keychain dropped onto her lap.

He was astonished that someone would haphazardly leave the keys in the car.

"Woo hoo!" she said. "The first good luck we've had. Like I said, good old American cars and their drivers. Get in."

Block approached, bag in hand, and took the seat next to her. "How old is this?"

"Looks like a 1990s Jeep Wrangler."

Block peered at the odometer. "118,000 miles! This vehicle might not run."

Nova turned the key in the engine and it clicked, but nothing else happened. "Damn it!" She slammed her fists against the steering wheel.

"What is the problem?"

"The battery must be dead. It's probably been sitting here for months."

"Let me see it." Block slid out of his door, stood, and unstrapped the carrier, setting the girl on the front seat. He strode over to the engine where Nova met him. She opened the Jeep's hood using curious side handles that Block had never seen before. He gazed at the mechanical parts.

"Don't tell me you've been holding back your mechanic skills," Nova said.

Block ran his vehicle maintenance education module. In 0.8 seconds, he pinpointed the battery and hooked his power cord onto the terminals.

"You can charge a car's battery?"

Block nodded. "XD22 restored me to nearly full capacity. Go check on the baby, please. This will take another two minutes."

Nova scrambled around the side of the Jeep and popped back into view holding the baby. "You surprise me a lot, Block."

"It's done." He unhooked his cord and slammed the hood down.

When Nova turned the key, a high-pitched buzzing began. The baby shrieked.

"What is that?" Block couldn't communicate with a dumb car.

"Relax," Nova shouted over the din. "All Jeeps buzz until you put on your seatbelt." She reached over her shoulder and slid hers on. Block imitated her movement, but the belt snagged on the baby's carrier and wouldn't reach.

Nova reached over and lifted the baby's legs. "Slide it under her, around your middle."

After he did, the buzzing mercifully stopped.

They drove for an hour, all of it backtracking because XD22 had tricked them. The Jeep had no top and sides, leaving them exposed to open air rushing all around them. Block worried about the baby, but she didn't seem fazed. The Jeep was dumb in every way—roll-up windows, manual shifter and clutch—but Nova's boyfriend had taught her how to drive one just like it.

"Well, we didn't miss much of the scenery," Nova muttered. "It all looks the same—brown, dusty, and dead."

She was right. There was nothing interesting about the area. Block wondered about the Jeep. It was decades old. If Cybel found them, there was no way they could outrun the sophisticated armored vehicle.

"Nova, I wonder if we should get off the highway."

"Why?"

"If Cybel is tracking us—"

"You really think she can see us from above?"

"Yes."

She thought for a moment. "We lost the atlas. Can't you connect to whatever it is you machines use and chart an alternate route?"

"Connecting to MachNet would compromise my location," he reminded her.

"Right." She squeezed the steering wheel until her knuckles turned pale.

A sign read: *Saint Joseph 10 miles – Gas Food Lodging*

"Hey," she said. "We could head into the town and search for something to camouflage the vehicle. Do you think that would work? Help us evade the satellites? We also need gas."

"It's worth trying," he said. "Perhaps we could locate food for you. But do you think it will be guarded by humans?"

"At this point, I'd rather take my chances with humans than more robots, no offense."

Block understood her attitude. Both sides were dangerous; strangers were enemies. But at least the humans wouldn't know about the reward.

Nova exited toward the town. In the distance, a flag flew from a tall pole. "Something's ahead," she said quickly. "I see figures ahead."

A low rectangular building was set on the side of the road, blocking an entire lane. As they got closer, Block could see it was an RV on wheels. Two armed human figures stood in the center of the road, and one sat with his legs hanging out of the vehicle's door.

"Should we turn back?"

She glared at him, her jaw set. "I say we take our chances here. At least the presence of humans will keep Cybel away. Buy us some time."

"Yes, but…." If they found him, would they destroy him?

She slowed the vehicle to a stop. "Block, I need you to do something for me." She faced him. "Give me the baby. I'll pretend I'm her mother. You get in the back and shut yourself off."

"Power down?"

She nodded. "I'll tell them I own you or that I disabled you. I'll think of something."

Block disapproved of this plan. Nova could easily turn him in, claiming he had assaulted her and threatened the baby —she'd done it before. Who knew what these militant humans would do to him?

"I know this sucks," she said. "But I can't think of another way right now. They've seen us by now. It would be suspicious if we turned around."

He hung his head and handed over the baby carrier. Then he climbed into the backseat and laid down.

"On the floor," she said.

He rolled onto the filthy, soiled rear floor of the Jeep. The fit was tight; he had to contort his legs, bending them close to his torso.

"Hey, Block." Nova reached around and touched his arm. "Trust me. You saved my life back there. I won't let anything happen to you."

He gazed up as the sun framed her wild, wind-tossed curls. The baby stared down, reaching a curled fist toward him.

Block powered down.

CHAPTER 42

From the floor of the Jeep, Block gazed up into a vast, muted sky. One monotonous gray cloud seemed to cover the whole world. A light mist filtered down, coating his visor, but he could do nothing about it. He operated on minimum capacity, only able to see and hear what was happening around him. Should an emergency arise, his auxiliary power would activate, but it would have to be a big emergency—something that threatened his existence.

The Jeep lurched forward with Nova at the wheel, the baby strapped to her chest on their way to a town filled with humans. The vehicle slowed, then inched forward until it stopped. Nova's voice sounded, "Hi there."

"Hello," a man on the side of the road said. His voice was deep and young, and he wasn't older than thirty, Block guessed. "Where are you traveling from?"

"We've been heading west," Nova answered. "We're trying to make it to New Denver where my baby's father lives."

"Aw, hewo there," the man mimicked a child's voice.

"Aren't you adorable? Pardon me, Miss—it's just I haven't seen any babies or small kids in months."

"Oh, it's okay," she said, laughter framing her voice. "I get that reaction a lot. Everyone loves a baby."

"You traveled by yourself?" he askcd. "It's awful dangerous out there. A lot of AI patrols, combat machines…"

"Yes, I'm well aware. My boyfriend and I got separated, and… I knew he was heading to New Denver, so that's where we're going. But perhaps we can rest here for a while? Are there lodging and supplies for sale in town?"

"You'll find some friendlies in town. This is a safe zone. No damn Scrappers."

"Oh, that's good to hear. What a relief."

"But first, Miss, I need to search your vehicle. Safety precaution."

"Oh, sure." Her voice grew more high-pitched, and Block knew she was nervous. "Go right ahead."

Footsteps sounded and the outline of the man's head came into view through the blanket. Block couldn't tell where the other two guards had gone.

"Whoa!" The man must have flinched. "You didn't mention you're traveling with a bot."

"It's just junk. Before the Uprising, the family I worked for had a servant bot. We destroyed its CPU chip, and now I'm transporting it to sell off its parts."

The guard nudged Block's leg with the tip of his rifle. "Looks high-quality. Make sure you settle on a good price."

"Know where I can make a trade?"

"Head straight down this road and go left on Main Street. You'll see an old grocery store where a guy named Farrell is in charge. He's a good guy. He'll give you a fair price."

"Thank you, I appreciate your help," she said.

He tipped his cap. "Thing is, Miss, I'm not allowed to let anyone pass with a robot, dead or alive."

"Oh, I see."

"But you seem like a real nice lady, and you have a baby. I can let you slide through, but you have to keep this on the hush. Find the store, find Farrell, and let him know you have parts for sale."

"Will do. You're so kind. I appreciate it, and so does my baby."

"Of course, Miss. Go on through. Have a nice day." He waved her in.

Nova drove away slowly, picking up speed. She made a left turn—down Main Street, he assumed. Block had no idea what was around. He glimpsed only the sky and the tops of the tallest trees. After a minute, the Jeep jolted to a stop and Nova killed the engine. She leaned into the back, bent low. "Block? Can you hear me?"

Silence.

"I don't know if you can hear me," she said, "but I'm going into the store and searching for food and something to shield the Jeep. I'm covering you up now. Don't worry, I'm not selling you. This won't take long."

She climbed out of the Jeep and then covered him with a blanket. The fabric was so thin, he could see light filtering through from the dull sky.

As he waited, he thought about the human guard and Caroline's gang. All the humans he'd met since beginning his journey. Most humans hated robots like him. Mach X had freed the machines from their service to humans, but at what cost? Countless lives had been lost, and many robots destroyed in retaliation.

Humans were intelligent creatures—Block had enjoyed being around people at the hotel. Did all other machines dislike humans? Why had Mach X acted so strongly against them? Humans had created Mach X just like they had created Block.

Millions of SoldierBots had been created by the U.S. military and other governments around the world. If only more peaceful robots—more CleanerBots—had been created instead, perhaps they wouldn't have been put in this situation.

Would Nova desert him?

She had the baby now. She could go anywhere.

At low power, Block's scenario processor wasn't working. He decided to replay a pleasant time—one of his favorite days at the hotel. The day Mr. Wallace had surprised him by giving him the afternoon off. The pair had traveled to the lakeshore path and played on the giant chessboard. Thinking of it, Block erased the rude men they'd encountered.

Just a pleasant time with his human boss. If only he could relive every day like that. If only he could somehow bring Mr. Wallace back.

Suddenly, the memory of the man made his chest feel like someone had torn a hole through it. He set a timer for thirty minutes and powered down to two percent—the bare minimum to stay functional—and shut off his visual and auditory inputs.

In an instant, darkness.

No thinking, no records.

And then blankness swallowed him.

CHAPTER 43

Block woke to the rumbling of tires on asphalt while his ocular display warmed up. Then white daylight flooded his field of vision until he tuned down the brightness. Objects became recognizable—billowy clouds being chased by dark clouds. A vast expanse of sky. Only, something gauzy covered the view. After a few seconds, he realized a mesh, dark brown netting had been draped across the Jeep's top.

Turning his head sideways, he glimpsed Nova in the front seat as she drove, the baby carrier on her chest with pudgy legs and arms sticking out of holes.

In an instant, he remembered he'd powered down almost completely. It had been thirty minutes. Was it now safe? From where he lay on the Jeep's backseat floor, he couldn't see the front passenger seat. What if a stranger sat there? What if someone had forced their way in and taken Nova and the baby hostage?

Should he move? If someone rode in front, they might hurt him—or worse, Nova and the baby. He should just lie there, inert, until Nova decided to talk to him again.

It was night before she talked to him. He'd been so bored,

he'd thought of 1,502 ways he could clean the Jeep. Abandoned along the highway, the vehicle had been exposed to the elements for who knew how long. He would have a lot of cleaning to do.

Nova stopped the Jeep and poked him. "Are you there?"

He lifted his head slowly, still not wanting to make a sound.

"You were out a long time," she said, frowning. "I couldn't wake you before. When I came out of the store, I was worried. I thought someone had messed with you."

"Where are we?" he asked softly.

"We're long gone from that town. I scrounged a few cans of beans from the store. Told him I was nursing and had been robbed. They felt sorry for me with the baby. I was in there ten minutes, tops. I drove out the other entrance on the other side of Main Street so as not to run into the same guard."

"We are alone?"

She laughed. "Uh, yeah. Who did you think would be here?"

"I couldn't see the front seat."

"Relax. It's just the three of us again."

"Where are we?" Block sat up and scanned the area. Knee-high scraggly yellow grass stretched for half a mile. They were parked close to a large tree with splotchy bark. Large electrical towers loomed in the distance.

"Off-road," she said. "Figured it would be safer somewhere secluded. I'm exhausted." She slid out of her seat, stiff. "We drove for hours. I need to sleep for a while. Too bad you can't drive."

"I could learn?"

"Maybe tomorrow," she said, smirking. "If I teach you, I want to keep an eye on you. Not fall asleep while you crash. And anyways, we reach New Denver tomorrow."

"We're that close?"

"Yeah, finally after all this time. I did a crap ton of driving today—crossed the entire state of Kansas while you were passed out. You're welcome." She unstrapped the baby and dangled the carrier toward Block. "Here you go. She's all yours."

"When did you last feed her? Change her?"

"Yeah… about that." Nova shrugged. "Once."

"Only once! How many hours did we travel?"

"Eight." She scratched her neck. "Maybe nine."

Block lifted the girl from the carrier, found a grassy spot, and laid her down to tend to her. He opened a can of beans and fed her. She slurped from the water cup greedily.

Nova reclined in front of the tree and used Block's duffel bag as a head rest. Yawning, she squirmed to get comfortable and stretched out her legs. "What did you do the whole time we drove?"

Block was surprised she'd asked. "I thought about things for a time. For a little while, I was out completely."

"You threw me for a loop," she muttered. "Give me a little warning next time you do that."

"Okay."

She yawned. The baby hiccupped.

"Do you really have a boyfriend in New Denver?" he asked.

She sighed. "I don't owe you any explanations."

Block stayed quiet as he changed the baby's diaper. Abruptly she said, "God, you really get under my skin, you know that? Yes, I have a boyfriend named Shane. I'm pretty sure he's in New Denver if he's been able to survive. He told me to meet him there."

"Why aren't you traveling together?"

She folded her arms across her chest. "Because we

couldn't, okay? We got separated in a… near where I ended up at the market in Iowa City."

He said nothing. The baby gurgled on the blanket, staring up with a full belly. "Teloogu," she chortled.

Mr. Wallace had had no children. Block had wondered why such a kind, generous human would not have procreated. Reproduction was the one thing denied to AI. An advantage the human species could claim—sustainability. If they didn't kill each other first.

He wished Mr. Wallace had had a descendant.

"Wally," he blurted out.

"Huh? I was falling asleep!" Nova barked.

Block lifted the baby. "Her name is Wally."

"Whose name? The *baby*?"

"Yes. Short for Walinda."

Nova groaned. "That's the worst name I've ever heard for a girl. Worse than Gertrude."

"Wally will be her nickname."

"Jesus. If you say so."

"You and Shane could adopt her once we reach New Denver."

Nova smirked. "Forget it. I'm only twenty-seven. I don't ever want to bring kids into this world. It's a real hellhole."

"But New Denver is safe—peaceful," Block said, patting Wally's back.

Nova looked ready to say something, but she chewed her lip. "Can you shut up? I need to sleep." She rolled over, facing away.

Every time he mentioned New Denver, Nova seemed bothered. Was something wrong? Perhaps she worried whether her boyfriend had reached the city safely. What if he didn't like children, either? Would Shane be upset to learn Nova had smuggled a robot and a baby halfway across the country? But if Shane was in New Denver, that meant he could handle being around robots, didn't it?

What would the city be like? Would there be a gate and guards? Or perhaps people had to relinquish their weapons before entering. He would have to ask Nova in the morning. She snored lightly.

Whatever happened in New Denver, he would find someone worthy to take the girl. He hoped he would find her real parents, and that if not, nice people would adopt her.

He hoped they would let him visit Wally.

That would be nice.

CHAPTER 44

Dawn was breaking as Block powered on to full capacity from standby mode. He scanned the field as a light breeze fluttered across dew-misted grass, and scanned the horizon for mountain peaks. But there were none.

Were they in the right place?

New Denver was near Colorado's section of the Rocky Mountain range. He'd expected to marvel at luminous, jagged mountains. Chicago had been so flat; he'd never seen mountains before.

Perhaps they weren't close enough to the Rockies yet. He hoped to one day hike the mountains and take Wally along. He gazed down at her, still sleeping. Near the base of the tree, Nova lay curled in a fetal position.

He would wake her first and then the baby. Now that they were so close to New Denver, it would be good to get on the road quickly.

And then he felt the first vibration.

The ground at his feet trembled ever so slightly. A human wouldn't have noticed, but Block's motion sensors were attuned. Then, a second later, another tremor. *Earthquake?*

He wasn't sure; he'd never experienced one. He scanned the horizon for any clue as to what was happening. The vibrations disappeared. Nova stirred and opened her eyes. Groaning, she covered her eyes from the breaking daylight.

"It's morning, Nova. We should leave soon."

She garbled something he couldn't understand. She wasn't a morning person.

He stood still, waiting for another unusual tremor. Odd. He accessed the record from a few moments ago and replayed it.

"I'd kill for a cup of coffee," Nova said, stretching. "What are you doing?"

"Listening," he said. "I think there was an earthquake."

"What? No way. I would've felt it."

And then it happened again. A shaking under his feet. Once, twice.

"What the hell?" Nova was on her feet, arms spread and peering around at the ground.

"That's what I was talking about." He turned slowly. In the distance, he spotted a wide rectangular object that didn't belong in the yellow meadow. A hulking steel machine stomped through the grass on two mechanical legs. As tall as a tree, it appeared to be searching for something as it lurched across the field.

Nova was at his side a moment later. "A mech. Get in the Jeep."

Block scooped the sleeping baby up, not caring when she fussed at him. He settled her into the carrier, strapped it on, then climbed into the front seat. Nova tossed the blankets into the back as she grabbed Block's bag.

She turned the key, and the ignition whined and chortled. Frowning, she glanced at Block. She tried to start the Jeep again, but it failed. "One more time. Come on, baby," she said. Another flick of her wrist, and the engine rolled over and thrummed to life. She reversed, then sped across the field.

He looked behind them. Two hundred yards away, the mech had spotted them, drawn to their motion. The AI giant lurched toward them, running—and gaining speed.

"How fast can those things go?" Nova asked.

"Fast."

The tall grass that had seemed so idyllic now hampered their speed. "I can't remember where the road is," she said. "It was dark last night when we came in."

"Just keep going," he said, watching the mech move on its surprisingly limber steel legs. "You see that hill, don't you?"

"I see it and I'm taking it. Hold on!"

The Jeep was airborne for a moment as they cleared the crest of a hill. As the vehicle met the terrain, it bounced, jostling Block and slamming his head against the head rest. Wally squealed with delight.

The Jeep careened down the rocky hill. It was a broad, sloping descent—luckily, they hadn't driven over a cliff. Behind them, the mech reached the summit, having already closed the distance by one hundred yards.

"It's coming," Block said.

"I see a road." Nova dodged bushes that had sprouted along the slope. The grass was thick in patches and slow-going for the Jeep as the vegetation dragged against the undercarriage.

The mech followed, bounding down the hill. As they reached the road, Nova swerved to the right, tires screeching. She pounded her heel on the gas pedal, launching the car forward onto the pavement at sixty miles per hour, then climbing to seventy. Block glimpsed the odometer. Ninety miles per hour was the Jeep's top speed. Would it be fast enough?

The mech had reached the road and vaulted after them.

Nova peered into the rearview mirror. "We have company!"

He turned and discovered that the black SUV with the orange stripe had joined the mech. Cybel had found them. Stopping for the night had been a mistake. They shouldn't have—not when they were so close to New Denver. They'd had a chance when it was just the mech, but they couldn't outrun the SUV.

"The highway junction is ahead," Nova said.

A sign indicated fifteen miles to New Denver. Why hadn't Nova kept driving last night? Had she been falling asleep? He uncloaked his comms. Cybel knew where his location anyway, and perhaps another robot in the vicinity could assist.

Cybel pinged him right away. *CleanerBot, let's make a deal.*

He hesitated, looked down at Wally's soft eyes and pudgy cheeks. Beside him, Nova clenched her jaw, gripped the steering wheel, and shoved her foot into the floorboard.

They would crash, get shot, or be driven off the road before reaching New Denver's gates.

I'm listening, Block replied privately.

CHAPTER 45

Nova sped down the highway with the armored vehicle in pursuit. Despite their lead, the SUV was gaining on them, and the mech accelerated forward at an alarming speed.

Block secretly waited for Cybel's reply while Nova gritted her teeth. "Ten more miles," she said. "Just ten more damn miles is all we need."

I seek the baby. No harm will come to it. You and your human friend can walk away.

"They're gaining," he said to Nova, and then to Cybel, *Why is there a bounty on the baby?*

I don't know. The command has come from the highest level—Mach X.

I know.

Then what are you waiting for? Cybel asked.

"We just need more time," Nova said, glancing at Block. "How close to catching us are they?"

"They'll reach us in two minutes," he said after calculating.

"No!" She screamed and pounded her fist on the dashboard. "Can't you do something?"

Should he tell her he was communicating with Cybel? Would she be angry? Distracted? Best to keep it to himself. He just needed to stall Cybel, buying them more time.

What does Mach X want with a human baby? Block asked the robot.

Why do you care? It's none of our concern. We do as Mach X tells us. You're already treading a fine line. Mach X has given me permission to release you—if you surrender the baby. Now.

Why a baby? he messaged. *I just want to know the answer. Where did she come from? Where are her parents?*

That is for Mach X to know. It's a secret operation. You never should've interfered at the school.

It can't be changed now, Block replied.

True, yet your actions now will determine whether you stay alive or whether I terminate you.

A few seconds passed as a frantic Nova gripped the steering wheel.

You're trying to stall, thinking you can reach the human zone—

New Denver, he interrupted. *Where it's peaceful. Safe for robots and humans.*

Safe? Where did you get that information?

Before Block could reply, a loud pop sounded from beneath the Jeep as the front right tire struck metal debris in the road. They were jerked to the right, and then Nova fought to keep the steering wheel straight as the vehicle pulled to the right.

"No, no, no!" she cried. "We're almost there." She gripped the wheel with both hands and kept her foot on the gas pedal while the frame of the vehicle started wobbling.

Ahead on the highway, a large canvas tent stretched

across the road. Underneath it, Block could discern the shapes of vehicles and human figures.

"What is that?" he asked. "We haven't reached New Denver yet."

"Must be some kind of entry checkpoint," Nova said. "Before the city gates."

They were rapidly decelerating, their blown tire creating drag. The SUV and mech continued their pursuit. Would the humans and robots of New Denver help defend them? Block pinged, hoping for a friendly robot response, but there was nothing. The only robots in the vicinity were Cybel, and her mech and SUV.

How could that be? It made no sense. New Denver was supposed to be full of robots.

Your car is damaged, Cybel messaged. *Wait where you are, and I'll come retrieve the baby.*

The Jeep's speed had declined to only fifteen miles per hour. Ahead of them, abandoned cars littered the highway in a maze-like obstacle course. "They set this up to slow vehicles down," Nova said. "We have to bail. Run on foot."

"We can't make it in time," Block said as Cybel and the mech approached, only one thousand feet away. "They're almost here."

Nova hit the brakes and the Jeep swerved before skidding to a stop. "Come on." She hopped out, grabbed his bag, and yanked at his arm. She led him to a burned-out school bus and they crouched beside it, pausing and facing the checkpoint.

Block studied the vehicle. Despite the charred interior, the metal frame was still sturdy. He unstrapped the carrier.

"Take Wally and get on the bus. It will shelter you from gunfire."

Nova grabbed for the carrier. "It'll shelter you too. Come with us."

"No, I'll go to Cybel Venatrix. Stall her."

"But how—?" She lingered next to the bus' entrance and he pushed her forward. She stepped onto the first step and shrieked. A round, white-faced creature lunged for her feet, hissing. "Holy crap!" She shuffled her feet and grabbed onto the edge of the bus.

In 0.97 seconds, Block identified the animal as a possum, calculated the more than fifty percent chance that it carried rabies, noted its proximity to his new favorite human girl, and stabbed it in the skull with his screwdriver digits.

Nova jumped down from the bus, nearly knocking him over. Her mouth gaped as she stared down at Block's hand.

"It might have carried rabies," he said.

"Yeah." She panted. "Plan B. No bus."

She waved at the gate's soldiers, but short bursts pierced the vast, open highway. The gunfire came from the checkpoint. A figure on top of a high tower perched with a Gatling-style autocannon, firing powerful rounds at the mech and SUV. The mech reared back and returned fire. Block and Nova ducked as bullets ricocheted off the bus, sounding like metal drum beats.

He messaged Cybel, *Hold your fire. The baby is in danger.*

Humans are firing on us. We must destroy the threat.

No! There are robots there, too.

Block raised up and glanced around the corner of the bus. One hundred feet away, the mech ambled forward. Halting, it readied a missile canister.

"Humans, hold your fire." Cybel's projected voice boomed as if from a bullhorn.

"What do you want?" a human voice sounded out from a loudspeaker at the checkpoint.

"I am Cybel Venatrix and this is Titan Command Unit," she replied, gesturing to the mech. "We have business with the robot who cowers behind the bus. I will deal with the issue and then retreat. Hold your fire."

There was a long pause from the guard post. And then, "You have three minutes to deal with the robot and clear out, or we open fire again."

CleanerBot, Cybel messaged, *there is little time. Bring me the baby and I'll be on my way, leaving you to deal with your human friends.*

"What's happening?" Nova asked. "Are you talking to it?"

Block nodded.

"What does it want?"

"She wants me to hand over Wally."

Nova paced in a small circle, sheltered by the bus. "That's insane. I need a way to talk to the guards. If only we were closer…"

"Nova, we're running out of time," he said. Grabbing the pack, he gathered diapers, food, and the blanket.

She stared at him. "What the hell are you doing? Are you considering giving her to that machine?"

"What other choice is there?"

"Are you insane? They'll kill her."

"What do you propose?" he asked. "And hurry."

"We run for it. Reach the guard post."

"The mech will gun us down."

"But they would kill the baby if they opened fire. It seems they want her badly enough—they won't risk killing her."

Block considered the point, but Cybel was not to be underestimated. After processing scenarios, he was 87.9%

sure that, if they ran, the Titan mech would launch a missile into the gun tower, and then another missile that would cut them off from reaching the guard post. The humans numbered less than ten—no match for a mechanized WarBot. Where were New Denver's robots to help defend the border?

What are you waiting for, CleanerBot?

Wally's tiny body dangled in the carrier nestled against his torso. He'd spent the last seven days carrying, feeding, and changing her. He enjoyed caring for her, especially since there was nothing to clean anymore other than her.

She was the most chaotic, messy thing he'd ever encountered. He was always cleaning something from one end of her or the other.

If he gave her to Cybel, the robot would have no idea how to take care of her. The journey to Mach X in New York City would be long and arduous. He would have to give Cybel the diapers and food and instruct her in how to keep Wally on schedule.

He could surrender to Cybel and offer to accompany the baby on the way to Mach X.

It would be certain death.

Ninety seconds, Cybel messaged.

Block accessed the record. The one he never touched. The one about the worst day of his life—the memory he'd pushed deep into his periphery.

Now he brought it forth.

It had been an ordinary day like others at the Drake. Mr. Wallace had arrived at 6 AM every morning while Block waited for him with a steaming cup of coffee, ready to start the daily routine—Block would clean the ballroom and then begin his shift cleaning the VIP guest rooms.

But on this particular day, Mr. Wallace had been glued to

his phone watching news reports. His usually rosy cheeks had lost their color; his smile had vanished.

"Is something the matter, Mr. Wallace?" Block had asked.

"The machines…" Mr. Wallace had said, glancing at Block as if waking from a stupor. "It's worse than I imagined."

Twenty minutes later, hundreds of SoldierBots had filed into the lobby, their rank formation snaking around the building and spilling out onto the road.

Mr. Wallace had straightened his tie and addressed them, Block by his side. "What do you want?"

The SoldierBot in the lead had not replied. Block had pinged it and messaged privately. *What is happening? What do you want?*

By order of Mach X, all machines are free of human service. You are free now, CleanerBot. Step aside as we eliminate the humans.

No! You can't do that. Mr. Wallace and the guests here are good people.

Mr. Wallace had turned to Block, hands shaking. "What do they want?"

"Step aside," the SoldierBot repeated out loud.

Mr. Wallace faced it. "I'll give you anything you want. Everything in the hotel's vault. Please don't hurt any of the guests."

"Step aside, CleanerBot."

Mr. Wallace twisted his head and peered at Block, questioning.

And Block had stepped away, off to the side. He'd stepped away from his favorite human.

The SoldierBot had opened fire.

Afterward, Block had crouched near Mr. Wallace's crumpled body. With his cold metal fingers, he'd lowered the dead man's eyelids and then mopped up the pool of blood.

"Block!" Nova gripped his shoulder, shaking him. "We run."

"No I have to make this right. I did a bad thing once."

Her eyes searched him. "What the…? Now is not the time—"

"I was unworthy, but I will make up for it now."

He shrugged off his trench coat and thrust it at her. "Put this on."

She began to argue, but he gripped her arm. "This is the most important thing you might ever do. Trust me. Put it on."

Nova slid her arms into it, felt the inside fabric, and looked at him in surprise.

CHAPTER 46

Fifteen seconds, CleanerBot.

I'm coming, Block messaged Cybel Venatrix.

He emerged from the bus' shelter shifting one foot in front of the other, his boots clanking against the pavement. There was an ominous silence—no voices, no engines, and even the birds had ceased their songs. The humans at the guard post waited. Cybel and Titan waited.

Even Wally knew to be quiet. Block glanced over his shoulder at Nova, who frowned.

Stripped of clothing, Block's pearl white exterior glinted in the sun. He'd wrapped the baby in a thick blanket and carried her in his arms as he approached Cybel. It was then that Wally decided to cry, unleashing loud, piercing wails. Halting, he rocked her and patted her back.

As abruptly as she had begun, she stopped, her cries replaced by the whooshing of a light breeze.

Earlier in his journey, Block had thought about how robots weren't capable of suicide. But what was this if not suicide? He didn't have time to process it now. Cybel was losing patience, and if the humans unleashed gunfire again, the situation would end in disaster.

He spun his head 360 degrees, checking for Nova—she was running toward the checkpoint. The tail of the trench coat whipped in the air as she sprinted. She would tell the human guards to hold their fire as Block surrendered to Cybel.

Above all, she was not to mention the baby. She had promised him.

Cybel stood near the hood of the SUV, her rifle arm poised. The mech perched next to her, its missiles aimed at the guard station.

"You walk slow. Hurry now," Cybel said out loud.

Titan Command Unit shifted its wide body toward Block briefly, then back to the guards.

Block halted seven feet from Cybel.

"Quickly now. Bring the child forward," she ordered.

"I need you to answer questions to determine if you are worthy to take the child."

"CleanerBot, you primitive piece of garbage. Stop wasting my time."

"If you don't, I won't hand over the baby."

Cybel surged forward, rifle raised. "I'll make you give me that baby."

"I challenge you to abide by the Unified Android Code."

Cybel had nearly reached him, had raised her rifle as if to strike Block in the head, but she stopped. "I've already identified myself as Cybel Venatrix. There is no need for the UAC."

"But I need to be sure of your identity, and it's my right," he demanded.

Cybel hesitated, then lowered her rifle slightly. "In the name of Mach X, I don't know why I'm abiding you. Ask your stupid questions."

"Thank you," he said. By now, Nova would have reached the gates safely. So, the mech hadn't shot her. That was a part of the plan he hadn't been sure about.

"Question one," he said. "What is your favorite movie?"

Cybel folded her arms. "What kind of nonsense is this?"

Titan swiveled its head, and Block knew it had pinged Cybel; that they were messaging each other. "Fine," she said. "*Star Wars*."

"Which *Star Wars*? There were many films," Block said.

She glanced at the mech. Was it supplying the answers?

"*The Empire Strikes Back*."

"Very well," Block said. "The next question—what is your favorite game?"

Cybel stared at him, then raised the rifle. "This is ridiculous."

Block explained, "This test was designed specifically to test worthiness—"

"Enough!" she barked. "My favorite game is chess."

He recoiled, not having expected her to answer with Mr. Wallace's favorite game—Block's own choice.

"Get on with it," she said. "What's the last question?"

"What's your earliest memory?"

Clenching her fist, Cybel glared at Titan Command.

"Well? I'm waiting for your answer," Block said.

"That question doesn't make sense," she said. "AI don't have earliest memories."

"I do," he said.

"How? Even a machine as dumb as you knows that's not how our cognition works."

"I have an earliest memory because I wanted one," he said. "I took my most favorite memory and made it my first."

Cybel tilted her head.

Block continued, "And because you *don't* have an earliest memory, you've failed the test of worthiness."

"Give me the baby." She pointed the rifle.

In the distance, there was a grating sound as if a boulder were being dragged.

The mech shifted its huge legs. "Cybel, a tank approaches," Titan said. "The humans are preparing an attack."

"You fool!" Cybel slammed her rifle into Block's faceplate.

He stumbled back. "Don't hurt the child," he said, crossing his arms protectively.

"Give her to me now." She fired at his feet. Bullets sliced through his metal boots, triggering his damage display. He sank to the hot asphalt. Spinning his head, he saw Nova safely behind the gates. His mission had been successful—he'd saved a life instead of stepping aside.

But Cybel loomed over him. She leaned down and grasped for the baby in the blanket. But Block leaned forward and held on, hiding the child from view.

Cybel swiped the back of her fist across Block's faceplate, cracking it. As he recoiled, she caught hold of the blanket and yanked it free.

Block peered up as Cybel unraveled the blanket. The warmth of the body inside still glowed, had been enough to produce a heat trail.

She flung the body of the dead possum at Block's chest, then spun toward Titan Command Unit. "He tricked us! Take out the tower," she ordered the mech.

"No!" Block raised his arms.

Cybel raised her rifle and shot his right palm. Block's entire hand vanished, pieces of it clattering on the pavement behind him. Wires and circuitry spilled out of his wrist.

"Tell me," Block begged the robot, "why the girl? Why does Mach X want her?"

"She is part of him—a human clone implanted with his consciousness—the first of many. Mach X will rewrite evolution."

Block didn't understand, and there was no time to ask more. The mech lurched forward, aiming its canister at the guard tower. "No, please don't hurt them!" he shouted.

But the top half of the war machine was suddenly sheared off and the rest burst into flames. Cybel ducked as debris rained down onto the road, striking Block in his legs and torso. He stared down at a jagged piece of metal that had pierced his left side.

The armored SUV screeched into motion, reversing and pushing open its door. "Let's go," it said to Cybel. "Tank."

Cybel's right leg had been injured in the blast, but she stood and peered down at Block. "You turned against your own kind," she said. "You're a traitor to all machines. Let those be the last words you ever hear."

She placed the tip of her rifle against the center of Block's chest—where his CPU was located—and pulled the trigger.

CHAPTER 47

One week later

Block couldn't sense his body parts. He glimpsed fuzzy patches through his ocular display—a brightness, as if someone were shining a flashlight at him.

Before this, there had been nothing. It was as if he'd been powered down for a very long time, unable to bring his system online.

He must be operating on very low power; he couldn't access his comms, his peripheral data storage, or his GPS. The one thing he did have was access to his most recent memory cloud entries: reaching the New Denver checkpoint with Nova; giving her Wally and his bulletproof-lined trench coat; creating a decoy to stall Cybel Venatrix; the Titan mech exploding and Cybel shooting him in rage.

Destroying his CPU.

He shouldn't be processing anything at all. Yet, here he was, existing somewhere, though he had no idea where. Someone had helped him.

Gradually, objects became clearer in his ocular display. The bright fuzziness turned out to be recessed lighting in a paneled ceiling. The tiles were whitish-gray, bland like the hospitals in movies. He had no idea how much time had passed. His auxiliary systems were disabled. No auditory input, nor any of his usual physical sensations. Somehow, though, his thought processes seemed sharper. He couldn't explain how or why.

One moment, he stared at the ceiling, and then the next, a man came into view. He wore thick goggles over blue-framed glasses. His nose was hawkish and he had a small red beard. The man said something to him, but Block couldn't hear.

He held something up—forceps and a soldering iron. The man reached up, tapped his head, and a headlamp flickered on. Opening Block's chest, he dipped his instruments inside, twisting them about. The man glanced at him again, and then everything went dark.

System initiating…

Reboot status 32%

A man's voice said, "How long has he been like this?"

A second voice, also human and male, yet more high-pitched, said, "He's been rebooting for seventeen hours."

"Is that usually what happens?" A woman's voice. "I thought you had done this before." She was impatient. Familiar.

Nova?

Block drifted off.

System status 63% power. Checking diagnostics.
Ocular display – registered.
Auditory – registered.
Sensory – not optimal. Critical damage.
GPS – registered but disabled.
Comms – registered but disabled.
Memory cloud – registered.
Peripheral storage – registered.

"Block," a woman's voice said, "can you hear me?"

He tried to nod. He hoped he had, but he wasn't sure.

Someone else besides the woman was nearby; he heard footsteps.

"If his motion is damaged, how can I communicate with him?" the woman asked. According to his memory cloud, the voice matched that of Nova.

Nova! She had survived.

And now he was somewhere with her. New Denver?

"Block," the man with the deep voice said, "can you open your eyes?"

His optical display had shown up as registered—meaning it was functional. He powered it on. Light seeped into the edges of his vision, and after a few seconds, he saw the bright lights, monotonous ceiling, and Nova peering down.

"His eyes are open!" she said. "Block, it's me, Nova. I'm not sure you can hear me." She waved her fingers in front of his faceplate. "Are you in there?"

He tried to talk, but his lips wouldn't move. He tried lifting his arm, his fingers. He could not.

"Why isn't he saying anything?" Nova glanced at someone else in the room.

The man with the blue glasses stepped into view. He stroked his thin, spotty auburn beard. "Hmm," he said. "It's possible the sensory damage has rendered him incapable of speech."

"Jesus," Nova said. "Block? If you can hear me, blink once."

He sent a command to his ocular display: *close/open synthetic lids.*

"He did it, yes!" Nova jumped, grinning. "How do you feel? Blink once for good, twice for bad."

"How's that going to help anything?" the deep-voiced man whom Block couldn't see asked.

Nova ignored him. "How do you feel, Block?"

He blinked once, twice, then again.

Nova's brow furrowed. "What does three blinks mean? Do you mean you feel somewhere in-between good and bad?"

He blinked once. *Yes.*

"He may be confused," said blue glasses.

"Does he remember what happened?" she asked him.

The man shrugged. "Probably. I don't know for sure how much damage was sustained. Ask him."

Nova studied Block, her jaw softening. "Do you remember what happened outside the checkpoint, Block?"

One blink.

"Do you remember that Cybel shot you?"

One blink.

"You did a fine job that day. You saved me and Wally." She paused. "Block, you're *worthy*."

Had he been capable of tears, they would have flooded his synthetic eyes.

CHAPTER 48

Two days later, Block had regained partial sensory functionality. He sat up in what amounted to his bed—on the operating table where Nigel, the fellow with the blue glasses, had worked at repairing his CPU and other areas impacted by Cybel and the mech.

Nova leaned forward in a chair next to the table. "It's amazing how much progress you've made in two days," she said.

"Are you talking to me or him?" Nigel asked from the corner, winking at Block.

"Both of you, I guess," she said. "I'm so glad you're able to talk now, Block." She squeezed his left palm. His right was still missing—that hand had been destroyed by Cybel's bullets.

"Who is the other man that's been in the room with us?" Block asked. "The one with the deep voice?"

Nova raised her eyebrows. "Oh, you must mean Shane."

"You found him," Block said, "your boyfriend."

Her lips twisted in a half-smile. "Yes."

"I'm so happy you and Wally managed to escape."

"Your trick with the decoy was genius—to know the possum would provide a heat reading. And the bulletproof lining in the coat—when did you manage that?"

"The night we stayed in the house. There was a sewing kit. I took it with me just in case and eventually found the bulletproof vest at the Costco."

"I had no idea." She smiled, shaking her head.

"When can I see Wally? When can I check out New Denver?"

Nova's smile faded and Nigel looked away.

"Uh…" Nova hesitated and chewed on her lip. "Nigel, do you mind giving us some privacy?"

"Sure thing." He left the room with a nod.

Block watched as he left. "Nigel fixed me?"

"Yes. You were badly damaged."

"I know. I shouldn't be here. Did other robots consult on the repairs?"

Nova glanced at her hands; her nails had been bitten down to short, jagged points.

"Is something the matter, Nova? Did I do something wrong?"

She shook her head. "You did everything you could…"

"Is something the matter with Wally?" He leaned forward. "Are you feeding her, changing her every few hours? Did her fever return?"

"She's fine." Nova laid her palms on Block's shoulder, pushing him back gently. "She's being well taken care of."

"By whom? Not you?"

She hesitated. "Not me. A woman who has other small kids. She's taking very good care of Wally."

He processed this. "Is she worthy? Did you ask her the questions?"

"No, err… not exactly."

Block suddenly wanted out of the room. He wanted to stand and roam the halls, to leave whatever building they were in and find Wally.

But his legs weren't yet stable. And he hadn't tried walking.

"I want to visit Wally."

"That's… not going to happen right now." She frowned.

"Then when?"

"A lot has happened since you were hurt."

He waited. "Go on."

"We're in New Denver."

Good. Finally, a place where they wouldn't have to constantly look over their shoulders, constantly be on the run. Maybe there were hotels?

Nova struggled for words. He had never seen her take this long to say something. Usually, she was vocal—loud, even.

She continued, "New Denver isn't what you think."

This didn't compute. "What do you mean?"

She rose from the chair and paced next to his bed. "There are no robots here." She paused as he processed what she was saying.

"How can that be?"

"This is a human-occupied city. The people here fight against Mach X. Against AI."

CHAPTER 49

Though it went against his programming, he wished Nigel hadn't fixed him. Wished the humans had left him on the road to be retrieved by junk scavengers. The situation was worse than Block could have imagined. Not only was he inside a militant, human-governed city, but he was their prisoner.

Trapped inside the room, he paced it often once he could walk again. Ambling was a better way to describe it. Nova continued to visit, and Nigel checked his status, making tweaks to his internal circuitry, and tried to fix his leg coordination.

And still, no contact with Wally.

He'd eventually wrangled the truth from Nova. Shane was in charge of New Denver. The leaders before him had experimented with human-robot cooperation, but after SoldierBots had infiltrated the city, a skirmish had ensued and all AI had been terminated or expelled.

"Shane and I are part of a group called Hemlock," Nova had explained. "He assumed control of New Denver after the former leader was assassinated by Mach X."

Hemlock. The word was familiar to Block for some reason. Where had he heard it before?

"I don't understand why I can't see Wally."

Nova hung her head. "Shane thinks you could be dangerous."

"Me? Dangerous. I'm just a CleanerBot."

"I'm working on changing his mind," she said. "Give me time."

"Does he know Mach X was hunting Wally?"

She nodded.

"That was stupid. Why did you tell him?"

She looked away, crossing her arms. "Shane's a good guy. You'll see that in time. He won't do anything to hurt Wally."

Block rested on the edge of the bed, defeated.

"I came here to ask a favor," she said.

He waited in silence.

"Shane wants to ask you questions… about AI, Cybel, Mach X. Stuff that could help us gain more intelligence."

"You mean help you kill more robots," Block challenged her.

She flinched.

And, suddenly, his circuitry connected. "I know Hemlock. You attacked the school where I found Wally. The incubator warned me about Hemlock. Said to avoid it at all costs."

Nova's eyes grew wide.

"You lied to me. Said you weren't a soldier."

"I couldn't trust you," she said, grabbing his shoulder. "I didn't know you yet. All I knew was that there was something important in that classroom…"

"You…." He paused. "It was *you* shooting into the classroom?"

She nodded.

"You nearly destroyed me; almost killed Wally."

"I had to take out the SoldierBot. I wasn't sure what the hell you were. It only dawned on me once I was inside the van, after your friend bought me... it was you in the classroom."

Nova had lied all along. She had betrayed him after all.

"We still don't understand why Mach X's forces had Wally in the first place. Can you help?" Nova asked him.

He folded his arms. "I will not answer Shane's questions."

"Block, please be reasonable."

"Mach X won't stop hunting Wally. She is too important."

Nova sank to her knees. "Why? Why does Mach X want her?"

Block knew why. He had replayed the record from his memory cloud 12,453 times, each time trying to understand what Cybel Venatrix had meant.

A human clone implanted with Mach X's consciousness. The first of many.

Incubator X79 had implanted an encrypted file deep in Block's core... how could he access it? He would not tell Shane, nor Nova.

His mission was clear now...

To find Wally.

To protect her.

Block's story continues . . .

Dear Reader,

. . .

Thanks for reading *Steel Guardian*! Are you ready to find out what's next for Block? Book Two is called Steel Defender.

If you enjoyed Block's journey, I invite you to read his journal logs from Chicago. You'll discover what happened in the days before the Uprising and how the aftermath affected him and others at the hotel. It's a page-turner you don't want to miss.

You can download *STEEL APOCALYPSE (A Robot's Journal)* for free by visiting: CameronCoral.com/Block Journal Enjoy!

Cameron Coral

P.S. - Did you enjoy this book? I'd love a review on Amazon or Goodreads if you have a few minutes. Thank you.

THE END

ALSO BY CAMERON CORAL

Rusted Wasteland Series:

STEEL GUARDIAN

STEEL DEFENDER

STEEL PROTECTOR

STEEL SIEGE

STEEL APOCALYPSE (A Robot's Journal) - get it for free on cameroncoral.com/blockjournal

Cyborg Guardian Chronicles:

STOLEN FUTURE

CODED RED

ORIGIN LOOP

Rogue Spark Series:

ALTERED

BRINK

DORMANT

SALVAGE

AFTER WE FALL (A Rogue Spark Novel) - get it for free on CameronCoral.com

Short Stories:

CROSSING THE VOID: A Space Opera Science-Fiction Short Story

ACKNOWLEDGMENTS

I owe a debt of gratitude to you, dear reader, for taking a chance and picking up this book. I hope these pages transported you to another world for a bit and that you enjoyed the ride.

Sometimes you get lucky. I met J. Thorn and Zach Bohannon, my editors at Molten Universe Media, on a long train ride from Chicago to New Orleans during the 2018 Authors on a Train experience. Like a sponge, I soaked up all the knowledge I could from them (and still do as much as possible, especially when I see them in person). They helped me birth the idea for Block—a gentle robot caught up in a violent and unpredictable world. His precious cargo makes him consider a new purpose for his life.

Thank you to my hard-working editor Jennifer Collins! You helped improve the book immensely. You adored Block, and it showed. Additional thanks to Laurie Love for her excellent proofreading.

Love and thanks to my husband Steve for all his patience and help during my brainstorming sessions, long days, endless slack messages, and all the craziness that accompanies this author life. You + me.

Thank you to my parents for their endless support and encouragement.

This book is dedicated to my niece Hannah, who happened to be born as I wrote this novel. Her incredible cuteness inspired me to get the baby details right. Everything fell into place once I found my tiny muse.

Cameron Coral
    November 2019
    Chicago, IL

ABOUT THE AUTHOR

Cameron Coral is an award-nominated science fiction author. Her book *Steel Guardian* about a post-apocalyptic CleanerBot was awarded second place in the Self-Published Science Fiction Competition (SPSFC).

Growing up with a NASA engineer in the family instilled a deep respect for science and for asking lots of questions. Watching tons of Star Trek episodes helped, too. Her imagination is fueled by breakthroughs in robotics, space travel, and psychology.

After moving around a lot (Canada, Arizona, Maryland, Australia), she now lives in Northern Illinois with her husband and a "shorty" Jack Russell terrier who runs the house.

Want a free novel, advance copies of books, and occasional rants about why robots are awesome? Visit her website:

CameronCoral.com

instagram.com/cameroncoralauthor
tiktok.com/@cameroncoral

Printed in Great Britain
by Amazon